Marcello surprises us with his honesty and his exacting self-critique. He dissects the classic entitled male, moving from condescension to humility, from objectification to compassion."

—Dana Spiotta, author of *Wayward*

"Imagine a Casanova who's outlived theory, therapy, and drugs to write a last tender and desirously wise volume of memoirs about the women he (mostly) hasn't slept with: his mother, his sister, his sister-in-law, his editor, his friends. That's Francesco Pacifico, whose *The Women I Love* will love you back, whether or not you deserve it."   —Joshua Cohen, author of *The Netanyahus*

Musacchio & Ianniello

Francesco Pacifico

The Women I Love

TRANSLATED BY ELIZABETH HARRIS

Francesco Pacifico lives in Rome. He is the author of the novels *The Story of My Purity* and *Class*, a *New York Times* Critics' Top Book of 2017. He is a frequent contributor to *La Repubblica* and *n+1*, and his work has also appeared in *McSweeney's*, *The White Review*, and elsewhere. He is a founder and senior editor of the literary magazine *Il Tascabile*. He has translated the work of a number of writers, including F. Scott Fitzgerald, Kurt Vonnegut, Henry Miller, Dave Eggers, Hanya Yanagihara, Ralph Ellison, Chris Ware, Matt Groening, David Mazzucchelli, and Alison Bechdel.

Elizabeth Harris has translated works by Mario Rigoni Stern, Giulio Mozzi, Antonio Tabucchi, Andrea Bajani, and Claudia Durastanti. For her various translations of Tabucchi, she has received an NEA Literature Translation Fellowship, the Italian Prose in Translation Award, and the National Translation Award for prose.

The
Women
I Love

The
Women
I Love

Francesco
Pacifico

Translated from the Italian
by Elizabeth Harris

PICADOR
FARRAR, STRAUS AND GIROUX
NEW YORK

Picador
120 Broadway, New York 10271

The Library of Congress has cataloged the Farrar, Straus and
Giroux hardcover edition as follows:
Names: Pacifico, Francesco, 1977– author. | Harris, Elizabeth,
    1963– translator.
Title: The women I love / Francesco Pacifico ; translated from
    the Italian by Elizabeth Harris.
Other titles: Donne amate. English
Description: First American edition. | New York : Farrar, Straus
    and Giroux, 2021. | Originally published in Italian in 2018
    by Rizzoli, Italy, as Le donne amate.
Identifiers: LCCN 2021032239 | ISBN 9780374292720
    (hardcover)
Subjects: LCGFT: Novels.
Classification: LCC PQ4916.A337 D6613 2021 |
    DDC 853/.92—dc23
LC record available at https://lccn.loc.gov/2021032239

Paperback ISBN: 978-1-250-85877-1

Designed by Janet Evans-Scanlon

Our books may be purchased in bulk for promotional,
educational, or business use. Please contact your local bookseller
or the Macmillan Corporate and Premium Sales Department at
1-800-221-7945, extension 5442, or by email at
MacmillanSpecialMarkets@macmillan.com.

Picador® is a U.S. registered trademark and is used by Macmillan
Publishing Group, LLC, under license from Pan Books Limited.

For book club information, please visit
facebook.com/picadorbookclub or email
marketing@picadorusa.com.

picadorusa.com • instagram.com/picador
twitter.com/picadorusa • facebook.com/picadorusa

P1

To Olivia,
Marianna,
Cristiana,
Francesca,
and Antonella

But after reading a chapter or two a shadow seemed to lie across the page. It was a straight dark bar, a shadow shaped something like the letter "I." One began dodging this way and that to catch a glimpse of the landscape behind it. Whether that was indeed a tree or a woman walking I was not quite sure. Back one was always hailed to the letter "I." One began to be tired of "I." Not but what this "I" was a most respectable "I"; honest and logical; as hard as a nut, and polished for centuries by good teaching and good feeding. I respect and admire that "I" from the bottom of my heart. But—here I turned a page or two, looking for something or other—the worst of it is that in the shadow of the letter "I" all is shapeless as mist. Is that a tree? No, it is a woman. But . . . she has not a bone in her body, I thought, watching Phoebe, for that was her name, coming across the beach. Then Alan got up and the shadow of Alan at once obliterated Phoebe. For Alan had views and Phoebe was quenched in the flood of his views.

—VIRGINIA WOOLF,
A Room of One's Own

Contents

Eleonora

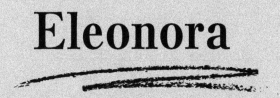

Now the end has come and I am filled
with sorrow that our ways must part:
the path I would rather take is the one
that leads to life.

—MURASAKI SHIKIBU,
The Tale of Genji
(trans. Royall Tyler)

*S*he was a natural: *she knew right away what a novel needed* before going to press. As soon as an author emailed her a final manuscript, Eleonora would print out a copy, silence her phone, turn off her computer, remove her shoes, tuck her feet beneath herself on her swivel chair, and start reading, crossing out lines, marking up the pages with an orange pen. Weekends, she'd work in bed, lying on two orthopedic pillows and scratching her flaky scalp. With those wide-eyed looks of hers, the sighing, the laughing, the "No way!"s that kept her company while she read, she'd hunt down the story's weak points and make her notes in the margins. When the main character was just on the verge of changing, but the writer was holding back, avoiding conflict or a major scene, Eleonora knew how to say, gently, over the phone or in person, in a honeyed voice (her written notes were also tactful): "After reading all these years, I've come to realize that I want to see the big emotions. Do the work. Show us who your characters are . . . I buy a book for moments like this: the son selling the house of his dead father. I don't buy a book for the metaphors. You're a great writer—you don't need me to tell you that—but I get the feeling you're afraid of something, you just don't want to write this part, you're practically begging me to ask for it, but you're not taking me there . . ." The authors, now convinced, would accept the idea of spending months longer on a text they'd thought was ready. I've been doing the same job as Eleonora maybe ten years longer, and I find myself imitating her methods.

She had an incredible ability to stay focused. Hours and hours on end, with stacks of printed pages, unearthing every typo, every awkward phrase, the fourth read-through no different from the first. We editors at the big publishing houses don't devote enough time to the text: we read agents' proposals, put offers together, hold meetings, concern ourselves with prizes—and neglect the book itself, that mass of sentences, paragraphs, each new start, each new page, what the reader's mind turns to a coherent whole. Eleonora practically stunted her career by prioritizing the prose over the book's public life. To her, a novel had to be prepared like a dessert. "The reader, discovering the book in a bookstore, has to feel like he's in a nice pastry shop: the cream, rich, the pastry, perfectly baked, each taste distinctive, perfect harmony overall." The rules she'd learned in editing classes at college—even now, when she was past thirty—she still treated like dogma: the proper number of letters per line to keep it from seeming too tight or loose, or the problem of orphans or widows, those lines at the start or the end of a paragraph that dangle onto a separate page.

She'd grown up with the young experimentalists who idolized the postmodernists, their stylistic bravura, yet she denounced every annoying metaphor she encountered both to the author and to me, her supervisor back then. Sometimes, on a late winter afternoon in the office together, or evenings at her place, she'd interrupt my work to read me a tortured phrase, and ask: "But do *you* know what this means?" It didn't matter if the author was a well-respected stalwart or some young hipster, already known for his grammatical acrobatics. Eleonora would take the offending page and start reading some long-winded digression about a certain kind of light that was compared, through four complicated relative clauses, to a laser beam and then to mercury; she'd look up at me, laughing, and say: "I'll tell you what—it doesn't mean a fucking thing!" And then she'd make a note. She was never aggressive—all she did was scrawl a question mark (a delicately shaped question mark) beside the passage, so that in the end, the author would find himself saying—as if it were his idea—that the metaphor in question had to go.

But no matter how much she enjoyed making fun of authors behind their backs, she never let them discover how unimpressed she was with their vague, unnecessary flourishes. She wasn't just polite on the phone: she was enthusiastic, genuinely so. She really seemed happy whenever an author called, even a nagging author—only after hanging up would she look at the ceiling and swear. What relationship was there between her warmth on the phone with the author and the weariness that seeped through her immediately afterward? It didn't seem like hypocrisy, more like a profound dialectic, evincing some general truth about all human relations.

After reading until midnight and feeling—like so many of us who've chosen to work in publishing—overwhelmed by contemporary books, which didn't always meet her rigorous standards, she'd put off sleeping and end her day with a great classic novel.

But she didn't boast about this, that would be pretentious—and she considered pretension a widespread crime in the literary world. I only knew she did this because I was fortunate enough to spend a few nights a month with her, in her room, in her bed, where we worked, after hours, for the same publishing house, and, also, made love. Since I needed at least eight hours of sleep per night, I'd accept the humiliation of wearing a sleep mask so I wouldn't be disturbed by her pleasure reading.

Yeah, she was great, truly inspired: I've never said this before, and it's liberating to set it down. [This attempt to clarify my thoughts and feelings for the women in my life began with the next chapter. I didn't have the courage at first to write about Eleonora, how much I like her, how impressive I find her. Now that I've gotten up the nerve, I'd rather just start here.

Perhaps I couldn't begin here initially because it's easy to forget how much you respect someone, how much you appreciate someone's sensitivity and intelligence, when you can only glimpse those virtues at a distance. A person's mind and what reveals it—laughter, syntax, running commentary—these are mainly what keep you company. When the people who've kept me company with their minds are no longer nearby, I force myself to forget what being near them felt like. I go out of my way not to preserve their memory and just turn them into bland copies instead.]

Eleonora started working when the publishing industry was mid-crisis, but she never allowed herself to be infected by its pervasive cynicism. At the end of the first decade of the twenty-first century, salaries were dropping rather than rising, counter to the expectations instilled by her middle-class upbringing. Eleonora didn't let the recession downsize the joy she felt in becoming one of the people able to choose which writers—whose manuscripts were piled up around the office and her apartment, gathering dust and making her sneeze—got to be called authors.

I'm using the past tense here, even though as I write, she's still an editor. The books she's worked on for a new publishing house continue to arrive at my door (packaged and stamped by a publicity department that has no idea that she and I were, until recently, whatever it was we were for each other for almost three years), but Eleonora and I are no longer on speaking terms.

She compromises less on her new books than when she worked with me. She continues to hone that ideal of hers, the vision she first had one morning in 2003 when an important writer, head shaved, wearing a fishing jacket, speaking to Eleonora's Italian class, revealed not only that he was friends with their teacher (*their* teacher, who wore pantsuits to school and left her hair gray), but that every time he had "around fifty pages ready to go"—what a marvelous image, a real, if unpublished, book—he'd print them out and bring them to their teacher, his friend, so she could "pick them apart." "With what color pen—red or blue?" one of Eleonora's classmates asked. It was winter, the overhead fluorescent lights were on and out the window, the cold cotton of fog was enveloping the trees one by one. And their teacher pulled a college textbook off a shelf, an anthology of contemporary Italian literature that included a piece by this author.

Encountering that college textbook at her godforsaken high school unsettled Eleonora so completely that she quit writing her own work and began to "correct" the writing of others. The following year, in college in Milan, she attended a meeting for a graduate-student literary blog and volunteered to be their "proofreader," a term learned, like others, that fateful day in high school. Meanwhile, she'd bought the Serianni grammar text and read from it daily. She commuted from a small town just outside Milan; her father was running for city council, and her brother was a policeman. The grad students had contacts who were real published authors; they interviewed them, and even went out with them at night. Eleonora began dating one of the youngest contributors, who hadn't yet graduated, and she moved to Milan after that first year so she wouldn't have to run home at dinnertime while the group was headed to someone's place or to a reading at a bookstore. But this decision made her mother stop speaking to her for six months, and as a result, Eleonora lost ten pounds. Her boyfriend began to look after her, and she lived in his room and off his parents' money; as a gift, he enrolled her in a short, introductory class on editing.

She almost never talked to me about those years: they were too hard, and every day, or almost every day, she wondered: When will I get to do real books, books that get excerpted in college textbooks? She detested how others found literature to be a nice way to pass the time with people they thought were better than average. She found it impossible to feel superior to others, to those who might be considered "average," and she hadn't rebelled from her "average" family, her politically involved father, her Catholic mother, her older, policeman brother—three people she considered honest and humane in spite of their ideological differences from her, along with their enormous prejudices. While she worked, she felt more like Montaigne than a modernist hipster like Fernanda Pivano, because only the logos, a force even older and more established than the grand narratives her family had suffocated her with, could allow her to choose her path with freedom.

As a result, she was ambivalent about the counterculture, with all its arrogant blowhards competing with her boyfriend, hitting on her to the beat of their musings on enormous tomes by Italian and American authors, all of them male—earnest, pretentious, and male—but deep down, she also knew she was lucky to have found a rich boy from Milan, a raft on the endless river flowing toward intellectual perfection. Around 2010, the couple moved to Rome because he was swimming in money and the blind faith of his professor parents, and so he enrolled in a creative writing workshop to make connections in the young, indie literary scene in Rome.

As Eleonora approached her goal of editing actual books, she added up how much time had passed: it was six or seven years since that writer in his fishing jacket had come to her school. For the first time, she felt like an adult—she'd never wanted anything for so long. In college, she found her high school teacher on Facebook, wrote to her, and learned that the teacher and the famous writer had only worked together on two novels, then lost touch, and that she no longer had any connection to the literary scene in Milan. From the teacher's nostalgic tone, Eleonora gathered that the two of them had been involved, and this explained, more than anything else, their collaboration. Eleonora hadn't been raised a feminist and didn't run in feminist circles, but she read this exchange with her teacher as a warning: she had to be careful about relying too heavily on sexual or romantic relationships to get ahead, because these relationships wouldn't last, and would only serve to trick her into believing she was making progress in the literary world, given that male intellectuals—including her own boyfriend—tended to imagine they had intellectual chemistry with the women they desired.

Eleonora couldn't help sparking men's imaginations—because of her looks, yes, and also because she knew how to talk to them. One Saturday, she went to her boyfriend's writing workshop and, after silently observing and listening for six hours (including at the lunch break at the small tables outside a bar in the historic center), when five o'clock rolled around, she approached the two teachers, both men and both published authors, and asked to be their assistant: "I promise I'll stay in a corner and be quiet the whole time," she said in a strawberry voice. "I'll keep all the student manuscripts and stories in order, I'll do your emailing, anything you want." And those two male teachers, both of them around forty, immediately said yes before they even consulted the school's director.

That's where I met her: a beloved girl with a gleam in her eye; there was a puppy's meekness to her, a beauty like a faded leaf. Her legs were slender, athletic, and her outfits were neat and perfect, bomber jackets and fancy sneakers. We talked about these sneakers, and modernist novels, in one of our first conversations: I was teaching a class as a guest editor, and like her, was involved with someone. She was bright, and one day I passed her a story by a young female writer who interested me. "Why don't you see if it needs any work?" I was curious to find out if she was any good, or if I'd only been charmed by her mannerisms, her clothes, her hair, and her voice. (It's always bothered me that intellectual desire and physical desire are so similar that they incite misunderstandings: like anxiety and allergy, united by hydrocortisone.)

After Eleonora revised it, the story was accepted in one of Italy's most important literary journals, and the day it came out, she invited me to have tea with her as a thank-you. She spoke in a different tone than usual—serious, stressed-out but not neurotic, and while she talked, I found myself thinking of the contrast Ibsen was going for in *A Doll's House* between the Nora who tries to coax her husband and the Nora who signs loan notes behind his back to save her family. "I risked losing my mother for books," Eleonora said to me, "and that period seemed endless. I didn't have my mother, and I didn't even really have literature. Since *2003*"—and she emphasized the year like she must have done in a hundred grueling conversations—"I've been trying to become a part of literature."

I told her that I found her devotion moving, and then she added: "I have to do it—I can't give up now."

Those were great days in Rome. The new independent music scene, romantic and electronic, its flashes of lyricism in sync with the young people of Rome and their struggles—those living as artists and those who dreamed of doing so, undeterred by the constant remarks about how the city was dying from ignorance and corruption. Eleonora and her boyfriend hung out with the producers of that music, the singer-songwriters, and also with young comedians, writers . . . but she was frustrated that her boyfriend hadn't finished his first novel, which she couldn't wait to edit: he seemed too satisfied with his lifestyle to dedicate himself to art. She found a little freelance work, some copyediting under the table, five hundred euros a month. As the months passed, her anonymous work started showing up in the bookstores she'd visit, and she was thrilled. So what if these novels weren't so great—just a bunch of genre fiction—it was fun seeing the paper fruits of her intelligence budding in the greenhouses of culture.

Another girl from the (now finished) workshop wrote me and sent me her first novel. I sent it on to Eleonora, like I had the story and again, I was pleased with the result, and this time forwarded it to my publisher, and they bought it.

I gave Eleonora the news over the phone; she burst out crying, apologized, and hung up. A half hour later she called back to ask if the colophon could include her name as editor. I told her the author could put her into the acknowledgments.

The publisher I worked for, one of the big houses, is located in Milan. I divided my time between Milan and Rome, where I'm from, because it was my job to work with our Roman writers. When I returned to Rome that day, I met Eleonora in a tearoom downtown: she seemed unhappy. She'd entered the literary world by truly, irrefutably helping a young, talented writer, and this had unnerved her: "I can't take it. It's over, just like that, there's nothing stable, no place to stand. Stefano's perfectly happy as he is, hanging out with singers, this endless Tartar Steppe is fine by him . . . this dream he'll never obtain. Marcello, I can't take it." And then she made this leap in logic that I still remember, maybe because I was so struck by hearing my name spoken in such an intimate way: "Do you think I used him? For his money? I want to start eating again, Marcello. I hate feeling so bad."

The next day, I recommended Eleonora for an internship at my publishing house, and when I told her the editor in chief had approved, she started crying again and gave me a big hug, because this time I'd told her in person, at a bar, and she glued herself to me. That night she stayed over at the young female writer's after breaking up with her boyfriend.

She'd finally gotten into publishing: she went back home to live with her family in the same small town near Milan; from there, she'd commute to the office for her internship, two points in orbit around Milan that held her exclusive attention until she was hired on as an editor. Her mother was happy to devote herself to packing a metal *schiscetta* with Eleonora's lunch and getting her healthy again. Early on in her internship, Eleonora regained the weight she'd lost, regained her figure, her red hair and freckles became bright again. She started seeing a young accountant in her town.

And that's when she and I began our secret affair.

I *haven't been able to figure out what this next part means,* and so I keep cutting details, pages, whole chapters, hoping to get down to the bone: the two of us standing by a glass wall on the sixth floor, admiring the torrential summer rain coming down, taking a short break from a meeting with the editor in chief, who'd been assigning books to each editor, our colleagues returning from their smoke break downstairs, or from the bathroom. I couldn't ask her outright if she'd gone to bed with the editor in chief, and I felt like an idiot, standing there, silent, thinking that since he'd just proposed—without consulting me— that she handle the autobiography of a very old writer who lived on the Lombard lake where the director also had a small villa, then this meant the two of them were lovers, because that writer was too old to leave the house and she'd actually be the one writing the book, interviewing him, putting the transcribed interviews, letters, and diaries together for him to work on. She'd stay over with the writer and his caretaker a few days a week. I could picture her scuttling out of the villa and into the editor's car.

If the illuminated part of me preserves the facts I've presented in the preceding chapter, the person I was that afternoon, that Marcello, enveloped in the white light of the vending machines glowing behind me, in the saturated air of that open-plan interior, with a piece of sponge cake in one hand, looking out the window at the rainy sky, the puddles in the empty garden, the sun turning the rain golden, I, that Marcello, felt myself reduced to a new low: I thought Eleonora had tossed me aside for her career. After her writer boyfriend, there was me, the editor-poet lover, and after me came the editor in chief. I attributed her career advancement to a strategy that was cynical, cruel. I was desperate because I sensed I was losing her, this fantastic, introspective woman. She didn't have the subtle fear of most women, who, when they possess a man's body, almost imperceptibly squeeze our hips with their legs, withdrawing from us when they are physically closest to us. Eleonora's legs, in contrast, spread open like a yawn, and then closed. I would never feel her thighs around my hips again, and I wondered if I could keep working in that remote, paradoxical place of glass and darkness, that sprawling suburban building, so far from downtown Milan, if I could keep taking the high-speed train every week, the train, too, wrapped in glass but so stark, so bright inside that when I returned to Rome at night, I'd sometimes break into a cold sweat looking at that screen by the ceiling that listed our speed at three hundred kilometers an hour, while looking out the windows I barely saw anything at all, and that big, lit-up, plastic and alloy canister, filled with men and women and phones, gathering speed, all of us exposed, all of central Italy watching. The soulless absurdity of that commute. And I'd spend a few nights in a hotel in Milan, garishly lit . . . Could I go back just to living with my real girlfriend in Rome, who didn't travel for work and who'd told me she couldn't take that sort of life with me anymore?

Standing there by the windows in the lobby area, swallowing my cake, I caught Eleonora's scent among the office smells of cardboard and steel, and I felt like I'd been jettisoned into space.

After the smokers returned, I didn't go back to the meeting; I set off down the hall that ran around the entire floor of this glass building, set like a jewel in the garden. I turned right, to the Italian fiction section; I sat down at my desk, one of five lined up like school desks in the waiting room between the hall and the offices of the senior editors and the editor in chief. Each area had been designed with panels at about eye-level, and reinforced with bookshelves: the office hadn't been reconfigured yet since the layoffs.

A man in front of me bent over a manuscript, head propped up on one hand, elbow on his knee, feet on a box of A4 paper. He was wearing earplugs. He'd been an editorial director and a publisher, and now was back to reading manuscripts, untroubled, not even going to meetings. He was bald, tall but not gangly; his neck was thick and tanned as hide, much darker than the beige jacket he wore. His neck was saying something to me—that there'd come a time when I'd give the same impression of strength and mortality.

No one came looking for me; I went back to the meeting. They were waiting to start, gossiping about an author and his literary jealousies: I joined in on the laughter. Everyone (or almost everyone) at that table was a published poet or novelist, and we all recognized the need for glory. I'm a poet, but I wasn't writing anymore and hadn't published in years. The editor in chief was a writer.

He began assigning books again, and one novel I admired went to Eleonora, even though I'd discovered the author and edited his previous book. Now sitting, rigid, I started to flush, and I asked myself what was going on. For three years, Eleonora's talent had been my privilege to oversee: she answered to me, got her assignments from me. She'd work with the text, while I'd work on the author's career, taking him to lunch when he was immersed in his book or suffering from writer's block, submitting the book to prizes, introducing him to other writers who might get him more exposure or help him grow. I wouldn't say I'd exploited Eleonora and her self-sacrificial tendency—because I also made sure my colleagues and the editor in chief knew right away how talented she was, that we'd taken on a thoroughbred—but even knowing she'd be free one day, I wasn't prepared for this pain, this blind jealousy.

Ambition is an iceberg submerged in a sea of solitude from adolescence—even childhood—on. Dating back to high school, Eleonora's iceberg had been submerged underwater, and I couldn't take credit for its surfacing, it had just floated my way: I'd been the first person in the publishing industry who wasn't in awe of her beauty, who treated her confidently. Maybe it helped that she'd been so thin, and not a noir sort of thin: she had the wide hips of someone built to be slightly heavy, she was a Botticelli-esque Venus on trim legs, almost always wearing running shoes, with a face—people might say she had a "creamy" complexion, but I thought she had a face more like shortbread, full of sugar and flour and raisin-moles and freckles. The first years we knew each other, I'd look at her as little as possible. If I stopped to examine her, I discovered irresistible details, like her lazy eye: her left eyelid was only half open from reading too much and keeping her nose in a book, in bed, on couches, and on buses, never relaxing, never finding a healthy position to read in (if those exist).

I haven't really expressed how pretty she was before, because it didn't have anything to do with her career, no matter what I thought that day in the office when I suspected she'd decided so coolly to fall in love with the editor in chief.

Writing this, I can feel that old knot in my throat that I used to get when I traveled up to Milan in the weeks before we'd become lovers and I felt the pleasure, not yet contaminated by sex, of having discovered a treasure hidden in plain sight, where no one thought to stoop and pick it up, at a creative writing workshop in Rome, where for a year and a half, no one had figured out how smart she was, maybe because she hadn't joined the chorus of praise for the four or five hot authors at the time; the pleasure of knowing that weekly, whenever the professional need arose, I could see her.

The downpour had slowed to a drizzle. The sun beat down on the building, but the panels dividing the hallway blocked out the glory of the clearing sky; the fluorescent lights running along the ceiling, over every cubicle and room, overwhelmed the grainy light of that summer afternoon. I was watching this play of natural and artificial light when the editor in chief asked me, for the first time, if I wanted to handle the covers in *Varia*—that miscellany category of cookbooks, coaches' biographies, etc.—since the editor was out on maternity leave.

"Okay, I'll do the promotional copy," I answered, my hands sweaty on the glass tabletop. Below the table, I glimpsed my colleagues' ugly shoes: cheap rubber, Roman sandals, the editor in chief's leather boot, firmly planted while he spoke—"Great,

Marcè, I feel better knowing you're on top of this"—his elbows on the table, that Treviso accent, his posing, with Roman slang and Anglicisms. He was small and round, and dressed casually, in tans and grays. He did have his charms—he was confident, polite—and over the years he'd perfected his style, understanding that with his secure position, all he had to do was try not to crush anyone. I removed my hands from the glass table and looked down at my own shoes, through the condensation left by my palms.

Eleonora's legs, across from mine, were stretched out, relaxed and open, like a man's; she was wearing a pair of turquoise capri pants and elaborate sneakers with white soles and black, synthetic-lace uppers. There was a love story going on between her sneakers and mine, in among all those other ugly shoes, like two lovers in a puppet show. Meanwhile, above the table, Eleonora was tapping her left index finger on the glass, her tic: slowly tapping, like there was a gratification button there. She pushed down, pushed down again, with hypnotic longing. She deserved to succeed, I thought, and this hurt even more; looking at the round face of the editor in chief I added to myself, I hope she ruins your life, buddy—but I knew she wouldn't. Eleonora's gift was in holding all of life's demands in balance, moving straight ahead, focused and strong, without distraction, through time's everlasting night, toward the great literature of the future.

We left the office together as a group and the commuter shuttle picked us all up in the spot out front, near the automatic doors. The asphalt was already beginning to dry. The driver dropped us off at the metro station at the edge of Milan, and Eleonora headed for her usual escalator, along with two older colleagues. The rest of the group scattered and I called Barbara, my girlfriend, then strolled around the bus terminal, reading a newspaper article on my phone. It was rush hour and the Milanese didn't linger: immigrants hauled their bags of merchandise; I focused on the girls and boys from the fashion world, their haughty gait in their expensive sneakers, and I envied the streamlined, violent way they lived through their beauty, never locking it away.

I had a room reserved at a *pensione* by the station, which I often didn't use: I'd agreed to settle up with the proprietor at my next visit. Sometimes I'd pay ahead, to stay in his good graces. I took the stairs down to the metro and traced Eleonora's steps; I was wearing my dark backpack, tapered and inconspicuous, bought just for these Milan trips, since I never knew where I'd be sleeping and didn't want to raise any suspicions if I ran into colleagues: it's a small city, and in publishing, everybody knows everybody.

To get to her place, I'd walk along a canal until the blocks grew less dense and the old converted factories and condominiums began to spring up. (I'm not sure if I'm describing this correctly—memory's map is imperfect.) Suddenly, I was in among the cocktail crowd, where the most attractive people in the world glide along, never mixing with normal folk, and the first group and the second both feel exquisite—the first by comparison and the second by proximity—and where the networking is relentless, as I saw one day, when a friend of mine in the fashion industry introduced me to some of her colleagues, and while I was getting up to use the bathroom, I noticed that one of them, sitting, facing me, was also checking out my picture online, reading up on me even as we spoke.

The apartment Eleonora rented was in one of the ex-factories:

a residential area now, with no open bars or restaurants and no nightlife. The factories had been divided into apartments that were elegant but not overly luxurious, for professionals in fields far removed from our own.

I rang at the freshly painted gate, and twin lights went on from the surveillance camera in front of me. She let me in! Her apartment was on the second and third floor of one of two buildings in this complex, surrounded by a wall laced with barbed wire; I rang again, she buzzed me in, I took the stairs two at a time and stepped inside the door to this apartment I loved so well, where tomorrow, while I made my coffee, I'd look down and see the morning light playing over the table and onto the floor.

The lights weren't on; the sun hadn't set, and from up the wooden staircase with no handrail came the music of running water, Eleonora's shower, which she'd stepped into right after answering my second ring. On this half-level there was a bathroom and the (empty) room of the man who rented to her, a friend of mine, a designer with his own line of streetwear shoes whom I'd met when I was writing a meaningless article on intellectuals and fashion and why the young entrepreneurs in design and similar fields didn't rouse the least bit of interest in Roman intellectuals (one of those suicidal pieces I insisted on writing to get a reaction, and that the intellectuals on the Roman scene took as something not all that far removed from supporting fascism; my former friend Leone, a character who'll figure into this story, wrote on social media that now he finally knew for sure that the roaring eighties were back and political commitment was dead once more). The stairs led up past that middle level, to Eleonora's single room above, furnished with just a mattress; this apartment and its jutting spaces were shaped by those of the apartment next door.

The euphoric sense of freedom inspired by these nicely juxta-posed spaces and by the owner's lifestyle—he was always travel-ing to Asia or the States to sell shoes—was something that she could only tolerate once or twice a month: she lived there, but when she was alone, she only worked. When we were there to-gether, though, we breathed deeply in that atmosphere, knowing we'd never get to live so brightly anyplace else. We needed our unhappy relationships, but fucking in the bliss of feeling single let us pilfer some of the designer's spiritual wealth. The cleaning and utility bills were two hundred euros a month and not a part of the lease, just what they'd arranged, because the designer wanted someone else to keep the place warm when he wasn't around, but he'd stopped letting girls in fashion stay in the sec-ond room: they were always throwing parties, inviting god knows who, making a mess, empty bottles of liquor they never threw out, saved, as if their touch turned these bottles into trophies.

I went into the downstairs bathroom, washed up with some soap I kept in my backpack, then I went to the kitchen, got some ice and a bottle of vodka, and I sat down quietly at the table to have a drink, feeling a tingle of anticipation.

If not for this apartment and the agreement Eleonora had with her fiancé—that she could stay here during the week—she would have wound up feeling stuck and breaking up with him for sure, and we would have wound up sleeping together so often that I couldn't possibly have stayed with Barbara. God knows what that young accountant thought of her. Why would anyone agree to such an arrangement? Barbara and I both honored our unwritten pact. Ideologically, we both hated the notion of family and couples, but we couldn't help ourselves: we didn't know how to live alone and preferred staying together to starting with someone new and winding up two or three years down the same road. But those two, what reason could they have? Maybe it was better not to wonder. I had an excuse for not sleeping with my girlfriend: I lived over five hundred kilometers from Milan. But how did Eleonora manage to convince her fiancé, whom she lived with in a rented apartment next door to his parents' house along a state road that headed straight into the fog, like something that was more terrible and psychic than a mere road? It was absurd. It was absurd that our generation believed in "the couple" and that to keep clinging to our belief, we chose not to see all the absurdities needed to preserve this illusion.

Her fiancé had never slept here, on that mattress on the floor. Our complete delusion when it comes to the institution of the couple can lead to such aberrations, such abstractions, we can only blink, denying what's plain to see. The accountant didn't even feel the need to lay claim to that territory, sleeping and fucking on that mattress upstairs, yet he still pretended that society viewed him as Eleonora's fiancé. When I was with her, after we made love, we'd both work for a few hours. We'd order delivery. Sometimes, if she worked too hard in bed, she couldn't sleep, and she'd pull small clumps of hair out scratching her scalp because her anxiety meds had stopped working and gave her migraines, and she was afraid to start taking sleeping pills; then during the day, at work, I'd catch her sleeping at her desk, head to one side, or resting on a huge contemporary Indian novel, the first galleys she'd worked on when she started at the publishing house. She was thirty (I was almost forty) and she hadn't considered whether or not she wanted children, or when, and if she did, if she'd go back to working at the same pace afterward. Her fiancé was the kind of man who told his partner that he wanted a family and then told his mother that they were still waiting, and that his partner was to blame: so her future mother-in-law, who had no other children, couldn't stand Eleonora, who'd sit watching the game with them on Sundays and, after ten minutes, pull out a manuscript and start underlining and annotating. And yet, no one ever blurted out: you're not a couple—this is fiction. And so, an entire family gathered in a living room in Lombardy defined the circumstances of my love life.

I heard the shower turn off, and Eleonora appeared at the top of the stairs in a towel and leaned over to see me at the table— "Bring up the bottle"—her damp hair dangling down.

I took my time, finished my drink in three slow sips, smiling all the while, because she still wanted me.

I climbed the stairs with the vodka and two glasses of ice, my backpack over my shoulder.

Her room had no door and was a depository for discarded belongings: shoes of various colors, T-shirts and blouses hanging on clothing racks, toys and pop memorabilia collected in Asia. The sheets on her mattress were soft, the color of marzipan. The left side of the room had floor-to-ceiling windows, and the setting sun dusted through the electric blinds with their wide, lacquer-wood slats. I was there once more, once more, and always for the last time.

The mattress lay on a wood floor that was so polished, you had to be careful walking across it in your socks. She was waiting for me, naked, on her back, propped up on her elbows, legs parted. What a joy it was to be there, she seemed so grown-up now, without me in charge of her assignments.

I knelt before her, and then, without speaking, gently slid into her. The room was warm, and soon, we were sticky with sweat. I loomed over her, on my knees so I wouldn't crush her. It was natural, the kind of sex that makes you forget hunger, thirst, and fatigue, a trance that swells and pulls you along, almost makes you want to say "I love you," though you know doing so would break the spell, which itself has nothing to do with love. The blue eyeliner smeared around her eyes, her wet bangs crowning her forehead and the long hair spread beneath her, over the pillow: she stayed like this, her legs splayed, never shifting her position. Our smells merged, mine yogurt, hers ginger. Her thighs recognized me. I had never asked her to leave her fiancé for me—I never thought she could understand me through and through. Early on, when our affair still threatened to end our respective relationships, I told her: "Can't you see—you can't build a marriage on what we have—there's too much passion!"

The long fall into twilight, cocooned in saliva and sweat.

Afterward, we lay on our backs. We felt around in the dark for our clothes. We cooled down, spraying ourselves with raisin-scented water. The smell of rain rose from flowerbeds outside through the open windows. We checked our phones; I texted Barbara.

After sex, we'd usually stay quiet until we got into the bathtub together, but now, Eleonora remained sprawled out on the bed, so I took my phone and walked to the bathroom alone, like I was protecting Barbara from Eleonora (whom she'd never seen). I threw away my condom, turned on the hot water, put in the stopper, and climbed into the tub. The tub was small, the window was open, and I could feel the warmth from the tub mixing with the cool from the rain, and I waited a bit to pour in the bubble bath, to preserve the smell of wet trees.

Still, she didn't join me. When I came out, she was in bed,

fidgeting with a dented plastic bottle on the floor, tipping it over, standing it upright. She was lying on her side, her back to me.

Then she turned, stretched her arm toward me, not quite reaching me; as she moved, her right breast rose, and two folds appeared at her hip. "Can you leave now?" she said. "I want to work alone."

I knelt, towel dropping, leaning toward her. She turned like she was about to kiss me, her mouth approached my bearded cheek, and she bit me—hard.

I yelped, rushed back to the bathroom, naked, and shoved my face under the faucet. In the mirror, her toothmarks were red. She didn't call out that she was sorry—maybe she thought I was exaggerating—I was so pissed off, when I finished pouring water over the bite I went back to her room (she was texting with someone and didn't look up), grabbed my clothes and backpack, and headed down the stairs, almost slipping, wet from my dripping hair. I got ready quickly and opened the door, my shoes still untied.

Before I slammed the door shut, though, I called up to her: "Congratulations on your career!"—a joke of ours—I'd heard a seventy-year-old intellectual say it at an elegant dinner while he was pumping away on the hand of another old man. Such a mysterious phrase. The perfect description of the foolishness of passing time.

[I began this chapter by saying I hadn't been able to figure out what this part means. It's a sentence I've kept since the first draft: I can't manage to cut it even though over time, writing and revising, I've pretty much given a meaning to what happened that night. But I'm keeping that between us, along with the other details that make up this section, as a reminder that only the imagination, not opinion, can express inner feelings.]

I walked back along the road, to the canals, and ran into two friends and stopped for a drink. One of them was a woman who at some point—when, I couldn't say—had gotten into the habit of emailing me without pretext and giving me extremely intimate hugs, more sexual than affectionate. When the other person left us on our own, I asked her to walk with me, and we wound up going to the station where my hotel was located, because she lived nearby. It was a nice long walk in that city that was always empty: on some of the wet, empty streets, the asphalt shone like marble.

She was a very pleasant woman, a PR rep, and very straight-forward, even if her job (which she was good at) required subter-fuge. A brief description of her—dark circles under her eyes, wrinkles, wavy hair, Mediterranean, languid breasts, sturdy legs but lush hips—harkens back to some fastidious nineteenth-century novel that points out a woman's wilting beauty at thirty, forty . . . Yet in spite of my description, I think the current social-financial continuity between twenty and forty is creating a world where a woman can still look and feel like a girl while already possessing that generosity and complicity, the gentle air, that real young women lack.

When we were saying goodbye, she pressed into me, and we hugged closely, as we hadn't done for a while. I smelled her hair, the only part of a person we can treat the way a dog would. She was wearing two or three layers of cotton, a dress and a cardigan, an impalpable, fleshy bundle, damp from our walk. She pressed against my erection, not pretending she wasn't. "Man, why are you married? You're not supposed to be married."

"You're so great. I'm not married."

"But you are extremely taken."

"True enough."

We said good night and parted ways, now hugging warmly, like old friends.

I arrived at the *pensione*, where I met the old proprietor. He was from Piedmont, an old guy with shining white hair and only one hand, who gave me my keys and reminded me to settle what I owed, including for that night. I found his sullenness disturbing and reassuring at the same time. The building was very well air-conditioned, and the rooms were small, half of them without windows: this evening, he gave me one without, because he assumed that I wouldn't be sleeping there, though he obviously didn't say this, I mused, as I stepped inside and set my backpack on the chair.

I turned on the TV, ordered food off an app, went into the bathroom to check the corona of bruises that had formed under my beard.

I ate my delivery sashimi; they'd dropped it off at the reception desk, and the innkeeper brought it to me himself. I drank the lukewarm sake, pouring the little bottle into a glass. The room had one small table, almost entirely taken up by the television set, which I turned off while I ate.

Behind me, the bedside lamp emitted the only light in this cramped room with its walled-up window: the overhead light was too harsh, and I never turned on the bathroom light, either—I preferred leaving the bathroom door open and showering and using the toilet to the light of the TV.

While I ate, I thought about the designer's apartment in relation to this room. I'd never gone from one to the other, from that big mattress on a wood floor to the single bed in this small, sterile space. When I slept here, I tried to arrive drunk, to just crash and sleep: in Rome, I often worked at night, but that was hard to do in Milan, in this depressing room. Now, I felt I'd fallen from grace: I'd never return to the designer's apartment. Congratulations on your career, I told myself, and took one last sip of sake to wash down the sliver of raw fish.

I had a meeting the next day at the office—I'd have to see Eleonora. With this thought, while I lay stretched out on the bed, the television back on, I asked myself out loud: "Should I go back there and tell her I love her?"

My phone was next to me, I picked it up and drafted a text: "Maybe we should try to stay together, because I can't be without you." I didn't send it. I went back to my messages and clicked on Barbara's, making sure I'd chosen correctly, rereading her name until I almost wasn't sure if she was really my live-in girlfriend; her name seemed funny, almost a stutter, like the word "barbarian," the Romans mocking the sounds those northern people made—*bar-bar*.

I wrote: "I can't bear coming up to Milan anymore. Find me a job in Rome?"

After I'd brushed my teeth, swallowed a half gram of a tranquilizer, and slipped my bare legs under the coarse sheets, she sent back a heart. With my meds kicking in and my eyes welling up, I decided I'd return to Rome tomorrow without going back to the office. The editor in chief would certainly understand: I would be doing it because Eleonora belonged to him now, and he'd forgive this rare professional lapse on my part.

Barbara

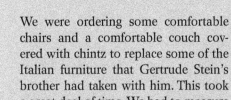

We were ordering some comfortable
chairs and a comfortable couch covered with chintz to replace some of the
Italian furniture that Gertrude Stein's
brother had taken with him. This took
a great deal of time. We had to measure
ourselves into the chairs and into the
couch and to choose chintz that would
go with the pictures, all of which we
successfully achieved.

—GERTRUDE STEIN,
The Autobiography of
Alice B. Toklas

S he was pedaling away on an exercise bike in one corner of the stage, while two actresses, one of whom had written the play, discussed their relationships with their mothers for the audience, drawing closer and connecting in a mirror exercise. It was a small production, a performance I found moving, that seemed to be about mothers failing to understand their daughters. A spotlight stayed on her, the short-haired woman pedaling on the bike. She wore a pair of old-fashioned Walkman headphones, the metal headband glinting in the bright light, and an aquamarine rayon tracksuit that was rumpled and hid her shape. She pedaled until she was breathless, singing the whole time, an Italian song I can't remember, a melody that rose and fell, like one of those blow-up air dancers in shopping-center parking lots: her voice, competent but untrained, so charming and enthusiastic, made me really want to meet her.

I got a closer look when she emerged, accompanied by her two scene partners, the playwright and the other girl: they were

arm in arm as they walked toward us. By us, I mean the playwright's parents, whom I'd begun chatting with in the fairly
uncrowded foyer. I'd headed straight for the only two older people, figuring they must be related to the playwright. My friend
Francesco had brought me along to see this show because the
playwright had proposed that they work on a project together,
but he'd just left, right after I told him I wanted to meet the girl
on the exercise bike. While I say "girl," she was really a woman
over thirty with the face of a girl: smooth and unlined.

The husband and wife were the same height, around five foot
six, both of them slightly heavy, and I remember that they both
wore brown jackets, his suede and hers vinyl, dressed warm for
the end of spring; they seemed to be very close and both seemed
startled by the performance. "You must be the parents—of the
bride." I blurted out this last part by mistake, but they found it
funny, and so we got to talking . . . That she'd never been "the
bride" was a problem for them, a problem—if you paid attention
to the version we'd just heard onstage—not unrelated to the
fact that at thirty-five years old, she was still paying for theater
space to produce her plays. They told me this with a sympathetic
and accepting tone that disappeared the minute their daughter
exited from the dressing rooms escorted by her friends.

"Hel-lo," she said slowly, and her friends kept holding on to
her. The girl in the tracksuit, now in a blue and light-striped,
eccentrically double-breasted dress, had honey-cream cheeks,
honey mixed with blush, swollen cheekbones like she'd been
punched: she had the face of a field mouse, an alien's high forehead, with a boxer's nose that looked broken, an Owen Wilson
or Belmondo nose, though her beauty wasn't androgynous and
in fact appeared carefully designed. She looked at her friend with

small, dark, loving eyes. The playwright and the bike girl were the same height as the older couple, while the third girl was almost as tall as me and seemed to know the playwright's parents, since she was slyly joking with them—"So, did you enjoy yourselves?" The playwright laughed and didn't comment.

My parents raised me to never feel inferior to anyone: the foreign publisher, the local administrator tasked with running some cultural event, the candidate for the Nobel Prize. If you're calm and humble and give people space, you'll feel comfortable anywhere. My parents never explicitly told me any of this, but there was something in the combination of my father's secular, sober confidence (he's an angel investor for young entrepreneurs) and my mother's deep Catholic faith: there's no one my parents feel inferior to because there's no one they feel superior to.

This kind of upbringing is useful when it comes to women: here I was in this intimate circle, and I felt comfortable talking to the bike girl, without knowing her name or even feeling the urge to look for it on the poster hanging by the ticket counter. I told her: "Maybe someone should write the parents' side of things . . ."

And she looked at me for the first time, her expression friendly, and said: "No, no—you've got it wrong. This is a comedy, and the mother and father are archetypes. Besides, you know—it's more based on my family than hers."

"My clients aren't the least convinced," I said while the others laughed, "it's more like a personal attack—and it warrants some kind of explanation."

And our little performance played out just as naturally as I'd hoped it would, with the two of us now continuing this conversation on our own, away from the others, as the parents said their goodbyes: "Yeah, that was something—her poor parents," she said. "But they deserved it, you know, they're pretty bad. Still, they're sweet. I kind of feel sorry for them."

The other two girls joined us, and then the four of us went out to the closest bar to buy the playwright a Campari; she wasn't laughing now; she kept thinking about her parents, saying, "Can you believe how they reacted?" to the other two.

The playwright insisted on buying for everyone and headed to the cash register, and I took advantage of the moment when the third actress went out for a cigarette to lean closer to this girl, whose name, I'd found out, was Barbara: "Let's go have dinner on our own," I said.

I stepped back, and she pursed her lips and looked away, smiling as she took her phone from her white patent-leather purse and typed in her code.

I wandered down the bar to give her some privacy—it was one of those long, narrow places that can make things awkward—and then the four of us went outside, split up, and as I headed to my moped, and, without any fuss or self-consciousness, Barbara came along, too.

We ate at an excellent Vietnamese restaurant owned by a man from Rome, who left off the "t" in "Vie'namese," and gave us our first inside joke. He stood at our table for fifteen minutes, going on and on—to the point that we stopped feeling embarrassed about our impulsive date—about his battles over social media with people who didn't understand that his restaurant served "regional Vie'namese, not national," because "talking about national Vie'namese food is technically incorrect."

He was so distracting that we could relax. I liked this woman, how she dressed, her earnest expression. Soon she was telling me about the "stagnant" phase she was going through: a boyfriend in another city who was probably seeing someone else by now.

I prodded her. "So it's been a long time since you went to bed with someone."

"Yup. You got it."

"What's that like, then?"

"Well, you know. It's spring."

"So, what would you wish for, to break this terrible dry spell?"

"Something ridiculously easy."

"Someone you don't know, someone who isn't dangerous, who can be traced—not like a stalker—just someone who does it all, takes you out, treats you nice, washes you, dries you, and sets you, all soft and ironed, back on your shelf with all your folded clothes."

She looked at me. "Boy, wouldn't that be fantastic."

"All right. First, though, you have to calm down."

"Oh, I'm very calm."

"Oh, yeah?"

"You are *very* calming."

"Well, good. Then I can calm down, myself."

We smiled at each other.

"Listen, Barbara," I said, "you're fantastic. You know what I'd like to be for you? A gay friend. I'd be a gay director, or something, and we'd have this extremely intimate relationship, because you wouldn't see me as a threat. You know—I'd get to be the gay guy in your dressing room."

"You don't seem gay to me."

"You know what I mean."

"Yes, I do."

"I'd get to be around you, but not like some vulture . . . I'd just want . . . while I'm checking out your tits, I'd want you to trust me."

We laughed.

"Marcello, you're great. I think I get what you're saying. And we can get to work on that."

"Nice diversion, don't you think? For the poor, unhappy girl-friend."

"Nice for you, too."

"Very nice indeed."

[I don't like long, drawn-out stretches of dialogue (as an editor, it just feels like a cheap way to add on pages), but I have to make an exception when it comes to the card game of seduction.]

The sun had set, and we'd finished our dinner. "These days," I told her, "I'm living on Tiburtina, a friend's ninth-floor apartment, I've just come back to Rome from Milan—I used to work there—now I travel back and forth. From my friend's place, you can see the mountains. The sky's pretty clear tonight. You know what I think we should do—we should go back to my place and make love on the balcony. My friend has a nice, big shower: you can wash up after, and then I'll take you home."

"Why wouldn't there be a shower?!" she said, laughing.

"Well, sometimes even the most mundane things are amazing. I want you to get the whole effect—like a brochure. Afterward, I'll take you home, everything all nice and easy and uncomplicated, and so you'll get to have sex with someone you feel incredibly compatible with (or maybe he's the one who feels it—he's been sucked in by your incredible charisma!), and you'll have given yourself this little treat."

"What an amazing proposal. Would you really do all that—

for me? Just amazing. And then of course, we'd never see each other again—so I wouldn't get stressed out if I ran into you somewhere." After this last absurdity, she called the waiter over for the bill and said: "You're the perfect man to see once in a lifetime."

"What a nice compliment."

We laughed.

"The poor girl who ever marries you," she said to me. "How will things ever go back to normal after the seduction?"

Then she gave her credit card directly to the owner, who accepted it with the utmost gravity, in both hands, Japanese-style.

It went as planned: we got on my Vespa, wrapped around each other, kissed for the first time in my friend's elevator—he was such a great friend, he left with only fifteen minutes' notice. I asked her if she trusted me, she said yes, then I got a condom from the bedroom, slipped it in my pocket, went out to the balcony with her, told her to hold on to the railing, and she bent over as I lifted her dress from behind, and that's how we made love, drunk and amazed with our realized fantasy, both of us mysteriously unaffected by vertigo. I came inside her, her knees buckled. After, she asked me where the shower was that I'd raved about, she had the bathroom to herself while I dressed without washing up, then took her back to her place, and I thought about her long body bent over, first on the stationary bike, then on the balcony, her small, pointed breasts, that buzzy laugh that had been with me all the way from the theater.

The next day, she wrote me that her palms had been scratched and that she liked how I took her home, even if she did have to walk back to the theater to get her moped.

* * *

The times we got together after that, I gave her what she wanted, and so those first weeks I felt pretty special. Barbara was ending things with her boyfriend, talking with him so much over Skype that sometimes she had to cancel on me. I felt so good, I stopped going out with the other women I'd been seeing. I was her pleasure, her solace while she broke away from this other man. For the time being, she had two lives: one with me that was almost entirely secret (though her roommate knew), and then another, pale and listless life with a man she'd been seeing long-distance for three years.

But if everything was going great, it wasn't just because I was fulfilling a fantasy role for a woman no longer in love or because I felt I'd found someone like-minded, whose vision of life was inspiring; there was a third and fundamental factor—her apartment, the last one on a dead-end lane, before the canebrake leading down to the boulevard.

It was a one-story building, square and white, of unknown origin, maybe a railway building once, or an abandoned warehouse, and rumor had it that drug addicts had squatted there, until finally an architect bought the building, stripped it, and put in modern insulation. The building was now divided into three units, each with a section of roof for a terrace that you got to by a spiral staircase from the small courtyard near the entranceway.

Barbara wound up there after living in various parts of Rome, always renting and subletting with various female friends; but this group of friends, including the two from the theater, had dispersed, many going off to live with their male partners, some of them breeding. Barbara didn't want children, and so she found this recently restored place; the area, around Via Casilina, was quiet, with no loud clubs, just a very quiet communist bar at the edge of the neighborhood. She'd been looking there awhile before she found something and had been in this home now for a few years, lately with a roommate.

I fell for the neighborhood the same way I'd fallen for her. On the piazza, the usual five people would be sitting in the bar and someone always sat outside the tobacco shop. A couple of people in electric wheelchairs would go by on the streets. Some didn't work because they were rich, some because they were poor. Nearby, in Torpignattara, the social mishmash brought on tensions and the fear of Islamic terrorist infiltration. But here, in this wedge between the consular road and the high-speed trains, it only generated a sleepy charm in a breeze blowing along this backstreet cut with dead-end lanes, like degrees on a thermometer.

I grew up in a Rome thick with large supermarkets and apartment buildings that were taller than the zoning laws allowed; I never expected my home or neighborhood to bring me any peace or pleasure. But here, a hundred meters from the projects along Via Casilina, you'd find courtyards and one- or two-story houses. The only disturbance came from cars driving through to avoid the traffic in Torpignattara.

The vast sky and the area's haphazard construction—former barracks and the occasional fascist-era building—inspired a calm impossible to describe without getting lost in this hypnotic perfection that somehow let you ignore the lack of parking or the uncollected garbage piled three or four meters high behind the dumpsters.

As soon as Barbara told her roommate that she was leaving her boyfriend for someone new, I started coming over before dinner, traveling along Via Casilina, by the light-rail tracks and the Roman aqueduct. If not for the traffic, my heart would have slowed down right then. The yellow and gray train cars, the stone pines, the ruins of arches with the barracks underneath, the Roman castles in the background that seemed distant with the sky a thin cobweb of pink and gray, or extremely close when it was clear out; sometimes, though, the sky was sticky with spun-sugar clouds. If there was a lot of traffic early on, then I'd only feel calmer once I turned right, by the carpenter's shop, the air sweet with sawdust. That street ran along the high-speed rail line, and an abandoned mattress, worn down by the elements, was always lying in that desolate space by the tracks. After a hundred meters, you entered the area of that district where a small community lived, intimate, Roman, where everyone had known each other forever; the community accepted the foreigners quietly living there, the Egyptians, Indians, Chinese, Romanians, who didn't go to the bar on the piazza and lived in the ground-floor apartments. You'd see them in groups of no more than three, private communities, invisible, never projecting hostility. Then, there were the well-off Italians fleeing their middle-class neighborhoods. Where I grew up, people were always offended when someone else was double-parked; here, you could stop the car a moment and greet someone, and not get scolded by car horns. [I know—this isn't the most urgent take on the complex issue of gentrification, by which I mean the bourgeois assault on working-class neighborhoods—but it does illustrate the feeling of paradise I experienced during those early days of love, even though the editor in me feels compelled to point out that I've painted this neighborhood like a colonial English gentleman might paint a "quaint" Indian village.]

The interior of the apartment was even better. Three rooms on the ground floor, and a steep wood staircase leading down to a basement room converted to a bedroom. This is where her friend lived, paying two hundred euros a month and still getting natural light through a glass door that led to a small cellar space dug out from the earth and covered in grids and glass panels.

The walls were all painted a soothing sand color. When the sun came in, the light was warm and comforting. It was always quiet, and the courtyard and terrace were filled with plants. Barbara had excellent taste in decorating. On the wall, beneath a skylight, hung an antique gray print-shop cabinet filled with coffee cups and glasses and knickknacks; during the day, this cabinet was draped in light. A beautiful, refinished 1960s Danish table stood beneath it, and across the dining room was an armchair where I'd sit and watch the sun from the skylight playing over the cabinet, and I'd relax and read a manuscript before getting to work.

After knowing each other only a month, I started paying half the rent, as soon as Barbara's friend took off, with the secret agreement—I learned about this much later—that she wouldn't look for another room for two months and would stay with someone else (I don't know who), waiting to see if things worked out between Barbara and me, or if she could move back in.

She never did, and in those first months, it felt like a miracle that I'd settled into that apartment with this woman who was living the good life. It was the happiest place I ever laid my head, and all it took was the lavish wooing of a stranger.

In the end, this was all a case of masculine pride. For a long while, having successfully played the peacock and won that glorious apartment, I completely ignored Barbara's life, her history, like this was all in the past, like the world starts over once a man struts around for a woman.

But the warmth and comfort of that place came from Barbara's past: from her misery at not having a room to herself growing up. Barbara's parents separated when she was two. When she was a teenager, an insensitive aunt told her: "You know what the problem was? Your parents couldn't stand two years of your bad tonsils: food would get caught in your tonsils, and you were too small for surgery, so you always had infections and your parents never got any sleep . . ." Her mother and father quickly built new families. Her father would have two boys and was extremely attached to her, his girl: but unfortunately, his new wife, when her stepdaughter was a teenager—especially after Barbara discovered her tonsils had been the cause of her family's being pulled apart—became a stepmother right out of a fairy tale, strict and mean, and with the excuse of making the girl more refined (she was a teacher at Barbara's high school), made her feel stupid, which was not how she treated her sons. Barbara lived at her father's every other weekend, and the rest of the time the family went on as a family, without her, and her room doubled as a storeroom, a place to iron, a bed for the babysitter. If they had guests when she was there, if a grandmother came to see her grandchildren, Barbara slept on a cot set up in the living room, behind a couch, by the window. Her brothers were two years apart, and she was older than the youngest by seven years.

At her mother's, it was much better—until middle school—when her mother had a daughter with her new partner, something she'd resisted for years, afraid of how it might affect Barbara, but finally she did get pregnant, and since there wasn't much money, when Barbara's little half sister was three, the two of them were put in a room together: the thirteen-year-old with the three-year-old in twelve square meters. Their place had two floors, and Barbara started staying downstairs, sleeping on the couch and keeping her things in the large drawer at the base of the bookshelf.

Lying on that couch, Barbara became an insomniac and an avid reader. As soon as she could, she worked in coffee bars and during the last years of high school, began traveling with her girlfriends. She started having boyfriends as a teenager, never staying with any of them more than three years. For college, she moved to Rome and joined in with some feminist-art circles, where *A Room of One's Own* became her religion, well beyond the subject of the female novel: you needed five hundred symbolic silver pounds a year and a room of your own, as Woolf said, to be able to do anything. Barbara never lived with a man— well, she tried once, but it lasted less than a month. She could only live with women, women who were "politically aware" and not inclined to invade her space. She'd go to the man's place, countering the old-fashioned belief that women should stick close to the nest. Barbara visited men in their neighborhoods like she was on a trip, so afterward, she could return to her room.

I'd led her to believe, though, that this time, she could open her home to a man and not lose her freedom.

She'd never let men into her personal realm, not even with long-term relationships, preferring to betray—and to be betrayed— to the intimacy of living as a couple, which would suffocate her, take away her room of her own. In private, Barbara was more closed off than she was in public or with her friends: in private, she wasn't good at asking, at getting what she wanted.

She considered herself to be someone who existed more in public than in private, and working in the theater, she could enjoy spending every night of her life far from home (right from the start, I'd ask to stay at her place and would eat dinner there by myself).

The evening after I returned from Milan with a corona of bruises under my beard—that bite—I didn't see Barbara at home; I saw her in a crowded bookstore.

The store was on a narrow road with hunched, early-nineteenth-century buildings, a neighborhood along the city walls, full of students and drug dealers. I was walking with Francesco, my best friend, a writer: we'd been drinking since four that afternoon, and balancing the two of us on my Vespa had gotten too difficult. We're both over two hundred pounds, he's taller than me, six foot two, and we both like to eat and drink. It was only after we'd been drinking and riding along on the scooter that he told me the magazine he edited wouldn't be renewing his contract as they'd promised. I arrived at the bookstore with this awful news in my heart and a pair of new sneakers on my feet. We stuck out: big, tall, almost drunk, him in baggy pants and a jacket, me in shorts and my bright-white shoes, and holding a plastic bag with the shoes I'd been wearing.

The street was crowded, mainly with people I knew. I'd worked with many of them but had either lost track or lost interest. Even just by the doorway, I saw two from publicity that I'd had affairs with at different times, never telling anyone; they were chatting with a journalist whose book I'd rejected ten years before. Sitting on the scooter of an old friend of mine was a guy I used to meet for coffee once a week, but then, after a summer of doing this, I just quit; there was a woman with whom I used to exchange book recommendations, but when she took a long trip to Africa, I forgot all about our shared interest: I watched her say goodbye to a former author of mine and then go off to talk with the guy I used to meet for coffee.

I couldn't seem to show up sober for these things. Plus, that evening, inside the long, cramped bookstore filled with the best picture books and bottles of Sardinian wine and carrot-cake cupcakes, there was a presentation of a book by one of my former students, Leone, who'd moved to a new publisher, leaving me after I'd acquired and published his first two novels. And not only that: apparently, one Sunday morning last spring, Leone and Barbara met up in Villa Borghese to discuss a theater project for high schools. I was still in bed when Barbara had left the apartment with a container of wild strawberries and chocolate drops; along the way, she stopped to buy a bag of *lingue di gatto*. Francesco had told me this a few hours earlier, while we were sitting, drinking sparkling Campari and negronis on the steps of a fountain in a small piazza in the historic city center: "Leone was sure they'd sleep together," Francesco let slip, because he was drunk, and obviously still shaken up from learning about his canceled contract: "And Barbara felt bad—it was a misunderstanding. So naive. Afterward, Leone insulted her behind her back to a few people and stopped talking to her. I don't know—maybe they've made up, since you're saying she'll be there tonight. He was super embarrassed about it, though. Because it really seemed like she wanted it. And Barbara, you know, she's getting bored with you, and she's thrown herself into trying to make things right with Leone. She thinks about it nonstop."

Listening to him was torture. I remember there was gum on

the seat of my shorts from the fountain steps, and I listened to Francesco while I leaned over and studied this mess on my shorts, standing up and twisting around, and what he was telling me, and this stickiness, and the sickening sweetness of my drink, all merged into one.

The most complicated thing for me to accept, while I opened the glass door to the bookstore, was that there, inside, way toward the front, just as I imagined I'd see as I moved forward with my bag of shoes, past unknown bodies, in the fall humidity, that person sitting there was the person who shared a bed with me, shared the bills with me, the person who stepped outside with me in the morning, and tossed the bag of cabbage and fish bones into the garbage.

There she was, at a small table up front. From where I stood near the back, I saw her in profile: her high forehead, her cheekbone, her undyed hair, sleek, dark brown, with thicker strands of white. That day, she exuded sex: this way, she truly looks the part of the actress; when she's nervous and withdrawn, she just looks old. That day, she was beautiful, holding a small glass of beer, her nails painted blue-gray.

She was very close to Leone, who sat on a stool while he spoke to the moderator. I was still toward the back, with everybody else standing, and I listened along with the others to the discussion about the Articolo Uno Movement, all the dead workers, Gaetano Bresci, the '77 Movement: and she was listening to him, her chin raised.

Had they kissed? Barbara knows how to kiss, even with those thin lips; she must have thought about how ever since she was a girl, how exactly to kiss with those lips. Did Leone think he'd be better at it than me—at living with her? Her severe profile, her confidence, the light way she carries herself, these attributes have attracted many who thought they could do a better job in my place. These suitors would text her for weeks or months on end about meeting for lunch or for happy hour; she wouldn't tell me outright when it happened, but when we argued, she let me know that she questioned if staying with me made any sense. This happened so often, in fact, that while I was seeing Eleonora, I'd tell myself that Barbara wanted a boyfriend just to have one—an adult pacifier. She said herself that she was afraid of chaos, and I was well aware that she always cheated on her boyfriends.

I stood at the back, admiring her and sweating. She was taking small sips from her beer in a manner completely different from how she drained her glass at home when she and I would down three martinis and fall asleep by ten, forgetting to eat dinner. She nodded, smiled along with the others to the rhythm of the conversation and the readings. She dabbed her forehead with a folded tissue; she applied lip gloss and dropped it back in her leather purse with the metal buckle, which scratched me sometimes when I fished for a phone charger or a theater ticket.

She was there for Leone, listening to him, looking up at him, like everybody else. I walked out.

I had dinner alone at a trattoria on the piazza down the street, where the waitress always called me "darling." She must have been about my age [since writing this I've discovered that she's ten years older than me and that the restaurant is hers—she's not a waitress—but I've left the previous, naive description in, because now that we're talking about women, it feels significant for me to make this blunder: she's the owner and she's youthful, not a servant and prematurely aged, like I made her out to be; she's aged well with her androgynous style, her dyed and streaked hair, and her bright green tennis shoes]. I leaned over my plate of spaghetti with clam sauce, rolling pasta onto my fork, trying to sober up, reading the sports page on my phone; and if I thought about my situation, I couldn't see a way out.

A few nights later, in a completely different frame of mind, I helped put on an event for one hundred people in a penthouse apartment in the historic city center. I'd asked the owner, a social-ite, to organize the launch party for a novel by a talented writer we were hoping to get out of her niche with a book that had both literary and commercial potential. This woman with the pent-house apartment was just getting into public relations, so it was useful for her as well to receive these people I'd invited into her home, these journalists, writers, screenwriters, directors, and crit-ics whose names she could save in her Rolodex. The writer had always steered clear of "salons," but she liked my idea, because the novel spoke of Tangentopoli, a familiar story, now modern-ized, without moralizing, about a man embroiled in the Tangen-topoli corruption scandal, and then exonerated in a typically Italian-Catholic way, in that he might still be considered guilty. The Roman world the book depicted—a world of salons like this one—was still talking about him, sketching him out in various conflicting ways: the novel was composed of three stories about him, interwoven, like they were entirely separate.

[Of the characters discussed so far, those participating that evening were Barbara, who'd come on her own because she knew her various theater and editing friends would be there, including

Leone; Francesco, with Giò; and then the woman I'd embraced near the Milan station just ten days before, the PR rep whose agency was in charge of the event.]

I made a few short introductory remarks in the spacious, minimalist room, with Petri's *Investigation of a Citizen Above Suspicion* silently projected onto a white wall. Half this space was given over to long couches beneath the sloping ceiling, the light harmonious, rising from unseen points, and the windows looking out over other fashionable evenings, both large and small, other roofs and terraces and large, indulgent windows. I finished by reading one of this author's old poems that began: "We are the ambiguous forms."

That evening, I wanted publishing to return for one moment to the search for pure pleasure and beauty, to distract itself from the domain of the literal content of things. Basically, I wanted to throw a party, and I had. I drank three gin and tonics before I spoke, hoping I'd stop at just the point of being free but not lightheaded. I'd succeeded, but right when I finished reading the poem, everything seemed to lose substance, because I was beginning to relax and my stomach felt empty and sour: so there's a decisive moment I barely remember. I was surrounded by several others, including Francesco and two extremely young, unpublished writers, and the PR rep stood in front of me, and she was endearingly unhinged: she was "so very thrilled" with how the night had turned out, and was staring at me with a look that I sort of understood and that I was sort of forgetting, it felt like I was being entirely embraced, unwinding after all the tension I'd experienced the last few days, and right at the center of this was her weak, smiling face.

She wore a white blouse open to the sternum; her nose was

slightly crooked, and she was perfectly elegant, the kind of
woman who in a different generation would have married a pol-
itician, but in this day and age was too elegant to concede anything to a man. She was brazen enough to wear silver: tight,
silver pants. I was dazed by her presence, and all I remember is
that I'd singled out Barbara, ten meters away, talking in a little
cluster of Leone's friends, maybe with Leone himself, and I was
drunk and relaxed from the success of the evening, and I hoped
she wasn't looking my way, because the PR rep was leaning into
me; while I stood chatting with everyone, she was right there, I
could feel her body touching mine.

We went up to the roof, up a stairway with no handrail.
To a small, plain room leading out to a balcony—small, square,
commanding—surely, Barbara wouldn't see us up there, but the
two writers, they would, they'd followed us, because for them the
big party was all about being young and newly on the scene and
getting to talk with the grown-ups and drinking (that was when
Mad Men was so popular, and every night when you lifted your
elbow, you wound up comparing yourself to that debauched,
imaginary world). Francesco and Giò might have left already: the
PR rep just kept leaning into me. I was feeling pretty compro-
mised. God knows what those kids thought, it must have seemed
so great, they probably spread it all around, the same way I did
at the start of my career, when I was thrilled if I saw some important writer arm in arm with his lover strolling around in some
town during a festival.

As the evening came to an end, this woman and I went down
the stairs together, and I discovered that in the meantime, Barbara had gone off to dinner with some group, so I thought I was

safe. I knew, before long, I'd have to leave that home where I'd been so happy, Barbara's home, because she and I weren't happy.

The rep and I walked down the wide, slippery stairs of the ancient palazzo, down into the Baroque piazza; I pointed to my scooter parked by a street just off the piazza. I unhooked my helmet from under the saddle; I laid it at my feet and sat sideways on the bike, facing her. She came closer, and we talked about work: "I want everything to be like this," she said, "all glamour, nerd-glamour, something sensual, something hot, not this endless, awful boredom . . ."

While we were celebrating our mutual professional understanding, I could feel myself swelling against the overly heavy cotton fabric of my pants, my hard-on pressed against the silver fabric of her pants and touched her; she was hot, electric. We weren't holding each other or looking each other in the eye. We spoke incoherently, groin to groin: "Let's agree to meet as soon as you're back in Milan, let's make sure that idiot boss of yours understands that this is how you blend high and low, how you lift your literary authors out of the mothballs . . ."

"No, listen, you make him understand—you'd say it better than I would . . ."

All this friction, me pulsing and feeling her shifting slightly, back and forth.

"We'll have a blast," she said.

At this point, I laid my hands right on her hips, to feel her jacket, feel her, her belt and pants, I held on to her while we rubbed against each other, and without moving away, I told her: "I really have to get going—let's continue this some other time."

"Sure thing," she said, and kissed the corner of my mouth.

She'd pulled back, paused, her hands on my hands on her hips, and then she was gone.

I rode cautiously, for an eternity, until I arrived at Francesco's eight-story building. I'd texted that I was coming back our way—we lived in adjoining neighborhoods—and that I'd stop for a quick visit. I saw their door was ajar, they were out on the balcony, I shouted up that my stomach was killing me, and I heard them laugh, "Come on up then." I went to the bathroom and to relieve my stress, I masturbated, sitting on the toilet. I'd never been indifferent to Giò, though we were like brother and sister, and I'd always felt Fra's sexual energy, he was a big man, his mouth always open, with his gritty, contagious laugh that at times cut through certain steep nights, seeming to make women fall all over themselves when they spoke to him. I washed up, splashed my face to wake myself, and joined them on the balcony, where they were sitting smoking pot and admiring the lights of the buildings that, with the occasional gap, led up the Appian Way to the Roman castles. The glorious view was their favorite pastime.

They handed me the joint, and after taking a hit, I became even more disoriented, and said: "I guess I'll be moving out. Did you see? We came by ourselves, and we left by ourselves. Me and Barbara."

"Poor thing," Giò said. "Has it really come to that? You two seem so great together, even when you're not talking. Tonight I saw you guys say hello—so private."

"At the party?"

"Yeah, at the party!"

"I don't remember." This surprised me—I'd come over because I wanted to know if the PR rep and I had been too conspicuous. I tried again: "Sooner or later, she'll catch me flirting with someone, and then she'll leave me."

"But she told me you both were free to flirt."

Francesco kept quiet. He was sitting beside the glass partition between their balcony and the neighbor's. My arm was hooked through the swinging chair, for fear of throwing myself over. "Fra, what did you tell me the other day, before the presentation?"

"That she was hanging out with Leone." He sat up, laughed. "It's over, Giò, it's over. Let him talk. Poor things. So much love. Now it's all over."

"Wait," I said. "Don't get carried away. You told me—your exact words: 'That might also be a way for you to get in touch with another part of yourself.'"

"What do you mean by 'that'?" Giò asked.

"I mean—what Barbara's doing with Leone."

"Oh my god," she laughed, "Franceschino, you know, sometimes you can really shoot your mouth off."

"Giò," I said, "the real problem is, if we break up, then I have to leave my home."

"Yeah"—suddenly absorbed—"but *she's* home."

"True," I said.

"*She's home.* Oh my god," she said. "I never really thought about it."

That balcony lent itself to existential conversations. My two friends were going through a period when the only thing that was certain in life was that unrenovated apartment, those ivory-colored outlets, the pink-speckled floors, the kitchen cupboards

lined with cherry-red contact paper, and the strangeness of a sofa
bed right next to the sideboard, where I'd sleep now and then if
Barbara had her girlfriends staying over.

Giò's grandmother had bought the apartment when the
building was under construction, but then left the area shortly
after because her husband, a railwayman, had a larger place in a
more central location. Giò was her favorite grandchild, and when
this area was becoming more hip, she invited her to move here.

In some ways, for Giò and Fra, this apartment was the only
thing they could depend on. They were two good writers who
hadn't published in over five years. During those five years,
they'd had two miscarriages. Once in a while, she wrote some
fiction with a friend of hers who had an in with RAI, and the rest
of the time, she worked with refugees, gave private Latin lessons,
and worked in the espresso bar in the bookstore from the other
night; for a year, he'd been the social media manager for a magazine, and the editor promised him a fixed contract but then re-
neged because the magazine was losing money on its website,
and so he decided to hire some viral content experts, so they
could focus on that along with their daily assignments.

You can project any thought at all onto another couple.
Watching them smoke their homegrown weed, rocking on their
porch swing, creaking, suspended in emptiness on their eighth-
floor balcony, looking out at the long trail of low mountains,
sometimes dark, sometimes light, and the tall buildings in the
nearby working-class areas, those built with a utopian vision and
those that had just been thrown up, and all the houses and pine
trees in between, and the splashes of green or cement, yellowish
in the streetlamps, you might conclude—and so what if Francesco sometimes shared kisses with other women or Giò did god

knows what (she was a street-smart woman, passionate about sex and drugs, yet she had her own fascinating, extremely private temperance)—what you might conclude is that this house, these two, were truly one. They made love seem possible. And I knew, in Giò's eyes, that love seemed possible for Barbara and me. One couple incites another, a mirror game where happiness truly seems in range, if for others then also for us, though it didn't feel within our grasp.

Days earlier, after leaving Milan, and then that long after-noon drinking with Fra, we'd gotten on my scooter to go to Le-one's event, and we struggled to keep the bike straight. I don't remember who wrote that drinking at lunch fractures the day into golden fragments—when you drink at five, those fragments are bronze. Fra was tall and heavy behind me, and the bike wob-bled on its tiny wheels. At the traffic light, I put out my arm to slip between the cars. Since my blinkers didn't work, at intersec-tions I signaled right or left with my hand, and in those few im-balanced seconds, the scooter turned to stone . . . And that's when he told me, and I had to stop: "I'm not getting a contract. In two months, I'm out of a job." I craned my head to look at him, risking our falling over; I felt him plant his feet on the road to keep us steady.

"That's awful."

"I'll start writing. I'll finish the new book."

I didn't see how Francesco could find something else in Rome. "Go to Milan," I said. "Go work for *Rivista Studio*." But going to Milan means Giò can't come, and they'll break up. I told him: "Commute, then, just try something," and I saw that secret look in his eyes, there was sand, something of the sea, the urge to do nothing.

For Francesco, a life entirely suspended was beautiful. His true task was to live well and he was doing that, with Giò: here they were, and they welcomed me in any day at all, with that affection. And here I was, still thinking, like everyone else, that other couples can be happy . . .

And so here I sat on their swinging chair, eyes closed to avoid the vast emptiness through the iron rails, Giò's head on my shoulder, while Fra ground more weed in his red pocket grinder.

*O*ne October Sunday, after seeing a dance-theater production that went on all night, I jotted down my first reflections about Barbara and me, and months later, these germinated into an idea for writing an entire book. Proof that our unhappiness was balanced out, in a fundamental way, by pleasure, though when I spoke with Francesco and Giò, I'd forget:

Me and her in a balcony box in the Teatro Argentina, at three in the morning. Onstage, six rectangular tables covered in large flower petals, an actress sitting on each table. The women have their legs spread for the audience, and with paint brushes, are gluing petals of various colors, shapes, and sizes all around their vaginas. Barbara and I drowsily watch from above: they're at enough of a distance that what's happening doesn't seem real. This part of the show keeps going, Barbara and I whisper to each other that we're excited and we talk about desire, and I say I'd like to fuck every woman on that stage; sometimes our eyes close, we blink, sip from our water bottles. The performers' concentration is putting us to sleep. An eighteenth-century theater open all night for us.

Later, before sunrise, we drive through Rome on my scooter, feeling electrified, happy. Our parents have never seen naked people on a stage.

In this darkness of balconies and orchestras, the stage lights reflect in her dark eyes, and I feel shooting pains in my back from my cramped position. In this theater darkness, I can accept that the world might be mysterious—until the next day, when I read the authoritative, scathing review in the paper and I start to think this excited dream was just trash.

(. . .)

Trash and masterpieces plunge us into a sensation that this life happening now is a representation, something secret between us, that's realer than real. Certain nights, for instance, her menstrual cramps transform her into some character, a dying person. She let me help her once, the bathroom door cracked open, everything spilling from her, into the toilet. I'd go by, see her sitting or on her knees, I'd help her, bring her a glass of water, a towel. She really thought she might die, though the next day it was as if nothing had happened. Our bathroom that night held the absurdity and solemnity of a long performance. She went back to bed, feverish, in pain, forgetting to flush, ranting she was going to black out, leaving me to the scene, to the sediment of her convulsions at the bottom of the toilet: grotesque, sophisticated, like a tour de force where actors and dancers end up sprawled and spent among shreds of beef they've had sex with, raw potatoes, feathers, un- wound videocassettes, tape pulled out, stage strewn with objects, greasy, wet, genitals rubbing on the piece of cloth covering the planks, the stench rising to the highest balcony ring . . .

At the show's climax, Barbara checks her watch and says, "I think it's about to end," and sits up straighter, preparing to exit the dream.

(. . .)

In spite of everything, certain things do exist between us. We each help the other to pursue a beautiful life, even if we both carry within us the injunction to cease: one day, sooner or later, we'll feel called to a purpose higher than pleasure, maybe we'll have children, adopt, be aging parents, legitimate people with the right to live, to be valued.

We own vibrators—one's remote-controlled. We know our liquor bottles on the tray on the Danish table. When she's out in public, Barbara's terrified of losing control, but at home, we get wasted on martinis and she asks me to go down on her, or we fight over things we forget by the next morning, or we really get down to it and talk about our past and there's always a moment when her eyes fill up with tears.

Maybe my therapist is right: I'm hiding from the fact that Barbara makes me feel good. I find it easier to talk about enjoyment with a lover than a wife: "Who is it you have to tell about your enjoyment?" my therapist asked me. "Who do you have to assure that you're not happy?"

(. . .)

This relationship of ours has reached the point where our shared pleasure feels incestuous—we draw close to it, then pull away.

Sometimes things don't work out with a woman because she begins to represent desire itself: a desire so strong it frightens us. We degrade the relationship and humiliate our own desire, and some part of us is happy about this—it feels right.

I try to pretend for a moment that Eleonora is my wife and
Barbara is my lover—Barbara eludes me far more than Eleonora.
She's too intense. Eleonora is like me: give her a manuscript and
she stops right there and the night is over. When I met Barbara,
I was convinced she was the love of my life. That's why I shut
down.

(. . .)

Her skin smells like mine, yogurt against yogurt, and early on,
we'd say that maybe the real reason we decided to live together
was that we smelled the same, and so we immediately trusted
each other.

To keep at bay all the pleasure our common smells might
promise, she has a ritual: after a weekend of tenderness, Monday
evening she'll be tense when she comes home from work: "Ah,
you're already back. Why are you on the couch?" Or: "Why are
you in the bathtub?" Or when a trip is winding down, the last
day, she'll find an excuse (turbulence on a flight, a downpour on
a drive) to put herself into a bad mood, so pleasure won't spill
over into normal life.

At our darkest moments, she says, "We're worthless."

(. . .)

[These pages were a first foothold. It was hard for me to seriously confront our problems because I'm a typical Italian who's
always got himself a steady, token girlfriend—guys like me are
incapable of truly being alone and analyzing our own emotions.

Francesco insists that in novels by real men, from Philip Roth
to Edoardo Nesi (only the best), the man must *endure* a woman's
incomprehensibility, as if this were natural, just one of the ways
life is unfair: for Francesco, these books don't portray real rela-

tionships between men and women who know each other deeply. In these great male novels, men are restless, they make mistakes, they struggle, and the novel is a pinball machine where the women are bumpers that ring and light up when touched— they're so striking, so crucial, that they seem like main characters, but they're really only a function of the man's little steel ball.

In spite of my own nearsightedness, I think I do know Barbara, and I have a relationship with her that I can describe, but in order to do this, I'd have to step outside of the mold of the man who makes mistakes, the man who bounces back.

On the other hand, there's no saying that by leaving the safe path—which I've urged so many young writers to do, sending them off to study the masters—I'll manage to land somewhere, in the unwritten androgynous literature that Woolf called for a century ago, but which, with the mystifying banality of prose, seems unattainable.]

Let's take a look at her, let's see if I can manage to get her down.

In front of the lady at the fish counter, the loudspeakers announcing the store would be closing, she stood comically straight, something she'd learned from her mother, that you stand up straight when you order at a counter: "And the gilthead? Is it locally caught?"

Barbara was a fish herself: from nose to chest, she was completely rigid, cold, symmetrical, shoulders defined in her sleeveless, red-and-white striped shirtdress. The woman behind the counter, with her white coat and big, black eyebrows, held up a farm-raised gilthead, and after weighing it, slipped her fist inside the belly to rip out the guts, tossing them down the hole at the center of the filthy counter.

I asked Barbara: "You girls planning your Christmas trip?"

"Oh, sure. But we're still waiting because Michi's not sure when she has off."

"Mm. I'd like to get out of town this year, too."

She pretended to concentrate on the shop assistant, blurry in the fluorescent lights behind her, who was scaling the fish with a grater, gripping the fish under the water, shifting the hose. I knew Barbara was annoyed by what I'd said. She paused, then replied curtly, "Good idea. You should get away."

"Yeah."

"Go visit your cousin, maybe—he invited you."

In the checkout line, she criticized me, saying that I was getting a late start, in her opinion.

The fish wrapped in blue paper proceeded down the conveyor belt, along with a bottle of wine, some bitter chocolate, not much else. "Can I kiss you?" I hugged her and gave her a kiss, which she seemed surprised by. I could taste her lip gloss. "Is that mint?"

"It's something gross—from a guy at work because I'm always losing mine."

I imagined this stranger kissing her. She was beautiful, and I wanted other men to think so.

While we walked up the street, headed back home with our bags, I said: "Where else could I go for vacation? Where are you all going?"

"You want to horn in on our trip?"

"Maybe. Me and all your girlfriends—we'd have a blast."

"Right. You could go hide out somewhere with three manuscripts. You wouldn't bother anyone."

"Really? Could I?"

"Come on. What would you do—go find someone else to 'work' with, and you two 'work' together?"

"So where are you going?"

"Not sure yet. Lisbon, maybe. So how much time will you have to spend in Milan over the holidays?"

"Actually, I'm thinking I won't go back between Christmas and Easter. Maybe not even after that."

"What do you mean?"

"I don't know. I'm just joking."

"Oh, sure. Joke all you want. You always make me sleep alone."

I stopped, carefully set my two bags on the roof of a car, and hugged her, lifting her off the ground: "You're right." We started kissing warily.

Barbara's mouth was dense, cool; her lips were chapped. When I set her back down, she looked me in the eye for a moment. A pack of rice and some zucchini dropped to the ground from one of the grocery bags. I told her: "What if you and I go away alone together, right now, and forget about Christmas? We won't take time off."

Her eyes shut down. I looked away; I squatted to pick up the fallen groceries. We started walking again, in silence.

By the time we opened the iron grid over the front door, I'd forgotten about her long silence; I filled the fridge, withdrew into the bathroom, turned on the fan, and put some music on my phone, because the bathroom door faces the bedroom.

Through the different sounds, I heard the bedroom door slam. I slowed down, kept sitting, listened to music, and after flushing, I washed myself with various cleansers, intimate, then facial, then a bar of soap for my armpits; before I left the bathroom, I put my shirt back on, cleaned my ears with a cotton swab.

I turned the key and looked in to find that the bed was suddenly unmade, and there was a wet blotch in the center. Barbara could cry quite a bit, and all at once. I felt my heart clench, and I didn't know where to go. I turned—I was in the doorway—and I opened the closet: on the highest shelf, where we kept our suitcases, the red roller bag was missing. I stepped into the courtyard and looked toward the street. Her scooter was gone.

The red roller bag has a symbolic purpose. Barbara looks at it to remind herself that she's free to escape whenever she wants. This isn't the only manifestation of her restlessness toward domestic life: at dusk, for instance, I can't lower the rolling shutters all the way, or she'll feel like she's suffocating. We don't lower them fully until she goes to bed.

Anytime at all, she could fill her red roller bag with her miniature clothes and run off. She'd done that with me several times. Each time was quietly revelatory: her escape expressed distance, but also measured that distance. As though our relationship had developed in such a way that Barbara had the right to be seen leaving, to be grieved for.

When she did this, I'd pour myself a drink—tonight, a whiskey soda—and lie down on the bed. Two drinks later, I picked up my phone and started writing her loving texts. I thought it was fine for her to leave, though I insisted she tell me which of her friends she was staying with. All of a sudden I missed her voice, and called, but she didn't answer.

I texted her that I had no problem with her staying overnight someplace else, it was fine.

She responded: "If you have no problem with me leaving, then why are we even together?"

"I like this about you—I like how you run away from home."

There was something, I wrote, that made me still have hope for our ridiculous relationship.

She wrote that my texts cheered her up.

It was almost two in the morning, we'd been texting for hours and from my bed, through the window and wisteria leaves, beyond the grate and past the low wall, I saw the front of two cars parked herringbone-style on the empty, dead-end road. I geared up to get out of bed, shut the glass door, brush my teeth, or maybe eat something.

Now Barbara was more present than ever, and I was like a scientist grappling with antimatter, reflecting on that sense of absence and tenderness, that momentary clear-cut distance.

It was early morning when we began our long car ride from a resort on the Dead Sea to Aqaba. First, we drove the winding roads into Jordan's interior, up to sea level and higher, above the pool of blue-gray haze where the salt lake hid. On the opposite shore, far off, was Israel, like a mirage, droves of men on horseback raising dust. Stepping outside the church of the Jerusalem mosaic, it was over a hundred degrees at noon, and we wandered a town's one-way streets, in search of bottled water and juice.

The King's Highway is famous for that section of canyon where people stop to take pictures of the carved sand formations along the curling road. Barbara managed to get a few good shots of me: I was sitting, hunched over, though she thought I looked glamorous, face in three-quarter view, hand propped nicely on my leg—a real, honest-to-god portrait. She hadn't taken my photo in a long time.

Looking through those pictures, I said something stupid, something languid and disrespectful: "So, are you starting to love me a little?"

She grabbed the phone away and kicked me in the shin, hurting herself through her sandal; she got in the car while I stayed where I was, drinking in the vastness of the canyon. I muttered to myself: "I think we're almost there. And it's not just me being stubborn, but for now"—I had no idea if she was looking at me through the glass—"one thing I know is, in another life, we have a great relationship, and it's not true that love is an illusion. But only in that parallel world. When she pulls away, it's like we're finally together . . ." I turned; she was reading the map. I wanted to kiss her, I got up, walked over, opened the car door, and leaned in to kiss her temple. "I really love you."

"I love you, too, my darling." She raised her hand, caressed my face, and drew me close.

"Really?"

"Yes, I do—look, though, don't we have a while left to go? I'm not sure—is this where we are now?" She was pointing to a spot east of the Dead Sea.

I sat on the edge of her seat and we studied the map together. She was right. We couldn't get to Aqaba, driving from village to village on that hesitating road where, not just in the denser areas—those lined-up villages and squares—but on the faster sections, too, kids stood selling tomatoes at the side of the road.

I got back behind the wheel and we sped off, without a clear idea of what to do.

"I don't want to wind up driving at night. That scares me."

"I know, honey. We'll figure it out."

Since we'd started our trip, we'd already been stopped three times by the highway police, and this filled her with anxiety. The rental car GPS kept switching off and the touchscreen barely worked. Still, she stayed incredibly focused, even if she wasn't the one driving.

We wouldn't figure out how long it was to Aqaba until we reached a turnoff that would take us along the Dead Sea. By that time, the light was golden. It was six-thirty—we'd screwed up on the distance. From the Dead Sea, we had to go south, toward a spot on the map that looked uninhabited, and Barbara sat rigid, silent for some time now.

She started talking again. [I'd written this in dialogue, then deleted it.] She said she had to be stupid to think she could take a trip with me, but even so, she still believed in us. The way she was sitting was ridiculous, at the literal edge of her seat, and since she couldn't grab the wheel, she was gripping the armrest to the door, and she looked pretty strange, from what I could tell out of the corner of my eye, while I watched the road: I didn't dare turn and look at her because that would scare her; she needed me to concentrate. I recognized the smell of her nervous sweat in the cold jet of the A/C.

I said that we ought to just accept that this relationship might end [really not the best subject given the circumstances; rereading this, I'm amazed that I managed to say it at all without bursting into laughter at my own ineptitude]. Right when I said this, I checked to see what her hands were doing, and I saw she was twisting up a pair of headphones that had been on the dashboard, the ones I'd been using to listen to my music. Still trying to watch the road, I snapped, "Stop it—you're distracting me! Put my earbuds down!"

"They're not yours—I have the same ones."

"Just put them down!"

"Stop shouting!"

She opened her window and tossed them out, into the sand. She was crying.

I let out a sigh. I was glad she'd thrown those earbuds out the window. It was only when Barbara disappeared, or she destroyed something, that our relationship found expression. In the past, if I wasn't sure whether or not I should consider her outbursts as something toxic, spreading, now that I was paying closer attention, her actions seemed to be clear indications, like warning lights on a dashboard.

Barbara seemed to be tossing those irrelevant things into another world, where they became real. That other world was where she went when she ran away, when she spent the night away from home. Now that I understood this process, I was able to say the right thing: "Baby, I love you so much. Don't be scared now—we're doing fine—it's a nice drive—we're just a little scared, that's all. Just don't be scared of me."

"No, no, it's not you I'm scared of. It's the desert. You're being sweet."

There were fewer and fewer houses along the road and possibly—or was I just getting carried away—each house was more ramshackle than the last. Finally, with a lot of fiddling, we managed to get the GPS going, which we'd basically ignored the entire day because we didn't trust it. We realized we had two hundred kilometers left.

The sun set around seven-thirty; the road was dotted with shacks; in the water, the plants made the Dead Sea look like a rice paddy. Twilight spread over the desert sky, and then it was absolutely dark.

There would be another intersection in about a hundred kilo-meters. Now that the problem was solved and we were really in the dark desert, and Barbara could indulge her death fantasies, I felt a strange mix of pleasure and concentration. I was certain we had enough gas and I felt confident, in spite of my tired, aching legs. My task was straightforward: I had to take her to the end of that ribbon of road, and in front of me was a scoreboard ticking off the remaining kilometers before the woman beside me gnaw-ing on her hangnails would be happy.

"I don't think I'm cut out for this trip." Her voice was soft. "The car scares me, and this is no country to drive in."

The desert went on so long that the fear of running out of gas kept us from talking. Barbara's hand was on my hand, and my hand was on the gear shift, though it wasn't necessary. The road was smooth, but we were fixated on the idea that if an animal ran out, we might have to downshift, a safer option than braking. We were convinced that at the first sign of trouble, our lives would be in danger, and both of us were imagining, on our own, the car stopped, our holding each other through the night. Every ten minutes a car would approach, and we concentrated on the white headlights.

Her hand was frequently on mine. The lightness of it, the cold sweat . . . Then, when she'd return her hand to her lap or raise it to her mouth, to chew her nails, the back of my hand was wet.

We reached a pass where there were houses and then we saw, emerging before us, a coast alight with human life. It took a while to figure out what this apparition was; then we realized it was a twin highway through the desert, which, according to the map, had to be the Israeli road along the opposite shore, drawn close now, separated only by a strip of land. The two roads would join at the gulf. That mirror gaze, between the cars over there and us, was comforting after that black darkness.

We stopped at a checkpoint for entering Aqaba's special economic zone. When we rolled down our windows to show our documents to a soldier, we felt the nighttime chill. The wind on our faces, the joy of brilliant streetlights. After customs, there were still streetlights; city palms, groomed, lined the road.

Now we faced the city's complicated ring road and its unlit intersections. Sometimes a reflector shone off the large stone barricade of a construction zone, but nearly all the barricades were dark; we drove cautiously to avoid them, exhausted from this new stress and feeling like we'd never reach our hotel.

Before getting to the resort area, just outside the city, along the coast, we almost collided with a semitruck. Two major roads, ours and the truck's, seemed to be merging in an elongated X that was difficult to navigate in the dark: my first thought was that there had to be a ramp and the semi was about to go by above, on some unlit overpass.

The semi was like a hallucination: high headlights from an angle I'd never seen before while driving. Like a joust, it seemed to be charging our left side. I slammed on the brakes, certain we were about to die, but our giant opponent braked and let us go, with a blare of its baritone horn.

Our hearts were in our throats, but soon we were laughing, our fear dissolving, also because we caught sight of the resort, its proportions comically grand, immersed in clouds of blue and purple light, and divided into all these various sumptuous shapes, from cottage to Corbusier house to airplane hangar.

We were still smiling in our room, when we stepped into the bathroom naked and discovered the shower was a room itself, walled by glass, with four stone seats and two large, square showerheads: we sat down side by side to slowly wash away the sweat, wondering how much water this desert might hold.

She asked me to go get my phone. I left the clean heat of the shower, slipped on a soft white robe, went into the bedroom for the phone, switched it to airplane mode, set it up on the sink against the toiletry bag, and turned on the camera. Then I took off the robe, stepped inside and we started making love in the shower, on the seat. She was into it, didn't kiss me, or kissed me a little and then stopped.

I often got the feeling from Barbara that what was happening between us wasn't intimate. So I won't talk about our limbs; I won't talk about heat; I won't talk about sweat. Like I wrote before, a good way to understand my situation is to think of Eleonora as my life partner, and to think of Barbara as my lover. She once told me she enjoyed it that I didn't fuck her like a boyfriend, and that evening in the shower, on our first long trip together in quite a while, it really felt as if she were fucking me like a stranger, with no intimacy, and so she liked it that I wasn't feigning tenderness. Now that there was no Eleonora, Barbara's disengagement interested me more; previously it had felt like the punishment of a woman who somehow knew I wasn't hers. I was hers, now, and she was fucking me like I was someone she'd picked up at a bar, someone happy to satisfy her without expecting any warmth in return.

The water off, we got into our robes, then into bed, and we watched our video before we started making love again and I held back from saying I loved her. Later, when she was nearly asleep, I told her: "I love you so much."

"Oh, me too."

And it sounded like it looks here on the page, inexplicable, lacking subtext.

When we turned off the lamps to go to sleep, she held on to me and said: "What a lovely trip."

I wrote my first poems when I started college and fell in love with a high school girl who had friends that found me annoying. This was my fault—I'd go to a party, corner one of them and talk her ear off for half an hour. My listener would sort of accept this and sort of complain about it later to the girl. Here's how I operated: I'd isolate my listener and tell her that her life was not going well at all, that it needed to change. I'd loved that girl for three years while I was involved with someone else, and maybe it was unconscious on my part, but I was going for a scorched-earth approach. Faced with her and her friends' indecision, half paying attention to me, half rejecting me, I came up with the idea of writing these friends poems inspired by Nietzsche and Jünger. So all these kids—well-read high schoolers and grad students—all of them with a season theater ticket, got a poem from me, about the fact that they had no future, that due to conformism and their lack of will, they'd soon be defunct. I'd type up a poem, cut it out, glue it down on cardboard, draw on a daisy, and hand-deliver it to the person, like a love letter. One guy who hung out in that group (I hadn't actually written him a poem, but he did get a hold of a couple, because my letters became notorious) said I was a poet. A few years after he graduated, he contacted me wanting to know if I still wrote: he was now on the editorial staff at a prestigious literary journal and remembered my nihilistic poems. I was just finishing my degree in political science; I liked to read and I had no clue what else I liked. I'd written some rap but quit because I didn't like the rap scene. I was thrilled to receive this note—I wanted to do something—I was an aesthete, I was conflicted about religion, and I didn't believe in the novel even if I was reading its most important examples; I felt like an artist. I submerged myself in a three-hour bath and reread my favorite poet, Guido Gozzano, then my favorite contemporary poet, Valentino Zeichen. I set a pad of paper on my bathtub bookrest that my parents had bought me because I was always reading in the tub. I left that bathroom with three poems about failure, about my directionless life; they were light, and they were warlike.

I was no expert on syllables and meter, but I did have an imagination, and those poems impressed my old acquaintance and his colleagues. They published them and showed them to Zeichen, who read them and very kindly suggested that we meet. We did, in Luigi Ontani's studio, a real *Wunderkammer*, on a weekday afternoon, and it all seemed like the ideal I'd been pursuing ever since I was a teenager. Lounging around, contemplating. Hanging out. In the editorial office, I met writers and critics; later, these editors would give me books to review for my first ever newspaper pieces. At the literary journal, they realized I was meticulous and set me up to work with my friend, who'd been made assistant editor. My first jobs outside of this were with independent publishing houses, and eventually I was hired by the largest publisher of all.

And that's my career. One day I didn't know where to go—six months after undergrad, I still hadn't enrolled in a master's program and my father hadn't spoken to me in two—and suddenly I was dining with writers found in the culture section. I'd always been afraid of ending up a bum, since I'd never been able to imagine my future. "A bum"?—like that would ever happen. Luca, my brother, got along nicely in the center-left world, well-suited to that combination of optimistic Catholicism and hints of communism; my sister had chosen the strange, parallel world of fashion; while I was too much of a snob to do much of anything, and so in the end, I found the perfect job* for a snob: I was a poet—a published poet—who corrected writers' books.

I moved to Milan for three years, then they let me return to Rome and work with Roman writers, because I didn't want to stay in Milan and someone was needed in Rome. I was good with literary authors, but I was always searching for other ways to make myself useful, as though I had to justify my position. I felt privileged they'd allowed me to stay in Rome. A few years ago, erotic women's literature became popular and I got an idea for an Italian trilogy of erotic novels. I found a female author willing to write it, helped her develop the three story lines, it was a success, and her debut made this writer a millionaire. From then on, I found myself working on commercial books just as frequently as literary books.

It was around this time that Eleonora received her new book assignments and I began to think she might be sleeping with our

---

* "Job" here refers to "status," not economic subsistence.

editor in chief. The more I grew, the more she eclipsed me in the narrow field of "literary" authors: those writers who didn't sell well, but garnered prestige in the publishing world. Then again, Eleonora's dream was to make books that eventually appeared in textbooks. My dream had been to express myself, to live as an artist, and with my four poetry collections, I'd more than expressed myself, but as an editor, I'd mainly tried to survive.

And just like that, I'd worked nonstop for fifteen years. And what happened to the wholesome snobbery that brought me to Zeichen, to Ontani's studio, on that perfect afternoon at the beginning of my adult life?

In our time, capital, they say, has been sucked up by a very select few. So today, the capital investment of the single individual—and let's still say he's middle-class—has a subtler quality: what he invests now is his own time, his own labor, his own ambition. And all he can do is ask himself if others are fulfilled. While I grew up with the crazy fear I might "end up under a bridge" (an insult to anyone actually at risk of this), I've always insisted—contradicting myself—that being fulfilled really only means you have an answer to the question: "So what do you do?"

Then a man approaches forty, and another axis is added on, one of duration, of accumulation: Have I done enough? To provide convincing answers for strangers, I (the snob) worked hard. Faced with the problem of social identity, the same man can seem cynical, then noble, then fragile and lost.

One day shortly before Christmas break, I was promoted to director of *Varia*. This didn't happen in front of Eleonora, though I had seen her in the office that day, after a long spell of not seeing her at all. We barely spoke. It happened one afternoon, when

I left the building with the editor in chief, who was giving me a lift to the station on his way to the historic center.

I've thought about that moment so often it's no longer a living thing, just the silhouette of a story, wordless. A man in crisis, a poet, about to turn forty, sitting in the passenger seat of the director's roadster, hearing that he's been promoted. The boss—the writer-manager—talks and his hands leave the wheel as he emphasizes what he's saying. The poet's only reaction: to roll down his window and stick his elbow out and raise his fingers to his neck.

This news comes as they're leaving the enormous parking lot of the publishing group; the employee turns, and through the rear window, stares at the enormous glass block rising up out of the wet greenery. The sky looks yellow, seems lit with three suns. The car, a responsive cube, turns and enters the street.

I could run *Varia* commuting from Rome, because the politicians were in Rome, and many of the talk show hosts. Maybe the pattern of going up to Milan would be more unpredictable, more hectic, but the raise was eight hundred euro a month. I carried this secret with me onto the train, where the air was dry and the seats didn't recline and a stranger's feet blocked my way. I took an anxiolytic, but the bright light and my high blood pressure kept it from helping much. My head throbbed.

The first person I told was my father, while I was getting off the train. After three air-conditioned hours, I thought the heat I felt rising from the underside of the train was the natural heat of summer: it dispersed at once, devoured in the cool.

"Dad, I have good news. I got a promotion."

"Tell me the exact words."

"My boss said, 'You're great. You want to be the director of *Varia*?'"

Lines like "you're great" I'll quote exactly. My father is fascinated by the allure of my job: his son, the poet, who can handle the most intricate power relations just like he does the challenges of Italian and who goes to dinner with newspaper editors and publishers.

I filled him in on the details while walking along a side street leading from Termini Station's east exit. Homeless men with ruined shoes were watching me. A mean-looking woman asked me for money; I shifted my phone from one hand to the other so I could use my right to touch my wallet in my pocket.

My father was calling me "honey," his voice tender.

"Dad, I'm not sure I'm doing the right thing. The truth is, I'll have to do Christmas books, cookbooks."

"Yeah, but how satisfying, honey. You've made it to the top."

"But what if I lose my reputation?"

"You're a poet—how can you lose that?"

"It's a blow to my ego."

"Take the weekend—relax a little with Barbara."

"I'd be giving money, visibility, to people who already have it or don't deserve it."

He grew impatient. "Come on now—you can't complain when things are good. These are terrible times. You should be proud."

"I'm tired," I apologized. "I'm really tired. I just need the weekend."

"I can tell, honey."

"I'm so tired."

"You're doing great. You're really amazing, honey."

My scooter was parked in front of Banca d'Italia, in a row of about thirty others under the security cameras. The young guy parking on the opposite sidewalk, looking at me funny, had done the same two days before, when I left. My Vespa—a beat-up Indian copy—took off, coughing smoke. My heart was heavy. I couldn't reach Barbara, who was at a block party on the piazza. I drove along by the aeronautical building with the enormous Rationalist-style eagle that was lit up at night with the three colors of the flag.

I've always been in debt to my father. In spite of my career, it was only four or five years ago that I stopped asking my father for money. The industry doesn't pay well.

He has this method, a computer file of all the money he lends us. It's a professional hazard, since he's been an angel investor for twenty years—before that, he was an entrepreneur. He invests in startups, which he began doing when we—my brother, my sister, and I—were in college, because he felt he needed to help our generation that's been "raised in a Europe with no political leadership." He offers grants to entrepreneurs and economists who don't have the backing of family capital. His world vision is capitalist but anticorporate.

He's a member of a group that helps connect startups with foreign investors: this model, Singapore-inspired, schedules meetings between investors and entrepreneurs who gather to listen and discuss ideas and projects. He also helps young people come up with business plans. Then he helps them expand, obtain more money; he withdraws his investment when foreign assets arrive: he'll bank double or triple the amount he put up and leave the young people in the hands of those with more money.

Before the 2007 crisis, these earnings occurred at least once a year, at fifty to a hundred thousand euros a shot. Now they've gone down and he feels it but continues to invest because of all those in his generation who know they've "robbed" ours of a future by adding to the national debt.

He's a man who doesn't spend his money; he treats it like it doesn't belong to him (maybe that's why he treats it like it doesn't belong to us either, and, for that matter, never will): he buys houses and rents them to ensure a monthly income, a psychological anchor, but he doesn't have significant expenses, and after the financial crisis he stopped leasing big sedans and trading them in every three years—he didn't like the idea that the kids with their startups might think he wasn't being frugal while their own efforts often went unpaid. He doesn't live extravagantly; he has a beach house that requires significant upkeep, but he doesn't collect wine or own a sailboat. Any thieves breaking into one of his houses would find only computers to steal, and some rococo knickknacks, and my mother's jewelry.

None of his three children decided to follow him into his career, but we're all good at "advancement"; we know how to "feel out a situation," set goals for ourselves, and keep our head down. And we respect his austerity, have always accepted the fact that it was his professional habit to record our every "loan," since we first started asking for support in college. I owed him over one hundred and thirty thousand euros; I would never be able to repay that, and I doubt he expects me to. The only one who did manage to wipe out her debt was my sister, Irene, whom we hardly ever saw, since she lived in Milan and had lost touch with us. He'd bought her place for her, but homes, my father said, weren't part of the bill.

This agreement, which made money even more abstract than it already was, grew surreal due to the fact that we had no idea how much he'd accumulated. Someday Luca, Irene, and I would become well-off; for now, we were entitled to enough money to support our professional dreams, but not to live like the rich. Or, we were rich but couldn't live like we were.

Being rich meant not being afraid of ending up under a bridge. Ending up under a bridge has been an absurd fear of mine ever since I was little. We "knew" that anyone could lose everything in an instant, because "the economy isn't something that's fair" and "when you play with investments you're engaging in the riskiest parts of the economy." But this isn't the story of a son who discovers that his father has debts: it's just the plain, ordinary story of how three kids and their mother lived peacefully thinking they had nothing and everything at the same time.

And it was only through this, I knew, that I could become an editor at an important publishing house. And here's what's really warped: I never even wanted to be an editor—I just couldn't help trying my hardest to succeed. Plus, what's the point of accruing debt if not to succeed? You go into debt to work to pay off your debt—I still find this idea bewildering. My father gave away his money, earned in a different world, in the seventies and eighties, to help me in this new century to realize a dream that wasn't exactly mine, or his.

I was living on the bourgeoisie's trundle seat, acting carefree, like I didn't belong there, when I'd actually worked pretty damn hard, like every true bourgeois, like Papa Grandet and Robinson Crusoe.

Anyway, I was thinking about my father on my way home: an entire library of thoughts evoked in one form or another between

Termini, Porta Maggiore, Via Casilina, then along by the light-rail tracks and the Roman aqueduct, where my heart began to slow. I turned right and caught the smell of fresh-cut lumber off the sawmill. On that always empty street, a high-speed train sailed by. Up the street there was a somewhat irregular intersection; tonight it was crowded with pedestrians.

The residents' association was throwing an antifascist street party. I reached the intersection, but the police had blocked it off to traffic. I parked my scooter, hooked my helmet under the saddle, and walked through. I greeted a few association members I saw in among all the people drinking wine, lemonade, and beer, the stalls of T-shirts, purses, and books. In the piazza, I found Barbara listening to a rockabilly-patchanka band. I walked up and gave her a hug, then took her cell phone out of her hands and put it in my pocket as a joke. She hugged me back and sent me off to buy drinks.

In the crowded bar, the waitress called me "love," I got some beers, left, handed them to Barbara, and looked around. Barbara hugged me around the chest like a kid, and put her leg between mine, and I started to feel aroused. My overnight bag was still on my shoulder. I decided to bring my bag home and take a shower, find some beer in the fridge.

Once inside, I started undressing, dropping my clothes on the floor, and I shivered from the cold, maybe the first time since before summer. I went to turn on the shower.

Barbara cracked the bathroom door open: she'd followed me, she wanted to surprise me. She asked if I minded and undressed, slipped under the water with me. We turned and faced the gray-tile wall, one behind the other, and made love until the water grew tepid.

While I sat on the bidet to wash up, I started to cry; Barbara knelt down, naked, and held me, stroked my hair and asked me what was wrong. I told her what had happened in Milan and she stiffened. "Do you have to move?"

"No, no."

"Well, okay then. Is it more money?"

"Yeah."

"So why are you upset?"

I was still sitting and she, standing now, had my head against her naked belly.

"I disgust myself."

"Why—because of your promotion?"

"Yeah."

Her fingers slid along my bare back, about halfway down, then up to my hair again, slowly caressing me.

"So what do you think?" I asked.

"What'd your parents say?"

I frowned into her. "You think I'd tell my parents before you?"

She laughed and held my head against her belly: "Yes," she said.

I laughed, too.

Barbara spent Christmas in Anzio: supper on the twenty-fourth with her mother and the noon meal on the twenty-fifth with her father. Though it was painful for her, she felt she needed to go home for Christmas, and so she spent three days and two nights planning everything out, like someone afraid of flying yet preparing for a flight: rituals, wary distractions, silence, alcohol and anxiety meds, and constantly adding up how much time was left, like she was responsible for pushing the boulder of time into the future. If I went with her, she'd feel forced to be more open, more vulnerable.

I didn't mind being on my own at my parents' for Christmas, like a teenager unable to see his girlfriend.

My parents were working away in the kitchen while I kept my nephew company in the dining room. The four place settings were for me, my parents, and Gionata, two and a half years old, who had his strange recurring fever that evening. For a couple of days now, if the cough syrup wasn't working, he grew despondent. As soon as his temperature dropped, he went back to being sweet. With the final dinner preparations, he had a high fever and was crying, sometimes enraged, sometimes confused. His eyebrows weren't sure whether to arch or knit: it was so unfair—no, it was madness—that his mommy wasn't here when he was sick, plus it was Christmas, the first Christmas when he seemed to understand its significance.

You couldn't leave him alone for a second because a few times this past year, his temperature had shot up to a hundred and four within fifteen minutes, and his eyes would roll back in his head, he'd grow pale, and start to convulse. His health problem, still unexplained, and lasting half his little life now, consumed his grandparents. According to his pediatrician and a succession of doctors at admissions, it wasn't anything; it might go away before we even discovered what it was. The pediatricians' approach was one of magical thinking, with the baby something less quantifiable than an adult.

Ever since the day my sister-in-law, Daniela, fled outside carrying her lifeless son, running into a Chinese coffee bar, screaming, "He's dead!," then racing by cab to the emergency room, her baby's care had become a collective effort. When he had convulsions, we needed to remove all his clothes and lay him on the floor, to lower his temperature. He had to be propped on his side so he wouldn't swallow his tongue.

Daniela and my brother moved to our parents', into one side of their apartment taking up the entire fourth floor of a building with long balconies and shaded by the pine trees in the public park below. Each place had a separate steel door on the landing, and then an interior glass door connected the two. The apartment overlooking the street had been rented out for over ten years but wasn't under lease when Gionata started developing fevers every two weeks. Our parents gave it to Luca and Daniela free of charge; they moved there, from a small house with a yard in a former working-class neighborhood near us to an upper-middle-class neighborhood, with its empty nights and expensive food markets.

That Christmas Eve, Daniela and Luca were on the hospital ward because their twins had been born the night before. Boys: healthy, tiny, hairy. My parents hadn't gone to see them yet. I'd visited my sister-in-law that morning, and she'd cried with me because her parents had been so cold, staying only a short while: they found the twins alarmingly small, and it made them uncomfortable. "Can you believe it!" This was Daniela's favorite expression. It wasn't cold and the sun wasn't out; on the ward, with its ancient walls and warm lighting interrupted here and there by a mirror or the fluorescent glow of some piece of equipment, she felt "suspended and useless" but also "protected in a cocoon."

At the table, I sat by Gionata and kept one wet towel on his forehead and one on his neck. Actually, for his neck, we were using a clear blue gel pack, like those for keeping wine chilled. The little guy was wearing mismatched clothing and looked a bit like a circus clown; he had crusty cheeks the color of ripe medlar fruit, and sad orphan eyes. I sent pictures to Barbara, and she kept writing back, full of empathy, so much so that at one point she sent me a picture of her eyes tearing up.

My parents started carrying in around ten different plates of antipasti. The dinner hadn't been scaled back after Daniela's water broke, at the noon meal on the twenty-third; and now that the dinner was here, the ten courses of fish and shellfish were absurd. My father uncorked the spumante, we raised our glasses to say grace: my mother said this was a depressing Christmas; I told her I thought it was sweet and Dickensian. We'd dressed like it was any other day. My parents started talking together about how the fish had turned out, bickering, not angry, not cold, an inexplicable middle tone, grating at first, then slow and mournful, like they both were sad. We ate the gilthead almost suspiciously, not able to tell if it was any good. It was. The homemade mayonnaise was exquisite, pungent fresh lemon enveloped in the rounded flavor of egg.

We cleared our plates, were in the kitchen. Gionata was happy at the moment, but his eyes were still brimming from his last cry. I wasn't applying the compresses because he'd had his medicine. With his constant state of emergency, we all knew when he'd taken his various medications, what his temperature was when he'd had his cough syrup, sucking it from two syringes, which I then rinsed and slipped back into their vials, still in their boxes. I wrote the times and doses in my phone notes, to update his parents.

His grandmother took care of him the most, and sometimes she could be thoughtless. While he wove in and out of the chairs pushed away from the kitchen table, she asked him, his back to her: "So are you happy your little brothers were born?"

I was kneeling in front of Gionata. At his grandmother's words, he sucked in his cheeks with a solemn expression. He narrowed his eyes, and his gaze seemed sharper, yet hollow. He pointed to the oven, which stood at his height. He was pointing it out to me, and I knew I'd been enlisted into his diversionary tactic: I opened a nearby cabinet, pulled out an aluminum pie tin, got the big pair of oven mitts sitting next to the burners, and I slipped them onto the baby's hands, then entrusted him with the pan. The solemnity at his grandmother's question never leaving his face, Gionata put the pie tin and an invisible main course into the oven, then pulled them out, saying, "Burning, burning!," blurring his consonants.

Gionata's pain touched a part of me I hadn't known existed before he was born. We kept playing ovens for a few minutes and I took my phone off the table to snap some photos that I went back to the entire night, when his crying and his grandmother's attentions would wake me. Being woken up like this, getting out of bed, phone in hand, seeing if I could help, I felt exposed to a blind limbo, suspended between life and death. Every reawakening showed me a reality that was unbearable: the baby's crying so counter to my senses, sluggish from lack of sleep; the docile willingness of the baby's grandparents; the fact that those grandparents were my parents, that they knew the secret to my loneliness and had never revealed it to me.

At night it was even harder to get him to take his medicine from the syringes, by propping up his head. He rebelled, squirmed in his sweaty clothes, wet blond curls, disdainful look. His eyes were gummy, his eyelids, eyelashes, crusty.

How strange it was to wake up in my brother's marriage bed, while the baby's grandmother slept next door, and his grandfather, that mysterious man (nervous around my mother, incredibly gracious to me, almost a stranger), lay abandoned to the twin bed in the guest room—too tired even to put on pajamas, sleeping in his undone, corduroy pants . . .

I thought about that Christmas for weeks—I still do: me and Gionata in our role as children; my helpless parents, upset, withdrawn, kind. In early January, terrorists bombed the editorial offices of the French satirical weekly *Charlie Hebdo* in Paris, throwing Europe into chaos. Shortly after, I spent three days in a hotel in Rome's historic center where I instructed the regional promoters on the new books they'd be proposing to bookstores. That experience and the attacks are linked for me—we were scared the hotel might be a "real target." After the final book to be promoted, the editor in chief, sighing, laughing, ordered the packed room: "Everyone, fall out! ISIS has spared us." As he stepped away from the PowerPoint screen, I approached him, and he looked at me, eyes completely blank, and I said: "Sorry to tell you now, like this, but I'm leaving—I quit."

His lips parted, he sighed and tilted his head to one side; then he straightened up again, took off his wire-rimmed glasses, held them delicately in one hand, and with his other, covered his eyes with his thumb and index finger. "Marcè," he said. And then he turned and walked off, shortsighted, to wrap things up with some promoters, and when he reached them, he put his glasses back on and was smiling once more.

My father's negative reactions come in three types.

The first is simple: he'll raise his voice, saying something like, "Oh, sure," then stop participating in the conversation.

The second is stronger: when something awful happens to his children, he stops speaking to us. When my fiancée left me, he didn't speak to me for three months. Then, just like that, we were talking again, and he gave me some good advice about getting over her, but he didn't apologize for disappearing. At home, we knew he was "so gentle he couldn't bear to see us suffer," but when he was ready, he'd come around and be available to us. He advised me not to attempt to get back together with that woman—she'd just leave me again.

The third type is the most subtle, and the most difficult to try to get down in writing: he becomes invisible.

Like when I resigned. He didn't stop talking to me. But he didn't *talk* to me.

He avoided me the entire time I was out of work. I'd go see my nephews fairly often, and he'd say hello from his easy chair, smile timidly, but avoid my eyes. I know he must have been ashamed that he couldn't seem to speak with me. I felt I'd done the natural thing, in a city and time when being unemployed or underemployed was becoming the norm, especially in those social classes where, between the scarcity and difficulty of work and then the abundance of one's family resources, the pursuit of a career had become an increasingly precarious notion. For my father, who reached adulthood in the sixties, this was blasphemy, though maybe, in his way, he did realize that the two of us were condemned to different moral paradigms.

(I remember one summer, during one of those times he wasn't speaking to me—that must have been ten years ago—I was shut up in a public library working on some galleys, and I left for lunch, it was July, and I caught sight of him, maybe twenty meters away. He was in the middle of the street, standing on the traffic island, talking with two guys my age. All three of them were wearing jackets and ties, my father in a beige suit. It was ninety-five degrees out, and I had on sweats, a white T-shirt, and sunglasses. I didn't know he went to that neighborhood. He'd left a restaurant with those two kids, who were talking to him like they were friends and constantly touching his arm.)

I didn't start looking for work after I quit—I started after I told my father. After hearing, then forgetting his response: maybe one of those "Ah"s of his, looking down, shifting, turning away from me. The next day, I'm sure, I "put my mind to it"—something we say in our family and that means a lot for our pragmatic *côté*—and I decided that my first move would be meeting with the newspaper contacts I normally sent our books to. I'd always written for the rival Milan paper, but to start this new chapter in my life, I thought a Roman paper might be better, where I could just drop by for lunch or coffee.

My closest contact was a friend my age on the assignment desk, who after asking about all my latest professional news told me that due to budget constraints, for the last few months they'd mainly given editors the assignments, but he'd find me something when he could.

I was like a student again, directionless, wandering around Rome, or like a recent graduate, new on the literary scene, running from one bookstore event to the next, to hear writers and try to meet them. Since I was no longer the disproportionate competition for the smaller, "quality," independent publishers, I noticed that those who'd shunned me for years now stopped to chat, curious about the decision I'd made, just when the rumors about the merger of the largest Italian publishing groups were proving true. And it was on one of those public relations mornings, among the Roman hills, an ordinary January day, with the first hints of spring and my coat unbuttoned after an hour's walk, when, over coffee in the public park by the Colosseum, a publisher of a small press asked me to translate the unpublished diary of a great mid-twentieth-century American author.

I let my parents know what I'd be doing for work now. "Seeing how things are," I explained to my mother at dinner, so my father would hear, "maybe it's for the best. Everyone's reacting really strongly to the merger, and in the end, if I really think about it, if I truly want to be a serious intellectual, it's better just to step back now from that *Varia* business."

My mother forgot this was more of a personal decision and started discussing some political aspects of the merger, something she tended to do when one of us discussed our job: she couldn't stay focused on the personal. But at least my father knew my situation now, and in the weeks that followed, he started contributing again to the conversations concerning me, even if he wasn't speaking to me yet.

One evening, as we crossed paths in the hallway, he reached out and stroked my cheek.

That spring, during a lunch under a restaurant pergola, I convinced the rich owner of a small publishing house to hire me. I'd been to his barely furnished office in a palazzo in the historic center, had advised him on foreign books to buy, and helped procure a story collection by an English writer friend of mine. Now one of his staff, an aristocrat named Asia, was pregnant and about to go on that sort of maternity leave which, for well-off women, was code for not returning to work. The publisher wanted to capitalize on this, to hire someone to help raise his profile, and so he offered me a temporary replacement contract that could develop into something else. He wanted to concentrate on the business, not the books: to come up with ways to generate new revenue, to open a writing school, maybe. He wanted me to take on some of his responsibilities as editor in chief, and also get him into certain circles.

Afterward, I drove back in a warm downpour, completely drenched, and I was shaking profoundly with endorphins, an internal rain that went along nicely with the rain hitting my skin, and my yelps in the traffic on Muro Torto: "I am so cool!—so cool!" At home I stripped at the door, left my wet clothes in a pile, and raced to the shower, and I remember two different sensations of heat, inside and out, and my cold hair as it warmed.

*S*ome details about my father. [It might seem like I'm going off-topic by dwelling on him, but the more I reread these pages about us and my relationship to his legacy, the more I realize that a man's carelessness toward women has a great deal to do with what form his obsession takes toward his father.] He's a sweet, private man; giving of himself is painful, depresses him, but he has no choice—he does nothing for himself. A mother who died young, and an elderly father, middle-class assets divided between too many heirs; a loveless marriage, I think, the only son. I've never written a poem about him, but recently, I find myself saying he's an interesting and decent man, though also strange. He's opened up to me about ten times over the course of my life, and that's been to give me some good advice or to cry in frustration over work. But then it's as if these discussions never took place: "It helps to talk with you—we understand each other," he says every time. "I should do it more often." But then it doesn't happen.

Now I don't ask. I've started giving him presents instead:

I'll order him useful accessories online that I buy for myself, too: charging cords, extra batteries, elegant key cases, Japanese stationery.

I've never heard his genuine fatherly voice, the voice he uses with the startup founders (they're often younger than me now) when he's advising them, supervising them. I'll go by his office sometimes and hear him talking on the phone. An authoritative voice, unwavering. I have heard him attempt that voice with me, though, when he's given me advice.

Like I already mentioned, ten years before all this happened I took a shot at getting married, but she left me the week before the wedding. When my brother came by with the news that the wedding had been "postponed," my father couldn't talk to me. My mother, too, was very sad; she drifted around me like she was in mourning. Those were rough months because my fiancée couldn't make up her mind, but she also didn't want to break off our engagement, in spite of the scandal. I left for Turin—I was working freelance then for the publishing house but didn't want to move to Milan, where I'd feel obligated to live at my sister's— and there in Turin I just tried to keep busy. I wrote a book of poems: *The Merry Widower*. After two months, my father came to see me in Turin, to start talking again; he came with my mother and a couple of their friends. We had lunch together in the Langhe wine region, and then dinner in the city. "He looks good," my father told my mother: "Doesn't he?" he said, pointing to my cheeks. In private he told me: "You have my full support. Don't see her again. There's a wound here that can't be healed. Don't talk yourself into getting back together—it would just be the same thing all over."

He asked me if I felt like "playing a little joke" on my ex. He'd taken it upon himself to pay for the reception instead of the parents of the bride, as tradition dictated, and he'd never told me what it cost. After this ugly event, he learned from his lawyer that there were rulings in favor of reimbursement for someone left "at the altar," specifically, after the banns were published, without probable cause. My father had put together a list of expenses for the reception, my wedding suit, and some furniture in the apartment where she continued to live. I just wanted to leave her everything, because I loved her and because, after the shock, I realized, with my sense of liberation, that our marriage was stillborn after years and years of being a couple. Even if the appeal that inspired my father's actions required a "justified reason for not fulfilling the promise of marriage"—something she couldn't offer—I knew a reason did exist. The lawyer managed to get this money back for my father, who once again kept the amount from me. With a mixture of kindness and sadism, he negotiated a monthly rate of one hundred euros, interest-free, with the would-be bride, a debt which, at the time of this story, I'm guessing probably hadn't been paid off yet. Naturally, after this joke, I had no chance of ever talking with her again; and my father never mentioned her.

I needed to spend a few pages on him because his style and success start to matter now in my story.

It was still spring when I learned from my mother that some entrepreneurs my father had helped, a group of twenty-five-year-olds, had wound up in the newspaper, because an important Norwegian investor had confirmed his "soft commitment" after exercising "due diligence," and these guys, inventors of an app to monitor the stress level of small-business employees, had closed an "investment round" at over two million.

All of this was realized in the group that paired Italian start-ups with foreign investors, and my father had offered to be their initial backer: now he could sell off his own investment for a much higher yield than normal. My father loved projects that combined IT and health; he'd been tempted to go into business with these kids, had proposed being their principle investor, but then—my mother was telling me this by the window in Luca and Daniela's apartment, one quiet day, a car zipping around the corner by their building, cracking the silence like a gunshot, with the brief stink of exhaust fumes before the warm air smelled again of pine trees and geraniums—but then my father decided not to go back to being an entrepreneur; still, owing to the cruel, Übermensch magic of capital, he'd earned four hundred thousand euros from this operation. And the beautiful thing, my mother said, a hand to her damp neck, is that he was "just about to pull off" another deal, for a machine that diagnosed osteoporosis: it was "a good year."

While she spoke, I was kneeling by the living room door, taking apart and oiling the door handle: it squeaked at night and woke my brother when Daniela got up with the kids.

"In this awful decade," my mother said, "we could really use a nice, solid payment. Poor Daddy—thank goodness—a little satisfaction."

My mother was more terrified than any of us that somehow our fortunes would change, and we'd "end up under a bridge."

While I was screwing in the plate on the edge of the door, I asked her: "So when's Dad getting back? I'd like to congratulate him in person."

My mother said she didn't know and changed the subject; with her quick mind, she's easily bored. I stopped listening, let my mind dwell on something else. That money, I thought, could buy Barbara's apartment. My parents had bought a place in Milan for my older sister, Irene, and it had been years since I'd asked for a dime, unlike Luca—he may not have asked for the patriarchal purchase of a home, but he lived with our parents and received help with the expenses for the newborn twins, this financial assistance starting from the moment his wife, Daniela, began staying home and he was earning the fixed salary of someone working for the governor of Lazio—not much, because he didn't steal, and he didn't steal because he was rich, and my father had always spoken calmly, persuasively, and with utter contempt of people who were rich and took the liberty of stealing.

I stood up to go put the tool bag back in the closet; then I washed my hands with dish soap in the kitchen, listening to my mother talking with her grandkids. Maybe, I thought, my father had realized that I was leading a life with Barbara lately that was based on frugal pleasures, dedication, and community, ideals he'd passed on to me.

On Saturdays, Barbara and I would drive to the nursery to buy plants. That spring we put a leadwort into a long, deep planter outside the dining room, and in the morning, we'd take our coffee outside and look at the sky-blue discs of petals. Up by the rooftop terrace, we were training a duranta plant to climb the wooden posts of the structure supporting the solar panels. We'd bought two wooden lounge chairs, a bench, two armchairs, and a small table. I'd go up there before nightfall and have a drink and watch the duranta grow, the small leaves and the lilac petals bordered by white.

In the courtyard below, the flowering sandeville fuchsia spread at a slant over the white wall, escaping the jasmine vines. A wisteria grew outside our bedroom. And for the courtyard, we'd just bought a lantana, red, yellow, and orange, covered in clusters of tiny flowers like fly eyes. This was the idyllic good life that my father believed in.

Of course, Barbara and I got there with plenty of turbulence. I've said in the past that my relationship with Barbara had a parallel dimension where we were already happy: if we fought and I threw a book of hers over the courtyard wall, into the rocks, it was as if I were reshelving it in a beautiful bookcase in a home where we already felt the plenitude of time and things. When Barbara left for the night with her red roller bag, she was actually headed off to stay in a place where our love was already complete. Now, though, I was beginning to sense a continuity between these two dimensions, as though certain situations didn't have to reach their limit for me to start feeling close to her.

We threw glasses, the ashtray, heavy photography books, handfuls of ice. Right when I saw these things go flying, slamming into the walls or the floor, I felt connected to her; I didn't need for her to run to the closet anymore, to pull down her roller bag and spend the night someplace else.

Once, she was so enraged, she tore loose the bedroom door, which didn't have the usual two hinges but one very long hinge held in place with rows of small screws. I saw that white slab at an unnatural tilt, impossible to close, and could feel time itself inside me and how every existing thing contained its own ending, and my whole being desired this unfamiliar form of Barbara, this vector constantly hurled at objects, unable to control herself, to not react to the world, this vector condemned to hurtle into the future, if not handled with care.

And she, eyes round, looked at that tilted door as well, and said she loved me.

"You want to go stay with one of your friends?"

She suggested we go for spaghetti with clam sauce on the piazza.

Before we left, I took out every screw from the two parts of the doorjamb and leaned the door against the wardrobe. It felt like the first time I'd ever really seen that door. The next morning, I called to get some workers over to hammer in new metal hinges, the same lightweight hinges that ran the full height of the door. Now, this tall door (without a mark on it) sounded different when clicked shut, because it was slightly out of alignment. That new sound won me over.

I'd never seen a woman from so close-up. Sometimes I'd recall my old lovers with a sense of heartbreak, as though only now could I feel what I hadn't really felt in the past for these other women I'd lived with, though perhaps these feelings had been there all along.

That's how things were during that period, and the news of my father's money coincided with seeing Barbara, like the door, as if for the first time.

I propped my elbows on the kitchenette windowsill, waiting to catch a glimpse of him while I kept my mother company.

The sun hadn't set, and it was that in-between weather, too cold for a T-shirt and too warm for a sweater; everything was suspended, elusive: the urge to beg for that money might vanish if I gave in to the feeling that I had to go home for dinner, that is, to the feeling that I had to disentangle myself from my present state.

After a short time standing watch, I saw him, in his raincoat, with his briefcase, coming down the sidewalk toward the entrance gate. I interrupted my mother: "I'm going out for a sec."

I can't find a realistic style to talk about this episode. I tried writing an actual scene, but I'm overwhelmed by how false conventional narrative feels: sentences alternating between facial expressions, gestures, a detail about the weather, the study of a tenant either exiting the building or coming home.

An important event is like a great soccer match, the confusing, incomplete commentary on the moment and what follows: observations, reenactments, instant replays, and all the talk.

The commentary on those fateful minutes:

He's on the landing! He's pressing the button for the elevator to go up to the third floor so his father can't get on! He wants them to talk face-to-face! He hurtles down the stairs, his heart in his throat! His father's there, waiting for the elevator! He comes toward him—he has to decide if he'll kiss his father or not! His father is carrying his briefcase, he looks happy! The son blurts out: "Way to go, Dad!" The other man answers: "Yeah!" "You coming back from a meeting?" "Yeah, at the club!" "Great!"

Now he needs to get to it, before they go upstairs to his mother, because around her, there's no talking about money! But his father's clearly weak—he's exhausted—he can't possibly propose they go back outside, up the steps, to the gate, and take a stroll along the street. He'd have to wait for his father on the

sidewalk, like the Bravi, with Don Abbondio! But in a flash—
they're on the elevator—he instinctively acts: the son quotes a
line he's used ever since he was little, the day his brother, Luca,
was born: "Dad, I have a great idea . . ." And what came after:
"How about we take Mommy and Irene, and we all go home?"
"And what about your new brother—can't he come, too?" "No,
he can stay here."

His father laughs! He's touched by this! And the son jumps
in with: "How about we buy Barbara's place?"

The elevator goes up, there's no escape—it's so small!

And his father says: "Hey! What a great idea! I'll come take a
look!"

The elevator reaches their floor! The idea's been approved
before his mother and father see each other again and the son
finds it impossible to talk, because his mother gets very worked
up over money!

They step off the elevator—it's over! He's not sure how, but
he's won!

And then, what I'd call "the post-game analysis" kicked in. My
father and I decided not to tell my mother that evening; probably he wanted to enjoy the triumph of his lucrative investments,
and he knew the timing always had to be right when talking to
her about large expenses. So I grabbed my jacket and backpack
and left, truly the prodigal son, who could go his entire life rejecting his old neighborhood and his father's world and now return
when he needed to and find himself bestowed with the gift of the
fatted real-estate calf . . .

On the bypass, riding my scooter to the right of the cars stuck
at a standstill at various places in the tunnel, I reflected on what

had just happened. How was it possible to be worth so little, that with no effort whatsoever, just by sincerely expressing something instinctive (Please, sir, I want some more), you could wind up with such an expensive yes?

Had I congratulated him enough? Had I explicitly said I wanted to speak to him without Mom? I had. Had he found it unpleasant, his success linked to this idea of a purchase? His yes had been so free, so natural. Let's take a look at that instant replay: yes, the paternal yes that opens the coffers. Sweetness, the land of milk and honey. I'd said the right thing: a home! Not filthy lucre—*a home*! For him, money didn't exist as money; for him, so-called *disposable income* (the pulsing heart of this capitalist period), namely, pleasure-spending—on Amazon or at a restaurant—is peculiar. For him, what you should do with money is shift it to some new territory, like tanks in Risk. Money's a nice roll of the dice, not a cause for celebration in and of itself, but serviceable for the proper move on the board of the game of wealth.

I'd made the best possible move. Since no one would give a loan to an editor, not one bank, all that public relations work in my fifteen years in publishing meant nothing in comparison to that pounce of mine down the stairs.

The biggest financial decision of my life was pushing that elevator button so my father couldn't get on before I met him on the ground floor.

When I left, I felt like someone used to feel who'd just graduated, or obtained a full-time position, or gotten married. I remember my churning emotions while I drove along through the bypass tunnel—I felt like I was choking—and I had to stop myself from thinking too much: it was overwhelming. In the cars there were all these men and women, and I had no idea of their financial situation, but many of them were thinking of their homes and their possessions.

And I felt ashamed by this idea. I owned nothing, had built nothing. The largest thing I'd built was my job for a large publishing house, which I'd just destroyed like it was nothing, and truthfully, didn't miss at all.

And what if the elevator had gone down to the main floor with someone on it, and I hadn't managed to catch my father away from my mother? I wouldn't have told him my idea, and maybe after a few minutes, I'd have found it ridiculous, shaken my head and smiled, embarrassed it had ever crossed my mind.

My phone dinged in my pocket; with so much traffic, I pulled in between two stopped cars and read my message—two little hearts from my mother. I started to cry, and I cried until I reached my neighborhood, the instant replay still going of those few life-changing minutes. Their glorious generation that had made money, suffered, explained, sacrificed themselves, gone into debt, been self-congratulatory, that had ceaselessly produced new visions, new worlds, that glorious generation that had fed me one bite at a time was now finally offering me an entire slice of its delicious pie.

I'm recalling this period in my life to see if I'm capable of describing the women I love or have loved without turning them into caricatures, into saviors or sirens, into wives, mothers, or whores. I've grown tired of the comedy of the clumsy man who always makes the wrong move, and since I returned home and made the wrong move, informing Barbara of my project without any preparation, any strategy, I'll just avoid that trite scene of the man who makes a mess of things through sheer gullibility—the neurotic, obsessive, childish point of view of the typical male narrator—and I'll tell the story instead through Barbara's eyes. Also, because she and I discussed it so long afterward, I'm fairly sure I can reconstruct—as they say in video games or pornography—her POV.

She was out watering the courtyard plants and wore a short dress and light wrap. As she stooped over the sandeville, the shadow of her enormous boyfriend engulfed her from behind, and he held her tightly, hugging her, squeezing one breast, then grabbing her hips, fondling her rear. She nearly fell over, but her boyfriend held her up, and she laughed, found it touching and also slightly annoying that her space had been invaded while she was lost in thought.

From point-blank range she heard: "Let's buy this place."

Confusion. The first precise thought she managed was that she had only thirty thousand euros built up over ten years in an insurance fund and that she couldn't ask her father for money. Barbara's father had ruined the family business that her grand-father had handed over to him unprepared, throwing him in, when for years he'd only been assigned menial tasks. Since then, he hadn't worked, and had paid what he owed by selling off all his assets. He lived in the family home of his second wife. Barbara would never be able to buy a house. Then, getting up, trying to turn off the hose, she said: "Buy this place? Who?"

Her boyfriend took the hose out of her hand, laughing, and pressed down hard on the nozzle trigger. "My father. There's enough money to buy it."

Who is this little prince, coming here, completely under the thumb of King Dad, and proclaiming he's seized my little dukedom,

and proclaiming it like it's my victory? This is awful—here I am,
a woman who's struggled to build a life for herself, and now these
two men come riding in with their sack of florins . . . "But you
don't even know if the owner will sell!"

"Sure, sure, we have to find out."

The courtyard, the flowers, it was all being commandeered.
"God, why are you like this!" she snapped. "You're so spoiled!"

And she stared at that son, his nearly hairless body but his
face covered in beard, overweight, someone who'd never had a
real job, never worked in a restaurant, who'd never been actually
scared, who now looked shocked: "Sorry . . . then we won't do
it . . ."

She said something she'd learned from one of her feminist
friends, who'd been through a similar situation: "No, no—buy it.
But my name has to be on the deed."

They continued talking in that semi-flooded courtyard, because the watering hose was still running, she didn't want to be
shut up inside—if they took this topic inside, she'd feel claustro-
phobic. Her boyfriend explained that it wasn't for him to decide
whose name the apartment would be under, since the money
wasn't his.

"That's bullshit!" she said. "You're putting me in a terrible
position!"

The idea that came to me then—and I can't write this down
like it was the confirmed truth for both parties involved—was
that her flirtation with Leone wasn't over, that she still wasn't
sure she was going to stay with me, in spite of our renewed feelings for each other. Then again, maybe this is my first thought
whenever a woman has plans that I don't factor into—take

Eleonora—I'd attributed her increased (and much improved) editorial responsibilities to an affair she had with the editor in chief.

We stood there, our voices down so the neighbors wouldn't hear. At one point, feeling sad, like our relationship was ending, I said: "Okay, that's it. I'll look for an apartment someplace else."

"No," she said. "No. Now that you've made me start traveling with you again, start really living together, now that you've made me think we're really serious about this relationship—you can't just leave . . . buy yourself another place . . . in the past, I thought I'd always feel sick when I was with a man, but now I like being with you. You can't just buy yourself an apartment someplace else and leave me like that."

Putting this dialogue down, I feel like crying: her declaration was so beautiful and so ambivalent. But here comes the instant replay, as usual. Right then and there I said: "Sorry, Barbara, but I could never buy your place after what you've told me. And I want to buy something now, because my father said yes, and I'll never be able to purchase an apartment without him. I have to look out for myself, I want to settle down." I didn't know what I was saying—I wanted her to feel bad for humiliating me. "So I'll buy something and I'll head out, and we'll just have to see what happens."

That was it. I went inside and put some red cabbage on to boil and whisked together eggs and parmesan for a frittata.

She stayed outside, in the courtyard, sitting on the front steps, her knees drawn up to her chest, fighting back the urge to run away, because if she did, she was afraid she'd lose her home.

I brought out two plates of frittata and vegetables, two sets of silverware, nothing else, and before I set the food down on the wooden table, I told her an idea that had come to me just as quickly as the one I'd had that afternoon when it occurred to me to take my father's money: "Let's get married. Then, if we separate, everything will be divided in half. And I'll make a will, and if I die, you get the apartment."

Our hunger disappeared. We let the frittata and cabbage grow cold, there on the wood table.

For a long while, we didn't speak, we just sat at the table, silent, staring at the plants, feeling the cold and the night coming on.

Marriage, I mean the legal act, not the reality, was that threshold beyond which we were still chucking objects at each other while we fought. Maybe, over there, we'd recover our torn-up books, our shattered glasses, as if in a ghost story.

For our party, my parents suggested the beach house, which was actually located in Anzio. It would be the first time we'd invited her family to my parents': our families had never met, not on the beach we all went to, and not because of Barbara and me. It wasn't so strange that we'd never met in Anzio over the summer—I don't recall making more than a couple of friends there, and that was just in elementary school; plus, her family lived outside the city center, while my parents, like all their friends, had bought a place high up on the hill overlooking the train station. The station cut this long, sloping town in two, neatly dividing the port area from our neighborhood on the hill.

We decided to throw our own party at the end of September: no reception, just a lunch on the side—but in Rome—for maybe twenty relatives and some friends.

And so, at the end of August, I was driving along Via Pontina, the car trunk filled with cases of liquor. Barbara had her knees up against the glovebox while she slouched, sweating in her seat, the window cracked open (she's phobic about objects flying in), and talked about her job, the event she was trying to organize.

She'd finally found an opportunity to plan a festival in a medieval villa she was crazy about, an enchanting place she'd made her early escapes to, with her grown-up boyfriends. For some time, she'd looked for just the right event, and she'd finally found one: an evening, next January, on the subject of violence against women. She happened to meet a member of the family who owned the villa, and this person told her about a recently discovered ancestral diary which documented the violence inflicted on this woman by her husband, and it was written with an "unusually modern sensibility" for the mid-nineteenth century. This noblewoman, Barbara explained, already knew one hundred and sixty years ago that this type of sex "wasn't a conjugal duty. It was murder without a corpse." They'd decided to hold this event on the anniversary of this woman's death, in January: a date that was alarmingly close, but that Barbara felt compelled to accept. The public notice of regional cultural activities could be modified to include this event. But it was a delicate affair, given that the Mafia Capitale scandal had been a main topic of conversation since June, and names related to this woman were under investigation: a change to the notice, though in good faith and with no personal gain, had to be carefully worked out so as to avoid being misconstrued. Now and then, Rome was keen on complying with regulations, and during these brief periods, you had to do everything very precisely, but doing everything very precisely was impossible. She knew that throughout the proposal process, she'd face all kinds of bureaucratic obstacles, lazy administrators, who, if they couldn't steal, wouldn't risk anything in the name of beauty.

Story over, she grew quiet, peeling the matcha-green enamel off her nails. "What?" I asked, and she said: "I'm thinking that hindsight's not the point here. From our perspective, we understand that was violence, but in the mid-nineteenth century, they didn't. The same way I think that in 2100, they'll look back, read your biography, and say you robbed me of my home, and they'll see this as violence, and will say you were a man of your time. Just a small-minded man."

"Fine," I said, "and you're completely nuts." I had one hand on the wheel, and I heard the click of the car lock, and then her door was opening. I was going only fifty because it was a two-lane road, winding, badly maintained, and those familiar with it were driving so recklessly, I slowed down even more. I had both hands on the wheel now, and I checked the rearview mirror. I was afraid of getting rear-ended, imagined the bottles shattering in the trunk. She had the door cracked open, was clutching the handle—I told myself she couldn't possibly want to throw herself out—the situation wasn't that dire.

She shut the door again, still clutching the black plastic door handle, ready to open it at any time. I turned off into an industrial area, and slowed down. When the car came to a stop, Barbara slowly opened the door and slipped her right leg out, grazing the asphalt with her bare foot, like a joke.

"What is it?" I asked. While I'd searched for a place to turn off, I'd felt a certain calmness; suddenly, her behavior felt normal.

She didn't answer.

"Come on. It's okay. Say what you want to say—go on, honey."

"I don't want to scare you."

I took her hand. "Come on—just say it."

"I have to be on the deed to the condo."

I rolled down my window. I'd been sweating the whole drive; the air-conditioning in my car no longer worked and hadn't for a long time. On the road where we'd stopped, I saw the gates to various small factories, all of which seemed to be closed that day; the pavement was worn and full of potholes. The sky was opaque; I was wearing my polarized sunglasses that made everything sharper, real and fake. I lowered my glasses and the street looked uglier. I put them back on and said: "Okay."

Barbara started texting with someone. I felt hurt that she hadn't thanked me, and silly for feeling hurt.

Outside Anzio, we stopped and bought a pizza and some orange soda as a snack to have with my father.

Getting out by the gate of my parents' beach house, Barbara said: "Now, let's see if your dad greets me." She set the pizza on the scalding-hot car roof, hoping he'd notice and suggest we talk, and she smiled as she saw him coming down the porch steps to meet us at the gate that he was now sliding open. I took out a bottle of beer. (Barbara and I were whispering back and forth: "You know we don't greet each other in my family." "Yeah, I know, I know." "It's not like he says hello to me, right?" "He's treating you nice these days." "He's terrified you're going to leave me the week before, too." "Poor thing.")

When he reached us, he headed straight for the trunk without so much as a kiss.

"Dad, let's have some pizza," I said, but he was already leaning over a case of liquor.

"Sure, sure." He lifted out the case, keeping his back straight, bending carefully at the knees. It wasn't exactly the best time of day for a seventy-two-year-old to be hauling cases of liquor, and I was worried he might hurt himself. I was caught between two lights in my life, each of them overly bright. My father was wearing sweatpants and the running shoes I'd given him for his birthday; he exercised, loved physical therapy, but he wasn't exactly fit enough to carry heavy boxes.

Barbara was fervently texting, drumming away with her thumbs, and my father rushed off for the stone walkway with the first case of vodka; he was already up the porch steps, my father, like he could barely spare five minutes to help us and hadn't seen that pizza.

Barbara slipped her phone in the pocket of her overalls and turned to open the pizza box.

"What, you want to eat now?" I said. I was standing in front of the open trunk, and I wasn't sure if I should grab a case and follow my father or stay here and support Barbara.

"I'm hungry," she said, chewing with her mouth open.

She was beautiful. Her short overalls that showed off her legs, her hair cropped, middle-school bully style. Standing between the flowering hedges and the varnished wooden rail, looking so sweet, and so stubborn.

My father trotted down the steps, hands empty, fingers splayed, breathing hard, ready for the next case. He shot a smile at his daughter-in-law-to-be, her elbow resting on the open car door: "Hungry, huh?" he said. "Fine, fine. Let's get this stuff inside, though, and I'll have a little, too." He got hold of the second case with my help, smiling to himself, not questioning why we weren't following him in with another case.

So he faced his second trip up the walk, slower this time, the bottles of gin clinking inside the box.

Our beach house was the most beautiful thing my family owned. Two floors stretching out, in wood and glass, with a sloping, asymmetrical roof, the steepest section over the porch. My father climbed the first step from the porch to the living room, the second, and then a stray cat scurried under his feet. He tried to escape it, gave an instinctive hop, then was juggling the weight of the case, off-balance, straining, screaming, "What the—!" Voice sharp.

Then he was lying on the porch, and he let out another scream, drawn-out, louder.

We ran to help, to see what had happened. The liquor case lay overturned on the tiles, the bottles unbroken. He was stretched out on his side, in a position I'd never seen him in before.

We yelled for my mother inside, but he said she wasn't home, and he started to cry. "It really, really hurts."

On his calf, I saw the knot of a second, smaller calf: he'd torn his Achilles tendon and the muscle had climbed, retracted. He kept crying as he rolled onto his back, beneath the porch ceiling. His elbow was bleeding, his arm twisted.

I looked inside the house: there were vivid shadows and the smell of pine resin. The yard was well-kept, but the grass had yellowed and coarsened in the sun. Small birds chirping, the quiet where tragedies occur, though this wasn't a tragedy.

I ran to the first-floor bathroom to look for a packet of analgesic, then into the kitchen for a glass of water. I returned to find my father's bald head resting on an outdoor cushion. Barbara knelt beside him, stroking his forehead.

We tried to get him to eat a little of the pizza we'd left on the car roof; the car door still hung open, the key in the ignition.

Instead, he wanted an antacid, and as he wiped the sweat off his forehead with his knuckles, he pleaded: "Don't call Mom. Just let me rest here a moment."

The day of the wedding, I told Barbara it was her zeal, her zeal while eating her pizza, that tore my father's ligaments.

*A*ccording to my therapist, a worn-out institution like marriage can still represent a rupture in a person's life. As I stopped feeling embarrassed by the idea that I was getting married, certain emotions of mine began to thaw. But freezing over had been my means of survival—now what?

It was pretty much the same for Barbara. So, in one of our honeymoon spots in Cambodia, we found ourselves sleeping in a raised bungalow over a green river, and we realized we were terrified of being together. In that remote and utter calm, we experienced a sense of horror we'd never encountered before: it was born from our harmony, perfectly formed and articulated, in sensations hitting us in the head and gut, a feeling of imminent danger, a weakness in the limbs.

It hit us one afternoon while we were swimming a couple of meters from the stilt house after a downpour. We were treading the water, heads raised, the ripples revealing a layer of clear water over a layer of green; on the opposite bank, the foliage murky and impenetrable and swallowing a windowless hut.

We'd reached this bend in the river the day before, coming by motorized gondola. The boatman picked us up at an open market under a high bridge, where a bus had dropped us off. We'd traveled for hours on a road riddled with potholes, the air heavy, past sugar palms, racks filled with bottles of gas, schoolchildren in uniform walking single file along the shoulder. The road had been mesmerizing, and we found the seclusion of this resort unsettling.

Floating in our swimsuits, we felt we were in danger. The manager-owner, a young Filipino, was sitting chopping up vegetables for dinner at the table that served as a docking station and restaurant for the place. He was a bodybuilder who'd been working at a multinational corporation in the Arab Emirates and one day struck up a friendship with a Russian who invited him to Cambodia to oversee his personnel in his resort a hundred meters up the river. After a few years, the Filipino led a mutiny against the Russian and his practices, and now he ran five stilt houses along with his wife, the chef, and his other mutineering colleagues. The huts were joined by a plank walkway that led down to the ground and to a kitchen and the workers' lodgings built in stone. We'd discussed his story; it was frightening and seemed impossible: the Arab Emirates, then this lost place, and all the while taking the bus to the Phnom Penh airport and flying out to international (physique category) bodybuilding competitions.

Barbara and I started kissing in the water. I slipped my hand into her bikini bottom. She swam to the wood ladder, with me following, biting her on the ass while she climbed onto the platform and grabbed hold of the two wood posts: the rotten taste of her sponge-like, soaking-wet suit.

She pulled me toward the bathroom. We stepped into the shower; there was the smell of sewer. In bed we made love in just one position; Barbara drooled a little. And we spoke during it, what would you like to do, I want to know who you are, what would you do. I always talked about my fantasies, not her. This time she said: "I want us to be watched."

"By men or women?"

"Men."

Our words slipped from mouth to mouth in saliva.

"I don't feel like your girlfriend."

"You're my wife."

"You don't make me feel like your wife."

We were sweating, our faces touching, our eyes stinging. I dried my forehead with one corner of the pillow.

Afterward, we lay breathing under the mosquito netting hanging from the ceiling. We caressed each other's hair, the breeze blowing in, and the green outside going gray. The river sliding by.

Barbara said: "I feel so strange. Like I'm about to have a heart attack."

"You're just too relaxed."

"Oh, you think so?"

"You're not used to being this isolated."

"Maybe."

I'd calmed her down, but her fear was contagious: "You sure your heart's okay?"

We held hands and were quiet a moment.

I got to my feet and went to the bathroom for an anxiety med. We took thirty drops each and almost missed dinner, where we sat, stoned, at a table for two, drinking cold beer and poking at crimson crabs.

That night we woke to boats dredging the river. The government had declared this a protected area, so they worked at night, as if they didn't want to be discovered. The stench of diesel reached the tents. The monstrous noise punctured the moist cool night, and I opened my dazed eyes in the darkness and couldn't remember where I was.

A few nights after coming home, I went by to see my brother and then my parents. It was getting dark when I entered my father's office: he was busy trying to reboot his slow tablet, and he hadn't thought to turn on a light. While the clocks hadn't been turned back yet, the days were growing shorter, and I'd ridden my Vespa with my parka zipped to my chin. His office was dark, but there was still color in the sky above the pines; some kids were shouting below in the park, forcing their nanny to lecture them in broken Italian.

I gave my father a kiss on the head, took his tablet from him, and knelt at his feet. The gadget in my hands now, I searched the menu for applications taking up the most space, got him to tell me which ones he didn't need, and deleted them. I showed him everything was working faster now. It was then that I asked if I could have Barbara cosign for the apartment, and he said yes.

I went to the notary with my wife—the first time I'd been to that office without my father. Barbara was dressed like a piece of candy, with me in a sweatshirt, jeans, and trainers with gold laces, and the notary, not much older than us, in a blue suit, no tie.

One November morning, the independent publisher I worked for just dropped by though he knew I was home revising a translation: he was in the neighborhood looking at houses for sale. He asked if he could come in; I made him an espresso, talked about the strengths of the neighborhood, but after these civilities, he told me the real reason for his visit: Asia would be reinstated at the end of her maternity leave. He had no choice but to "bring her back on board."

"And?" I pressed him, "What then?" I knew he liked my confrontational style: he was sly and rich and lazy.

"You would go back to . . . well . . ." His "we-eell" sounded something like a bleat.

"I *will* go back," I corrected him, offended now.

"To being an external consultant."

"To being a freelancer?"

He still held the tiny espresso cup I'd handed him. "Yes," he said.

What followed was a maudlin scene straight out of a Russian novel. I stomped out of the house, saying, "Come with me!" Surprised, the publisher obeyed, little cup in hand, as he walked after me, into the courtyard, then the street, awkwardly shutting the front door grate and then the gate to the yard.

"So meet me halfway," I said, speeding up along the narrow road, nodding hello to the man with his little granddaughter on his bicycle and to the lady letting her dog do its business practically outside my gate. "We'll do this: you keep paying me a salary. We'll do eighteen hundred euros per month, regardless, and I'll go back to working freelance."

We crossed the small piazza, not speaking; he couldn't seem to raise any objections. We walked past the full dumpsters. It was a bright day. I nodded to the baker.

"I can't, for tax purposes. I can't have you do the same work at the same salary but with a VAT number: there'd be an inquiry. Plus, you could sue me, you know." Under his hunting jacket and then his checkered suit coat, his white shirt was dappled with sweat. "It would be better to collaborate on individual projects, with you consulting, like before. Maybe in the end I'd be paying you the same amount, but I can't guarantee that sort of regular salary. I just can't."

"But I'm already meeting you halfway," I answered. I was headed for the grocery store. That ark of fluorescent lighting, linoleum, cardboard, plastic was the only place where I could get rid of him. "It would be a position as coordinator, not one project, as if it were one project . . ." We took the stairs down to the consular road that ran past the corner grocery store.

"Like I told you, I'm sorry," he insisted, "but I just can't."

"So, let me tell you what I think."

"Please. Thank you—please do—I know I'm asking a lot."

I forced myself to look him in the eye and to keep my hands in my pockets, so I wouldn't violently wave them around. He was still holding the espresso cup—it was empty—and now he was cradling it in one hand. I wanted to grab that cup and chuck it against a car.

"If you want to keep me," I said, "then make me editor in chief. You make me editor in chief, you write it down, send out an email announcement, all over Italy, then you can pay me whenever, with all the VAT numbers you want. No—you don't even have to pay me. But you have to say I'm editor in chief."

He just stood there, mouth slightly open.

"Work-for-hire, consulting on individual projects, no pay. But you have to call me editor in chief. If over the long haul you trust me and want to build your publishing house with me, you have to call me editor in chief. The only way I can accept this is if you call me editor in chief. I'll give you a few days to think it over.

Now I have to do my shopping." I held out my hand, he shook it, and not looking at him or taking back my espresso cup, I walked into the store.

Once inside, I glanced back through the glass doors: the publisher was still there, standing motionless, then he tentatively raised the espresso cup for me to see. I waved my index finger, letting him know he could return it some other time.

That fall, there were mornings when one of us would wake the other without so much as a movement or a word, like a fluorescent light clicking on, under the sheets. Facedown on the bed, arms numb up to my shoulders, unable to move, I woke my wife with my worried thoughts. It was Saturday.

Later, at a nearby plant nursery, I said: "They'll be upset. I shouldn't have lost that work. I should've kept it no matter what."

"Listen, I've been thinking about it." She was holding two chubby baby cactuses, each adorned with a lopsided flower, like toddlers playing dress-up. "Your job's so strange that there's really no point in going into so much detail like you always do."

"But I don't have a job."

"Do you get what I just said?"

"That I don't have to go into so much detail with my folks."

"That's right. Because tomorrow you'll take on an editing job, a translation, some proofs, and you'll be back at it. And in the meantime, write for the paper. Maybe you'll go back to working for that moron on his terms and you'll tell your parents you're still an editor. How you work is your business and no one else's! You're an intellectual—you can always pretend you have more work than you do."

The guy from the nursery came up to us, and Barbara and I

joked about the discount he gave us last time: "Maybe this time, you won't make us pay at all, since you're such a nice fellow?"

At the checkout counter, we added a bag of fertilizer. The girl at the register handed me the bill, and Barbara took it from me and paid.

Up on our roof, we tended to our plants: it had rained hard all week. Then we carried up some laundry to put in the washer in the cement shed and afterward, we caught our breath a moment while we lay on the wooden deck chairs, in the shade of the solar panels and Barbara said: "You don't need to tell your parents anything at all."

On the surrounding lower rooftops, laundry hung limp in the sun; we heard the sound of a power drill, carried in the chilly air.

What bothered me the most was that I'd lost that work just after meeting with the notary to cosign for the condo, but I didn't tell her this because I didn't want to sound passive-aggressive.

Barbara got up to look at something, and after a moment, she spotted a small gap between the wall and the metal windowsill, at the top of the spiral staircase, a crack, and a line of ants streaming in. She told me to go get the hose lying filthy and tangled on the roof terrace. We swept them away in a jet of water. Then we went down to kill all the ants bustling around the foundation: outside, black armies had built fortified paths into the bedroom and living room. Our coats off, our sleeves rolled up, we took a bottle of whitewash from the cupboard and let it snow down through the perforated cap, onto that flood of ants—all of them, bleached white and dying.

I always insisted on going with her for breakfast at the coffee bar and while we walked, I kept her from reading her phone.

Sitting there on her plastic chair, facing the traffic on Torpignattara, dressed up, in among the old-time regulars and a few Chinese kids.

Then we'd walk back to our neighborhood, a small flow of people heading out for the day, on foot, on scooters, in cars, greeting one another, stopping for a quick chat. Finally, I'd watch her drive off in her subcompact, her seat pulled up to the steering wheel.

After she left, the clouds lifting, revealing the sky, the temperature unchanging. Mornings at ten, my face feeling oily, I'd wash the dishes while two small birds sang back and forth on our dead-end street and the sun laid its rippling jasmine wallpaper over the walls.

I'd go up to the roof with a bag of dirty laundry and hang out the wash from the night before. I'd add softener, stain remover, sanitizer, a color-catcher sheet. The horizon beyond the houses, the stretch of sky, cloudy or clear. At these moments, I was completely alone.

I'd walk down to Casilina to buy lunch and dinner and poison for the ants, and in every muscle of my body I sensed what my wife thought of me.

In the grocery store, wiping my face, which I'd forgotten to wash. Composing lines of poetry on my cell phone: about additives, cold-water detergent, sinks. A man kneeling beside a car. Two old women commenting on a panhandler behind his back. Mornings with no work—as an editor I'd cut these details from a novel, but they were moments of love.

A boy hiding at the back of an aisle, playing a prank on the friend he's talking to on the phone. Laughing like crazy because he alone knows they're both in the grocery store at the same time.

While I recorded this image in the notes on my phone, the yellow screen disappeared and a call from Barbara came in. She was stressed, locked in a bathroom with a stomachache. A regional administrator was causing trouble when it came to modifying the public notice to add the event at the medieval garden. The women she was working with had made a proposal to a councilor to modify the events calendar to allocate around thirty thousand euros for this evening on violence against women. The problem was, if it wasn't announced in time, one of two things would happen: there'd be no texts from invited authors, so the festival couldn't go on, or they'd have to let the grant winners know secretly before the official date so the festival could go on, and doing that would be illegal. The public notice wasn't ready yet because the administrator was questioning the phrasing in the document.

"They're driving me crazy. We'll never finish it in time to get people to participate."

"Are you crying, honey?"

"No. A little. What are you doing now?"

"I'm at the store."

"I'm sick of this—I want to stop working, too."

I stepped into the checkout line. An old alcoholic kept telling the cashier to give her twenty plastic bags for free.

"I'm sick of this," she said again. "I'm quitting, too."

"Poor little bubble."

That evening she came home early, no cocktails with colleagues, no theater. She didn't greet me right away: she glanced up from her cell phone, then looked down again; transfixed, she slipped on her moccasins; with every message she let out a "Oh, Christ, what now" or a "Oh, Christ, not this, too."

She started looking around for something. She must have found it: "Must this keyboard always be on the couch?"

She picked up the cordless keyboard I used with my laptop and carried it into the bedroom, and I followed behind her. She hadn't looked at me yet. I followed her into the bathroom, too, where she pulled down her wool boot-cut slacks; they dropped lightly to her feet and she was left standing in her underwear.

"You want a gin and tonic, a martini?" I asked.

"Do we have beer?"

I went to the fridge, then returned to the bathroom, and found her sitting on the toilet in her wifebeater, holding her pale breasts up with one hand while wiping with some toilet paper.

"Is the announcement still being held up?"

She stayed seated, opened the can I'd handed her, and took a sip. A few sips later, she seemed to come up with an idea that gave her some relief. She got up, and setting the beer on the wide, flat sink, she knelt by the hamper where I'd draped the bath mat; she gave the heavy material a loud sniff, said it was filthy, and stuffed it inside an old chamber pot we used as a basin.

"You're losing it," I said.

Finally, her laughter. Guttural, eyes half closed. But after her beer, she stretched out on the couch and complained with a vengeance: the Roman council was destined to fail, soon she'd be out of a job, politics and culture were collapsing, money for cultural activities was so limited at this point, the dream was over.

I brought her some stuffed pizza, and she ate it, breathing hard, her head on a lumpy pillow. I finished a beer and opened another, checking if she wanted some. We went to bed before nine and I started reading her a Japanese story.

It was about a couple on their honeymoon, and they were so

anxious, they couldn't let go and enjoy the trip. Barbara listened, hands on her stomach, and started muttering to herself; then she was snoring. I felt a shiver of pleasure that she was asleep, and I kept reading in a monotone voice so my silence wouldn't wake her; another half page on, my voice grew quieter; a few paragraphs after that, my voice turned to thought and I continued reading to myself. That passage from voice to mind was magic.

My wife's position, faceup, so dignified, was entertaining, and watching her, I felt a tickling throughout my body. Her narrow hips in her faded pajamas, her feet, her bunched toes peeping out from under the jumbled quilt: I laughed at her, silently, and that laughter was good company.

Daniela

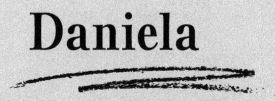

And women don't count in this family.
I mean that our women stay home
and bring us into the world and say nothing
and count for nothing and we don't remember them.

—CESARE PAVESE,
"Ancestors"
(trans. Geoffrey Brock)

It was midafternoon, and my nephew Angelo stood on the tall kitchen table, gripping my hands up high. He had on a pink, long-sleeved jumpsuit, a gray onesie underneath, and white wool socks with no-slip soles. I sat on a barstool, facing him, while he tried out his muscles, his motions sometimes voluntary, other times reflexive. Angelo's chubby knee would give, buckle, he lost his balance, almost fell backward or forward, and I'd save him. Reassured, he'd immediately try again.

Since I'd stopped working, I spent one afternoon a week helping my sister-in-law, Daniela, on her nanny's day off. And over the weeks, I saw my features emerge on Angelo's face: he sometimes felt like my son, with his big dark eyes, squashed nose, and the lovely hollow between his mouth and nostrils; the little hair he had was dark, sleek, and combed down—he looked like a mini fashion model; his forehead was twisted into three worry wrinkles; his skin was pink, with a few little red allergy bumps. The way he most resembled me and his father was that he had his grandfather's same dignified sadness: lips pressed together, the downward slant to the eyes, the tension in the curved brow ridge, balancing some overwhelming, internal weight.

His twin brother, Giuseppe, resembled Daniela, so when we were together, the five of us—me, her, the three boys—we looked like the typical bourgeois family, with one son entirely his father, me, and the other two entirely their mother.

One cave-in after another, Angelo's knees grew tired, and I sat him down on the table, legs dangling; worn out, he studied me with approval; then a look came into his eyes, some sad memory that made him withdraw into himself: he tilted his head and gazed off with a desolate expression, his chin beaded with sweat; he smiled, showing his gums, like his grandfather; a ghost gave him some bad news that pressed the corners of his mouth down so far I felt pervaded by pain; we looked intently at each other, and he grew calm; he reached out to pull my beard and his round eyes were soothing.

He received more bad news from deep inside: I figured he was about to vomit on me, so I grabbed him and leaned him to one side and watched the vomit spurt out of his mouth, onto the floor.

He was inconsolable, his screams carrying to his mother, who eventually strolled in, holding Gionata, her oldest boy, by the hand. Gionata, face perfectly round, with his long curls and my mother's beautiful cheekbones, was emitting falsetto screams, trying to compete with his little brother. His screaming was stylized, though he wanted to believe it was real, which made the sound even more annoying. But after spending this Christmas together, Gionata and I had developed a bond: I sometimes almost teared up showing Barbara his photos; when he grew sleepy, he'd call my name.

Shortly after Christmas, we discovered that Gionata's fevers were caused by food allergies. By eliminating preservatives and processed foods from his diet, his fevers stopped—he only got sick if he was allowed to have these. The year and a half he'd been shut up in the apartment with his exhausted mother had been for nothing, since his illness wasn't due to the cold or germs—he could have lived normally, gone outside. Now he did, he just couldn't eat cheese or regular sweets. Daniela had bought some books on vegan pastry-making and for the first time in her life, she'd grown passionate about cooking. Since this new eating regime coincided with the birth of the twins, Gionata blamed them; he hugged them too hard, like he wanted to strangle them, and when his mother gave them a bottle, he shrieked with jealousy (sometimes, watching him suffer, I'd search—and not find—a way to explain that since his mother wasn't breastfeeding them, that meant he was her favorite). He was mortified that he was being deprived of the tastiest foods, and he repaid this insult by sulking and hitting anyone who ate cake in front of him. I learned this from Daniela, whose love for her oldest son was so intense, I got the feeling, watching them when the three of us were alone, that I was a private witness to the force that drove the world.

Describing that "sweet girl," Daniela, "the angel of the hearth," after writing about Barbara and Eleonora, working women, who wouldn't have the faintest idea how to handle a child, I find myself compelled to judge (like it's an actual law of narrative physics, a gravitational pull), to decide which of them lives at a higher vibration: the mother or the woman with no children. And now we've come to the real point of the book: since it's not up to me to decide, what's left for a man to write when he's writing about women? Is there anything left?

I love each of the women who lends her name to a part of this novel, but when I look over what I've written about them, I find that, in a written work, these two types of women—who might live in nearly closed-off worlds, where they don't have to force themselves to question their every movement and choice based on the movements and choices of the other—still seem to compete in an incorporeal beauty contest where it's not legs and hairstyles that are judged; it's the soul. Is a man's prose a women's beauty contest? I can feel it, that everything leads to me lining up women, then holding up cards with a number from one to ten. If I force myself to stop rating them, is there anything left? Or is a man's prose nothing more than a fancy cow auction, with the best cows picked? And if I refrain from this, is there anything left?

One afternoon every week with Daniela, for a number of months, in her dim, badly lit apartment, the sound of rain on the windows, in the quiet after putting the babies down for a nap. Or out into the dazzling winter sun those days you could get to the park to air out the little inmates. Me and my sister-in-law, in an intimacy I'd stolen from my brother. I liked being there, in that apartment, immersing myself into a few hours of exhausting drudgery, mopping the floor washing the dishes fixing a toy or kitchen cabinet to calm someone down potty-training helping a kid climb the stairs: a whole slew of activities emanating from a calling that, because of my own psychological limitations, I'd been denied access to before.

The main room and kitchenette faced east: mornings were

sunlit and glorious, afternoons depressing. Further adding to the intensity of those afternoons with my sister-in-law was the fact that I grew up here. Forty years ago, my parents owned just this section of the fourth floor; thirty years ago, they bought the next-door apartment and combined the two, in part because my father wanted to see the sunset, and the abrupt darkness that settled over this side darkened his mood; he moved his office to the other half, where, at that hour, through the pine boughs, a mawkish pink or dramatic orange spread over the sky. The light my nephews were growing up with was the same light in which I learned how to obey, how to please others, how to leave projects unfinished. The square footage doubled after purchasing the place next door, this after my father started earning real money: they installed double-glazed windows, and added gilt frames around the mirrors, the first pretenses of a couple coming from two different backgrounds—my father more lower-middle-class, my mother more elegant and more religious—who had found common ground in their frugality in the seventies and in Catholic social movements; newly rich, my parents now felt compelled to invent a style that represented them, even if they were still socially frugal, because my father didn't wish to socialize with his work colleagues, and so my parents' dinner parties for old friends—not entrepreneurs or investors—just became more sumptuous, with chicken in aspic, silver dinnerware, sets of eighteenth-century glasses in a cabinet . . . that extravagant square footage had now disappeared between two families, and traces of the elegance demanded of the rich in the eighties survived only here and there, like ancient architectural ruins. My parents had an imperial age purely due to the demands of status, but they passed through this period with no ideology and therefore no great need to erase it completely. Now my parents and Luca and Daniela all lived surrounded by stucco and decorations and colors that contrasted with the new design sense that Daniela (a graduate in architecture) had brought to her side of the apartment and then to her in-laws' side, through her various presents. She'd scraped off the veneer, removed the gilt frames, the fake columns, the Greek-shrine bookshelves, the trompe l'oeil.

Daniela was ashamed to have a nanny, especially once her son's fevers had stopped: the ordeal of Gionata's first year and a half had forced her to have a nanny whose salary was covered by her in-laws, not to mention their free apartment, but now that she sometimes got a whole night's sleep, she was troubled by her own good fortune. It didn't seem right when so many mothers had to make do on their own.

I thought she was probably just exhausted, but no one discussed this, including her, just like no one discussed my mother's exhaustion when she was her daughter-in-law's age; Daniela didn't blame my family for this, though, not like she did with her parents, who had their life in Latina, were involved in the church or in academia, I forget which, and didn't concern themselves too much with their daughter, meaning, they thought she was difficult. Let the reader decide.

She felt my company was essential. I was the only "adult person" she spoke to—she hadn't had a night out in two years—first, it was Gionata's fevers, then raising the twins while Luca followed the regional governor around to every evening event. I asked her if she spent hours and hours watching TV dramas; she told me that I had no idea how hard it was for her to concentrate: "I've forgotten how to follow a plot."

She sat down to mix up a batch of butter-free cookie dough

for Gionata, whom she'd hoisted onto the chair beside her, so he could help; Daniela, Angelo in her lap, kissing the top of his sweaty head, didn't want to stop talking with me, but after a short while without us paying attention to him, Gionata started to whine. Daniela tossed some English in when she didn't want him to understand: "I never get to finish a conversation. I only get to talk *with children*. So *boring*."

"You or them?"

She sighed: "Both. But I meant them. See! You think I'm *boring*, don't you?"

"Come on! Not at all."

"My problem is, this seems fine for everybody else. Like my punishment is *that I can't have a life*. Plus, of course, my parents aren't around, which is both a blessing and a curse, and if they were around, I'd be even more of a doormat."

I was standing, listening to her while rocking Angelo—I'd scooped him up and he was now falling asleep in my arms, against my sweatshirt that he'd soiled with tears and sweat and a silent spit-up, so maybe the fabric had bothered him. Gionata saw me attending to Angelo far too much, and he wouldn't look at me. In the half-light, Daniela stood plump and chesty, in a gray wool dress; she'd put on weight but was still beautiful. She liked to have a water bottle with her to stay hydrated, and she went to the bathroom when the kids did, sometimes leaving the door cracked open so I'd hear her pee. She was telling me she couldn't seem to get rid of her belly fat; the rest of her body hadn't changed since giving birth: she'd always been beautiful, very curvy, a bit hidden with her retro fashion sense, swaddled in high-waisted skirts, dresses, peplum blouses. She'd rather ruin these clothes holding her children than tuck them away in her closet for some future use she didn't really believe in after Gionata's allergy and the curse—she'd never call it that in front of her in-laws—of having twin boys instead of the perfect little daughter she'd hoped to pair with her firstborn like it was a choice of interior design. She had red wavy hair that was dark and dull and reminded me of Eleonora when I first met her and her health wasn't good. [I've only just realized there's a triangle of red hair between Eleonora, my brother's wife, and then our distant sister, whom I'll get to soon.]

The living room–kitchen had three large glass doors, but there was little light coming in now, and Daniela was mixing flour in the dark, instructing Gionata, who obediently obeyed, anxious to keep this bubble of attention entirely on himself (the second twin was asleep at his grandparents'; my mother was watching him while she worked on a crossword). Being confined to home had put him behind: it was taking him a long time to learn how to talk, so even if he wanted to, he wasn't capable of expressing himself verbally and could only interrupt us by whining.

"Since *nobody cares* if I spend *all my fucking time with this little nightmare* . . . sweetie pie . . ." (she stroked his head) "I thought: instead of going back to work—yeah, right—I'd do something I like. No way I'm looking for a job, I've got another idea to get back a little shred of my life . . ."

"What's that?"

"I'm too embarrassed to say."

The cookies were ready to bake and now the oven was preheating. Daniela licked dough off her fingers and gave just a little piece to her son, kissing him on the ringlets of hair glued to his forehead.

"Come on—fess up."

"You're the only one I really should tell, but it's hardest with you."

I said I understood—an editor's the natural confessor for aspiring writers: "It's a common virus," I joked, hiding my surprise.

She told her son it was time to sprinkle sugar over the cookies, the last step before they went in the oven.

"I certainly didn't mean to hold her back, did I, Angioletto?" I told my nephew, his mother's synecdoche, his sleeping face against my chest looked so intense.

"You didn't?" She was tilting her head to one side. "So, what do you think then?"

"Let me get this straight—you want to be a mechanic, right?" She was silent, her back to me, cleaning up.

"No, of course I'm kidding. You want to write a novel, yes?"

"Is that so ridiculous?"

"No, no."

"What, do you think I should take a creative writing class first?"

"Oh, please. You take those to meet writers who can help you—I can introduce you to whoever." Daniela went to put the cookies in the oven while I was talking: "No, it's just—"

She set the teapot on the table and some little homemade butter-free cookies, shaped like letters. She gave me the *Z*, *I*, and *O*, uncle.

"Just what?" she asked, and pressed the button on the medical alert device. They used it to call my mother from next door: Daniela kept it in her dress pocket and could activate it with her elbow, too.

First my mother freed us from Angelo, then Gionata, who at this point was content because he'd been allowed to stay with us longer than his little brother.

Alone with me now, Daniela repeated: "What?"

"Well," I said, "I respect you—it's just, I hope it's because you're artistically inspired, not because Elena Ferrante's so hot right now. You know, the desperate housewife with a pseudonym, writing from a woman's point of view in a sexist society . . . It just seems like a fantasy, your fantasy of professional success, and I respect you too much to let you waste your time on something as serious as writing a novel, just because you have this revenge fantasy against your in-laws and your husband and your life."

[God, why did I have to treat her like that?] She went to check on the cookies in the oven, then left and returned carrying the other twin, Giuseppe, with his soft skin and kind, distant expression.

There was daylight out the windows; inside, it was dark.

She changed the subject: "Anyway, how's it going, this new life, not traveling up to Milan every week. What's Barbara think? Can she stand having you around all the time?"

"She likes it. She thinks I'm very helpful." I could sense the mood had changed and I was sorry. [Francesco, my reader and informal editor, said in response to this part: "After reading your whole manuscript and thinking about moments like this, I have to say it really surprises me more people don't just tell you to fuck off. How can you possibly treat people like this and still manage to land on your feet? Is it women's internalized sexism? Is that how you manage to get away with this sort of behavior?" It almost took my breath away. I'd been so focused on describing events rather than considering the morals involved, I hadn't even noticed how repugnant I was. Seeing my reaction, Francesco said: "On the other hand, you are the one who's reported these things and you seem to have remembered them correctly, so you do seem to know—at least on some level—just how disgusting you are, and maybe that's why people decide they're not going to tell you to fuck off. Because they really want to give you at least a little credit for having some sense of morality." This was Francesco, obviously drunk, not one to mince words, and while I was taken aback, he said it all through his laughter.]

"And what about you, Marcello, you like not working?"

"I love it. I'd like to never work again."

"Wow. And here I am, wanting to work. More than anything."

"You didn't let me finish before. I'm sorry—what I said before came out wrong. When something's important to me, I just have to say what I think, and obviously this subject is sacred to me."

"No, sure, fine, you're the expert here. It doesn't even make sense for me to talk about it: I mean, it's not like I have something to show you. I don't have anything down on paper."

I told her about the female author and the erotic trilogy, my go-to story on publishing—the best method for cutting off a discussion on books. "She was a nobody. She showed up at a dinner at a literary festival, we knew her through some mediocre stories she'd sent us, and then she just shows up, and with all the candor in the world, she announces she wants to write a bestseller. I thought she was awful, truly awful."

"Yeah, I remember you told me. But that's just one of ten thousand projects you've worked on as an editor. Besides, sorry, didn't you say I wanted to become a Ferrante?"

"Yeah."

"Well, her novels are beautiful. They make you want to shatter the world."

"But that's not why we write—to shatter the world."

She looked around: toys scattered between the two couches, still some light through the windows. She sat at the flour-dusted table, and I stood watching her; at seven, I'd go. She didn't answer, she just fled to her mother-in-law's next door, where she stayed for half an hour.

I knew she wouldn't be back right away, so I took a book of poetry off the shelf, started reading, silently composed a few lines of my own, wrote some of them down, and wound up using them in my description of Angelo at the start of this chapter.

When she returned to the kitchen, Daniela resumed the conversation with an opening statement that sounded rehearsed: "And so what if I wanted to be like Ferrante—didn't you start writing poetry because you read Gozzano's poems about *pastarelle*?"

This was partly true, something she must have found online that I told to a journalist one time. While I watched, my ego stroked, she took a piece of chicken out of the freezer and put it into the microwave set to defrost, then opened a container of formula.

I told her I didn't want to influence her, that she could do whatever she liked, and we changed the subject.

My father arrived in his wheelchair. He'd taken seriously the order of four months' complete rest to heal his tendon. He and my mother sat down on the living room couch, and they each took a twin in their arms and started talking about the Partito Democratico—the party my brother worked for—while Daniela tried to get them to tell her if they wanted to stay for dinner or not.

"Only if it's not too much trouble," they kept saying.

"Okay, so what would you like?"

"Really, whatever you have—whatever's easiest."

Daniela found it frustrating that my parents never had the guts to just ask her for something. In her view, professing to not have needs was a way of refusing her love. They could pop in for dinner on a Saturday night for no reason, yet never seemed to ask for anything. "We spend every single day together and they're always so formal," she'd say. "They make me feel like there's something wrong with me."

That day, there'd been another arrest in the Mafia Capitale investigation, and my father was talking about it because after that scandal, he could finally reproach Luca for always frowning on his business activities from his so-called moral high ground of political speech-writing. To my father, it wasn't so much that the PD was made up of thieves whose exploits were now being discovered, but of people like Luca, "too out of touch with reality to understand that Italy's a country of small entrepreneurs, and the PD can't lead if they don't accept the existence of individual or family interests, that these are the driving forces behind growth." He discussed my brother like his wife wasn't right there. "But that's not what's important to Luca because he's not truly passionate about the country. You can't say this to him, though, because he's a righteous man. And hiding behind righteous men, like Luca, are men who steal."

Daniela kept quiet and cooked. She was warm and obviously fragile, but no one ever hugged her: I sensed this, but I didn't hug her either, because I found her attractive, and I didn't want us to wind up in one of those full-frontal hugs that, for me, is a prelude to sex—maybe it was all those hugs around the campfire with girls smelling of grilled meat, all those girls I loved at scout camp as a teenager.

My parents took their plates of pasta with a cold sauce, a polished meal, despite the fact that Daniela had just thrown it together. They ate their dinner on the couch, on two TV trays that had become permanent fixtures in the living room. The twins sat at their feet, on a green rug with a soccer-field design. Daniela ate at the table and, though I was leaving soon to go play soccer, I sat next to her, eating orange marmalade out of the jar with a coffee spoon.

Once in a while I also stole a little taste off her plate with my spoon, and she'd shake her head and sigh, eyes down, smiling.

Gionata had learned how to climb up to the inflatable slide, but he was still afraid of the older children running around in the artificial grass, careening into the little kids like him, knocking them over. When they were on a rampage, these delighted barbarians, Gionata kept his distance and would walk in a circle, with careful, measured steps. But now the slide was free, because I'd threatened two older children, telling them I'd climb on, too, and play just like them.

Kids were scrambling up the rungs of braided rope again, up the middle lane now, toward the top of the blow-up castle. Gionata, learning to climb, though slowly, turned to look for me: I waved from below, where I stood shooting a little video. Once he made it to the top, he wasn't sure if he should go down the left or the right slide, and he studied the other children, worried, trying to figure out if they were going to leap on him, because they could easily climb to where he was.

When he landed, we chatted a little. He refused to speak real Italian, was more willing to use the play words he and his mother had invented to name things (the slide, for instance, was called a "wheee!"). It seemed only natural that he wasn't ready to be a big boy just yet: all those nights in the hospital growing thinner, paler, waking up with cracked lips. His favorite toy was his medical bag with the cartoon on the side; he hadn't had a fever in three months.

Of the neighborhood mothers, two were sisters who used to live in my building. Over time they'd merged for me and now I couldn't tell the older sister from the younger. They both had little girls they watched from a small colored stairway as they bounced on the trampoline next to ours. The women were dressed alike, in unzipped down jackets, white blouses, black pants. The younger sister had had some work done on her face, and now looked more like her older sister, who'd always been prettier.

Gionata shyly approached the other children, and was rejected, so he played by himself, once in a while mumbling the names of the children he knew. In my family, dwelling on disappointments means you lack restraint; sorrow is just a sign of ingratitude, not an emotion. For us, Gionata's melancholy was a new experience—perhaps he took after his mother.

He climbed onto the trampolines and fussed if anyone else got on during his turn, scrunching his eyebrows in mountainous concentration. He was figuring out how to bounce with both feet together, and his technique was paying off: his body ricocheted cleanly.

Daniela came down the steps, shoulders a little rounded, dazed, carrying a slice of white pizza, the sky above her full of high clouds. She didn't look like the other women in the neighborhood.

Her son wanted another coin for the trampoline, to show her

how he could jump and keep his feet together. We lovingly watched him while Daniela asked me about the talk show I was developing (with Francesco) for RAI. I didn't want to discuss the show—she'd resent me for it: she complained, sinking her teeth into her pizza, about how she'd love the chance to develop that show instead of me. She offered me her crust.

I felt a few raindrops. Daniela was worried Gionata's immune defenses were still down: she always worried when the weather was bad. A colored poncho went over her boy's head, and we set off toward home.

"You want others to really respect you and what you're going through," I told her. We were at the top of the stairs leading onto the piazza. "And you love me because I don't comment, I don't ask anything of you, and I let you vent—I don't bullshit you, like, I don't tell you everything'll be better in six months."

"What?"

"You said I'm the only one you can talk to."

"That's true."

"But you don't want to hear it when I complain about my life. This talk show I'm writing—I don't like it. Why can't I say that?—why can't I say I'm in a rough patch right now? Maybe I'm not an intellectual, but I'm too close-minded to be anything else."

"So?"

"So, what."

"So?"

"What? I don't understand."

"So, can't you see it's different?"

"No, listen," I said, raising my voice, "I'm going to stop you right there. I'm going to do what you do—if you say something

I don't want to hear, I'm going to stop talking and just wait till you're through."

"Is that what I do with you?" she asked. "Really?"

I put my arm around her waist a moment, then went to throw my ice cream wrapper in the trash. When I came back, I picked up her son, who started shrieking, so I handed him off to her. Then I said: "Your husband wants to leave the PD, my wife wants to quit, too, I'm not working anymore, and you feel guilty because your son got these fevers from his allergy. We don't think we're very likable."

"You don't like me?"

"I like you a lot. I just mean we both think we're assholes—we don't like ourselves."

"Well, at least you get to meet with RAI—me, *I just hang out with this little prick*" in English, again. "You get to try on a little *desperate housewives* of North Rome and then—lucky you— you're off to another job."

"Look, if you keep writing off other people's problems, you're just asking to be misunderstood. By your in-laws, for instance."

"No I don't, c'mon."

"Am I wrong?"

"Please. *What the fuck*." She kissed Gionata, then turned to me: "Your parents say mean things about you, you know."

"What do they say?"

"That you've always been crazy, but at least before, you had a job. Now, you're just crazy. Even if you are a good uncle. They do say you're a good uncle."

"Well, I'm simply speechless. How dare you speak such cruelty?"

"I didn't mean to." It wasn't raining, so we plunked down on a bench. "Please, I don't want to be shut up at home. Let's just sit here a little while."

"Yes, please. Let's."

"We're always shut up at home!" she complained.

"You never take me anywhere!" I complained.

It was great, the three of us sitting there under gold-rimmed clouds. In her book bag, she had unleavened pizza for Gionata and a peanut butter and blueberry jelly sandwich she'd made for me, because I love crappy American food. Not only had she remembered to buy peanut butter, she'd even cut off the crusts. I was so tickled, I grabbed my nephew, pulled aside his scarf—the baby scarf my mother knitted me—and covered his neck in kisses, but he was having none of it and slid off my lap to beg for bits of brittle pizza scrocchiarella: Daniela held a piece out on her palm, like feeding a pigeon, and he'd lick it off while we both laughed.

A woman and her girls were coming down the path by the piazza; she was a foreigner, Romanian or Moldavian, I recognized her, the doorman's wife, and she stopped in front of us and pointed to Gionata: "Look," she told her daughters. "He's eating unleavened bread." Then they walked off, into the light.

Daniela turned to me: "Why did you lock me away in this neighborhood, *my love? Get me away from here, I'm dying.*"

"My mistake. Let's move."

"And soon."

A dinner one night, me, Daniela, and my parents, my father worn out, aching from physical therapy, but delighted at its benefits, and full of endorphins. He was talking about the Greek crisis while Daniela and I listened and drank our white wine in sync, sipping in code.

"There's only one solution to the pension problem: people have to die sooner. And you watch—they've finally realized this. They're cutting health care. Where our friends live in Sabina, they shut down the hospital. Someone who's sick will think twice about going fifty kilometers to see a doctor at a different hospital, going all that way. You don't go today, you don't go tomorrow. Eventually, you die."

My mother cut him off, arguing only because she couldn't take his cynicism.

We heard Gionata start to cry. Daniela, going to check on him, brushed my neck with her hand on the way by, and I felt a trembling all down my back, like a lightning strike in a field.

My parents told me about Sunday at the beach with Gionata.

"He'll enjoy his private rubber raft from Rome," my father said, referring to the little gift I'd bought that afternoon at my neighborhood grocery store.

Intertwining lives on a cool, damp evening, various tendrils with different needs: the children down, now my parents went to bed, no sound of the TV, though—they streamed shows on their tablets, both of them wearing headphones, lying next to each other in their automatic, adjustable king-size, double-mattress bed.

My brother came home to me having a whiskey and soda at the living room table, the only light on, above the stove, and Daniela loading the dishwasher with the dripping plates she'd left to soak while we ate our slices of cantaloupe.

Luca sat down with me. He took off his jacket, folded it in two, and tossed it over the back of the easy chair behind him. He picked up my glass and took a sip; swallowing, he breathed in, then sighed. He got up and walked around the backless shelf dividing the living area from the kitchenette, got some ice from the freezer, and made himself a drink, chatting a little with his wife, without kissing her or hugging her hello.

They both sat down with me. I asked Daniela what she thought of the fact that my parents always changed the subject when I brought up anything that interested me: "That's been happening since I stopped working," I said.

In those days, if I'd noticed others' reactions, I might have behaved differently, but now as I write this, I can insert the strained expression on my brother's face, who hated when I discussed work with Daniela.

"I don't know what you're complaining about," she said. "My parents tell me I don't work because I'm too lazy."

"You, lazy? Yeah, right."

"Luca"—my brother was getting up to go smoke on the balcony—"your wife tells me Mom and Dad talk shit about me behind my back. Why didn't you say anything?"

My brother sat down and lit his cigarette at the table; Daniela stared at him, annoyed, then gave up.

"And they talk shit about you to me," I added.

"Yeah, I know," my brother said, "because they also talk shit about me to Daniela."

"So they talk shit about you to me and Daniela, and about me to you."

"And me," Daniela added.

"And do they also talk shit about you?" I asked Daniela.

"God, knock it off, Marcè!" my brother said. "Would you just go home already? Let me relax—you don't need to take on the whole family. I'll handle it."

In her tank top, no underwear, Barbara, wrapped up in herself, had been staring into the bathroom mirror for at least a half hour as I watched, picking up tweezers, clippers, makeup remover, cotton swabs. She had a big bruise under her ass, on her thigh, which she probably hadn't noticed. I was pacing between the bathroom and bedroom telling her about my day with my family, getting worked up at the sight of her back, her prominent shoulder blades. It was like her backside was speaking to me, without her knowing, she was so focused on her nails and cuticles.

Then I stopped talking about my parents and my brother and came up behind my wife. I grabbed her around the neck: "You're beautiful, so beautiful." I lowered my pants and rubbed myself against her, the tweezers falling into the sink, the clippers staying put on the edge. "Trimming your nails like that, a half hour of showing me your ass. You doing that on purpose?"

While we made love in the dark, in bed, I thought a little about my wife, a little about my sister-in-law, like all husbands with married brothers.

The program director didn't like my talk show pilot, the one I'd developed with Francesco. We shot it at my place, and the idea was to prepare a drink for a literary guest, then we'd discuss books, life, society; I drank one too many gin and tonics and proved to be such a novice that my guest—one of the most famous writers in Italy, who also wrote for television—had to tell me when to start talking and when to stop, and ever since I've been embarrassed running into him. I got myself involved in the project with the idea—that I obsessed over at every gathering—of making a "simple" show, like a video podcast, something popular now in America, just talk, no montage; Francesco and the other writers involved, all far more experienced, had wanted it to be paced for television. It didn't wind up fitting either category, and we came off as amateurs. The program director didn't even attempt to edit the raw footage.

"You must have been bummed," said Luca.

We were having dinner out, the four of us, including Daniela and Barbara.

"Yeah, I was pretty upset when they called to tell me. I'd wanted to be this scintillating talk show host, and I'd really thrown myself into it. Our place, all stuffed with lights and piles of gel sheets and cables. To get it all in there, I had to move the speakers and Barbara's trunk. And make sure not to scratch anything. I was the one in charge—and I got drunk. I thought maybe I could make some money as a talk show host—but now they'll think I'm this dumbass, bragging to the director, thinking I could teach him about modern television, inviting him to my home for this completely amateur bullshit I had no control over, and I'd refused to take any notes before the interview . . ."

My brother repeated: "So, you're bummed it didn't work out?"

I looked at Daniela, and she smiled back at me, stuck out her lower lip, and shrugged. "Whatever. Fuck RAI."

"Yeah," Barbara said, leaning over to give me a kiss. "Who needs them, anyway."

It was an unpleasant evening, and all of us got drunk. It was almost Christmas, which we also talked about, how much we didn't feel like planning anything. Luca was wearing a blue-striped shirt and a cardigan; he'd become a real spin doctor. Blue pants, blue docksiders. We were drinking a falanghina, Daniela and Barbara mostly talking to each other while my brother and I stared at our phones. Barbara asked Daniela about her father—he'd had his first chemotherapy a year ago and had started having fevers again: Daniela rarely mentioned this, so I kept forgetting. There was something inside me that prevented me from internalizing this information and acting on it. Similarly, Barbara's father had a genetic disorder that we rarely acknowledged, only when she grew pensive and left her food on her plate, her eyes tearing up, and she'd say she didn't want to lose him.

My brother cleared his throat: "Well, Marcello, I'm really grateful that, for once in your life"—he pointed to me—"you've talked about your failures without trying to pass them off as successes. I mean, you haven't tried to make them sound cool like usual—and I'm really impressed by your honesty, and so I've decided to make my own little announcement. I've just turned in my resignation."

I looked at Daniela, her mouth was hanging open.

"I don't want anything more to do with it. I'm sick of politics."

Barbara's eyes were wide, her head tilted toward me, studying Luca with affection, her lips pressed together. (She and Luca had met through me, then found themselves on the same scene, gravitating toward the last regional governor.)

"This is good news—really! I know I'm being a bit dramatic—it's just time to try something new."

"In that case," I told him, "you can watch the kids, and Daniela can become the next Ferrante of Agro Pontino and write a big fat novel set in Latina."

Luca turned to her.

Daniela looked down at her plate.

"You want to write a novel? Knock yourself out."

I took Barbara's hand under the table.

After a slice of cheesecake, I felt better; I drank five glasses of water.

Then Daniela said to me: "So, you think Leone's going to be as big as Camilleri?"

Barbara and Luca burst out laughing, and so did I.

"Let's change the subject," Barbara said, twisting around to give Daniela a look. (A few weeks back, my wife had learned on

Facebook that Leone's new agent, a woman from Milan—the best agent under forty—was working with a freelance press office, also in Milan; they were doing a full-on launch for Leone's new novel, a very different book from what he'd done previously: a family saga involving a murder, a bit more accessible without compromising his literary reputation; Barbara had thought long and hard about how to tell me, while I, unfortunately, had already heard the news from Francesco: he'd been fighting with Giò and after she went to bed, he kept texting me as he lay on his living room floor: "What a goddamned phony"; "No—now we're finally getting to see the real him."

"Did you hear about Leone?" I asked Barbara. She sat up in bed, slid over, onto my lap, on top of the quilt, and she raised her pajamas, showing me her beautiful, small breasts, swollen because she was ovulating. I'd laughed and said: "Okay, fine, I'll never be pissed at you over him again."

"Thank you." She lowered her top and leaned in to give me a long kiss, then rolled to her side, turned off the lamp, and was soon asleep. But I had to get up for my medicine, twenty drops, then I went and sat in the armchair in the dining room, waiting for it to kick in.)

"Oh, sorry," my sister-in-law was saying at the end of our awful dinner, with her jobless husband and her brother-in-law who maybe for once could stop hurting her: "What, are you jealous? You discovered him, no?" The "n" was faint, the sound of Latina dialect, "him-no?" "So when he wins, you win. Besides, you wanted out of that world, right, you didn't like it, and if you did, you'd be up there with all of them, right in the thick of it. You left, so what do you care? You're a poet, not a novelist—what's it to you?"

I puffed up my cheeks, and breathed out, my lips flapping in a *pff pff pff*, while I looked at Barbara.

Daniela rose from the table, took her purse, and went into the restaurant to pay for our meal, knowing I'd never babysit her children again.

Irene

"I therefore advise you to treat her gently," the notary concluded.

"But do you know what she did, Cruchot?"

"What?" asked the notary . . .

"She gave away her gold."

"Well, didn't it belong to her?" asked the notary.

"That's what they all say!" said Grandet, letting his arms fall in a tragic gesture.

—HONORÉ DE BALZAC,
Eugenie Grandet
(trans. Lowell Bair)

W*hen she moved to Bologna to study at DAMS, Irene* abdicated her role of daughter and sister. She didn't show up for my eighteenth birthday party, at the house on the seaside, or for my brother's, on a barge on the Tiber. Luca and I knew she had a fight with our father, and we figured it was her fault, for being so adamant about studying away from Rome even though she was sure to get a better education at Sapienza, according to an article our mother had read in the paper.

Through the events I'll discuss in this section, I've reconnected with Irene, and have finally learned why she left. Three years before her high school exit exam, she'd started seeing a therapist because she had low self-esteem, and wasn't doing well in school. I call it therapy, though Irene says she didn't lie on a couch. I was thirteen and Luca, eleven: for us, her appointments blurred with other extracurriculars our parents forced on her. In junior high, she'd become isolated, had gained weight and hated interacting in groups; the only thing she was passionate about was rock music—but she didn't play in a band—and she wore baggy pants that were frayed from wear. My mother, hoping to help my sister "find herself," told her that she should see both a therapist and a dietician. But after a couple of months, Mom told her, without explanation, that she couldn't do both and had to choose. Irene doesn't recall why, between these two solutions to her existential problem, she preferred dieting, or, for that matter, why a well-educated woman—our mother—would accept that her daughter preferred addressing the effect to discovering the cause. The truth is, Irene doesn't even know if she's the one who decided. We remember these things as if they occurred in a fog.

Grandma, my mom's mom, learned that Irene was about to stop going to therapy. Her proud religious belief was like an artistic calling; but unlike her children, her belief didn't keep her from being practical about life's problems, so she advised Irene to continue her therapy in secret, that she'd pay for it. Our grandmother was a widow and loved by all her grandchildren, and even though it was hard to get close to her, Irene had managed to. When Irene confessed this, she told me that she'd never told anyone, and she didn't want me to tell anyone. It was a sacrifice for Grandma—she had a lot of grandchildren and bought a lot of gifts. Through therapy, Irene realized she wanted to get away from the family for college. She was a tomboy at the time, and had never brought a boyfriend home, just some languid, continuously depressed girlfriends who offered soppy advice and a shoulder to listlessly cry on. Luca and I were into politics, were ferocious readers, and listened to alternative music, but we'd only just begun to dabble in counterculture, so we mistook the signifiers of lesbianism for sloppiness: short hair, stooped shoulders, chin raised in greeting, rejecting everything that could be called "lovely," because it gives off a meaning: a girl's surrender to the male world . . . Years later, looking back at family photos, the indications were so clear, I felt like a complete idiot.

When our parents insisted it didn't make sense for her to go to the University of Bologna, it was the same sort of dream I've called into question here about how Irene rejected therapy. It wasn't an order, wasn't advice, wasn't their opinion. It was the structure of the universe. "You don't go away for college." When a parent says that, it becomes natural law. That's the sort of family we grew up in: orders weren't doled out, but every declaration became fact. The talks my parents had with Irene were practical, reasonable; month after month she brought up her request and was told: "But it's not necessary, not practical." They were concerned about the university environment: "It's particular, the University of Bologna, it has a tradition . . ." My parents didn't devalue nonconformism, had been part of the spirit of '68, helping the poor and discussing Mao's Little Red Book with their parish friends (all future atheists, except them), and so they avoided overtly pious pronouncements and were always reasonable. Our mother's method was to point out what lay hidden behind a nonconformist choice: "Just having fun? Drifting?" In her opinion, it was "a kind of ideology that anything is possible . . . the flipside to commitment and open-mindedness is the myth of absolute freedom." These calm discussions turned me and Luca into two typical middle-class kids, romantic yet obedient, while Irene just wrote my parents off; androgynous, in her dark clothes, dirty red hair pulled back in a ponytail, by around 9:00 p.m., after exhausting everyone at dinner, then our parents on their own in the living room, watching the political debates, Irene would scream, "You're stonewalling me!," and she'd escape to her room or head out for a walk, sneaking a cigarette with one of her dreamy hetero girlfriends. In our eyes, by doing these things, she conceded the moral victory to our parents, so docile before this force of nature who was "dug in and there's no moving her." "But we're here in Rome—the cradle of education!" Luca and I kept insisting to her, parroting our parents.

Then just like that, shortly before her exit exam, my father gave his permission.

In Bologna, Irene immediately went into a state that even to this day she's never explained, and that we only found out about, one day around Christmas, when we discovered she was wearing a wig, that her hair had fallen out.

It seemed like drugs had to be involved, and yet they weren't. The truth is, we thought it had to be drugs, but we also didn't believe it: we needed to think this, couldn't believe this—

With her looking so strange, Luca and I, out of respect, to *give her space*, stopped trying to reach her. And she stopped coming home to visit—we became like distant relatives. One of our cousins suggested it might be stress: her hair loss was unnatural, it was thinning out, but it wasn't cancer, and it wasn't drugs; once that was established, we accepted the vagueness of the rest.

Meanwhile, Luca was going to meetings of the center-left and I was lying around in my room reading and listening to rap for entire afternoons. He read, too, and I'd go to his meetings like it was a religion I couldn't help but accept. Both of us studied at Sapienza and continued to live at our parents', sleeping in our small childhood bedrooms. Irene's name didn't come up. If Rome was playing Bologna, we'd find a reason not to watch the game at home; if TG1 programs discussed an underground comic-book writer from Bologna on the anniversary of his death, we'd get up to clear the table mid-dinner.

Irene was invited home for Christmas and Easter, but she never came, and for us, her steadfast refusal was an admission of guilt. She'd really gone to Bologna to satisfy some strange type of pleasure and was ashamed to be seen: she'd made "alternative choices."

As it happened, she graduated on time, with honors, and found a paid internship at a Milan fashion house. One night, my father announced, through my mother, that since the fashion industry was in Milan, they'd "be buying Irene a place to live." My father interrupted my mother to add that Irene seemed to be "nicely situated" in Milan, thanks to her "close-knit relationships from fashion school."

Suddenly we had our sister back, after years of not hearing from her, except the occasional phone call. We told her we'd help her move her stuff from Rome and Bologna to her place in Milan.

We rented a truck and loaded up what she'd abandoned in her childhood home; she came down to Rome in the morning to avoid running into our father, and she chose what she wanted, and afterward we left for Bologna. There, we emptied out her studio apartment. It looked over a street we barely glanced at, because it seemed like a street that had seen everything, a dangerous street, where wrong choices had brought so many desperate people together, at least that's how it felt to us. Luca and I were briskly courteous, unselfishly hurried, the style on our mother's side of the family, to avoid going where we didn't want to go. While we knew our sister wanted us to take a walk so she could show us around the neighborhood she was leaving, we were, no, no, "it's time to get going, dear!"

Our poor sister. Her hair hadn't grown back, and for the drive, instead of a wig, she pulled on a wool ski cap. And around that cap there rose a magnetic field that blocked her from our view. We could only sneak glances at her, at her and what she cared about, that neighborhood or that studio apartment and what I remember most about it: the lack of windows and the glass door leading onto a ledge on the second level that I found frightening, it was so exposed (and—I realize now—was a lot like the door to the apartment where I'll see Eleonora again, later on in this section). That our sister was virtually invisible still seemed like her fault to us, and our skill in maneuvering that big truck into merging and passing lanes and parking lots; pulling into gas stations to switch drivers; climbing down and back up into the high cab; all these things, to us, smacked of volunteer service.

We unloaded the truck in a suburban zone of a city we knew nothing about. Milan had produced the eighties—women with big tits on private TV, consumerism—only to fade when the nineties reinstated Rome, with its vibrant "grassroots culture" and center-left mayors: from Rome to here, a straight, flat suburb, a light bulb factory on a one-way street, and the gate to Irene's building, and beyond it, an enclosed garden leading to a printing works.

We brought each piece of furniture onto the main floor, scolding her if we saw her carrying anything heavier than a chair.

Through that reconciliation, incomplete but still significant, instigated by the acquisition of her condo, Irene started coming back to Rome three or four times a year, for work, and she'd go and visit our parents. Her hair was still sparse, but after this gift of the house she was showing it more, though not always, alternating with a startling wig display, maybe, when I think about it, to punish my parents. At times she dressed in a caricatural style, tailleur tone-on-tone, or like a lady right out of the fifties, with a wig done up in curlers. By then, she'd gotten a real job in fashion, and we considered her an artist. Luca and I still lived with our parents—we couldn't seem to move on, also because we couldn't make up our minds and go out and get any sort of job while still nurturing our abstract passions for politics and culture. At times, coming home for Sunday dinner, we'd find Irene in the living room, decked out like a respectable girl from the last decade, night-blue capri leggings, white tennis shoes, a bright green polo shirt, and a wig pulled back in a ponytail. Other times, she looked more feminine, in a tight-fitting dress and a black pageboy wig, while the sister we drove by truck to the start of her life in Milan was masculine, and seemed younger than us, with her basketball shoes, her hoody, and her deep-set eyes and natural makeup (we found these products lined up on a glass shelf in her bathroom in Bologna and had tossed them into a shoe box).

Irene's place in Milan struck me like little else in that phase of my life. I boasted to my friends that my father had pardoned his daughter. Her new home struck me for reasons I couldn't figure out, and it's because of that home, I think, that I went to Turin to do an internship, three years after graduation: to experience the feeling again of arriving that night with the truck.

While in Turin I didn't visit her nearby Milan home that had itself turned to memory over time—the road that went on for kilometers, empty, the large, damaged gate, the garden walkway and the three metal lattice steps, a structure that seemed built of Legos, two stories and a basement level . . . [Is it a coincidence that the condo I lived in with Barbara was like my sister's, with a ground floor, and then a basement and an upper level? I've only noticed the resemblance now that I'm rereading what I've written about both of them.] Again, though, even if my parents had pardoned her, Irene disappeared, so in those last years when I was working in Milan two days a week, I still only saw her three times, at various bars. She was always out with a girlfriend and wearing a wig.

A fter that first Christmas of unemployment, I felt the urge to go see her in Milan. My newfound intimacy with Barbara had brought up emotions I didn't know I had. At my parents', I looked through photos from when we were little, before Luca was born, and in these pictures, Irene was so vibrant—a messy little girl who played dress-up on her own, wearing scraps of cloth, bangles stacked on her wrists, red plastic roses taped on like brooches—so full of love and feeling that it made me feel unfamiliar to myself. I wanted to know her, I felt tender toward her, and I regretted never having known any other way to live than as I'd lived. Even at my wedding, such a short time ago, I hadn't managed to talk to her, to approach that gray-blue wig of hers, not even when she started flirting with Barbara, charming her . . .

Besides, I wanted to know if she'd felt the same sense of sadness and death that I'd experienced that winter, if hidden in her heart she felt the same happiness I did at the bare plants in the courtyard or the shadows on the walls from the weak morning sun: she must have experienced that same sadness. *Our extremest pleasure has some sort of groaning and complaining in it; would you not say that it is dying of pain?* The beauty of dead flowers, indigo yellow orange and white: I waited in the cold for them to bloom again in a few months, and for the first time in my life, I felt the passing of the seasons.

I wrote her that I needed to take my mind off Rome for a bit and asked if I might stay with her a week. She responded to say that she didn't have any business trips planned and would love to see me; if she had to go somewhere, I could stay at her place.

I arrived at night, like the time we moved her, fifteen years before. The light bulb factory was gone, replaced by a multilevel building with a garden out back. In the piazza on the corner, there was a bookstore-bistro that was well-known in my world. I'd always suspected it was near my sister's, so I'd never gone when they'd invited me to literary events.

I remembered how we'd thrown the gate open to get the couch through. I called on the entry-phone, then stepped into the garden area: the print shop had been torn down and the courtyard ended at the orange construction fencing for the latest town houses in this growing complex. On the right, I recognized my sister's large windows, low light coming through, her door open . . .

[In the Italian original, this passage is in the *passato remoto*, though these events are recent. Italian's literary tense is an old vehicle that will take you anywhere if you keep it well-oiled, but it's also, at times, a bit obsolete, when applied to current situations, for instance: while I'm writing, it's spring, I live in Milan with my sister, and I'm describing something that happened last winter. At this point, since it's the same setting and this happened so recently, I should use the *passato prossimo*, the present perfect, the tense I used yesterday when I told this story to a friend at breakfast—but writing in an unyielding tense makes even the closest things evasive: they've been tainted by what went before, like the photos of my sister, her therapy, funded secretly by our grandmother, the trip with the moving van, a memory so fleeting it almost sounds made up.]

I was by the steps to the entrance, which led to her condo, inside this old building that felt somewhat unstable, like an art pavilion—an impression made even stronger by the brightly painted interior seen through the high windows—when a man appeared in the doorway and greeted me playfully with those lines I'd heard so often from *La Dolce Vita*: "Marcello! *Come here!*"

My sister wasn't home, "she doesn't live here anymore," a second man added, smiling, wanting to get in on the fun. As a kid, she used to play these jokes on us: she made up entire worlds, tricked us into thinking we had aunts and uncles in the secret service, or that Mom had actually stolen her station wagon. I had dinner with this couple, uncertain if Irene was hiding upstairs or orchestrating this prank at a distance. I got drunk on Moscow mules, sucked on slices of fresh ginger, smoked some pot. My family had enjoyed Irene's good nature (Irene's name, by the way, means "peace"), but starting in high school, her humor grew more sinister, so I wound up forgetting how much we'd enjoyed her cheerfulness before.

As the drinks kept coming, the situation grew hard to read, I was texting with Barbara and chatting with these two television hosts while we passed around a joint. Maybe they were my age but that gray in their beards and their shaved-side cuts . . . After dinner, I fell asleep to a comedy on their smart TV and woke to a tapping on my shin. My sister stood over me, a tender look on her face. "What're you doing—I don't live here anymore!"

She had hair, real hair, thin like mine, but plenty of it.

I didn't get up. My body felt heavy, the pot hadn't made me paranoid, and right then just lying where I was seemed like a gentle, restrained show of affection and gratitude. The way she shook my hand was so bizarrely formal, I wanted to get up and give her a hug, then thought better of it. I saw the two guys lying together on the other end of the couch, and they told Irene they couldn't remember if they were supposed to explain the situation to me or not and decided it would be funnier not to, and I had just gone along with it, no questions asked: "He wasn't the least bit worked up—no, your charming little brother just went to sleep," and we all laughed.

[I promise this is so much sweeter in the Italian—it's lovely to keep using the *passato remoto* for something so close at hand. A fictional balm.]

We took a taxi across town. Milan is small, but it has a traffic light every fifty meters programmed to always avoid a "green wave," and so our driver didn't even try to beat the lights: he would approach the next red never going over twenty-five. He was listening to a commercial radio station, to the newscast between the music and other programming, an emotional piece on the Syrian refugees that European countries kept dumping on each other. No one considered them human, so much so that when the public learned they had cell phones, the response was bewilderment and suspicion. Our silent drive, where to, I couldn't say, through a Milan that was empty, rainy, unthreatening. It was a miracle, a pleasure to be considered human just for being

Italian, dressed, and clean: I could lean my head against the window, even if I wasn't sure where I'd be sleeping and I was in a taxi with a sister who, for a short while, I'd considered not inviting to my wedding, which might have made my attempt at reconciliation impossible.

(At this point, I'd say it was less reconciliation than rediscovery.)

The whole way my sister was texting with someone. The taxi stopped at the corner of Viale Gran Sasso, by an odd entryway, with a small gate to the left and a ramp to the right that dropped down into the belly of a building, below a glass hallway leading to elevators. It was a bold solution in this building that must have gone up during a time when cars seemed like something clean, potentially in harmony with man. The ramp was so much a part of the place, I practically perceived it as carpeted (I was still stoned). But the point was my sister really didn't live at her old place—she lived on the other side of town.

In the elevator, she watched me, excited, her complexion pink, almost golden, unlike the rest of us, and her eyes blue-green, also unique in the family: for a moment, as we stood in that cramped cherrywood box, which was manicured and polished by time, without so much as a vandal's scratch, I felt myself falling into her gaze; her eyes were wide, like she was frightened. And so we hugged each other tight, and for me, that embrace felt like it revealed yet contained within it the wet sensation of discovery: like a glass, the inside wet, the outside dry. When we reached her floor, I glanced at her, and she looked shy and sad, her eyebrows drawn together. "It's a gorgeous place," she said, "I'll show you around," and we stepped off the elevator.

"I've been living on my own here for four years." She opened the door. "Sometimes I'll have people stay for a few months, but the rent's a thousand euros, barely anything, it's huge, on the eighth floor, with views on three sides. It's a gorgeous building—I feel like I'm living in a novel."

"Sure. Milan. Twentieth-century Milan."

"Exactly."

"Show me around."

"You want another drink?"

"Let's walk around some. I get vertigo."

"So do I, so do I." She smiled and squeezed my elbow. "I have to look out a long ways, not down at the street."

"Yeah. Me, too."

She set me up in her guest room; she'd stopped renting it out because she made good money and liked being able to host her foreign colleagues when they visited Milan, or the initially straight female interns who, once they arrived in the city, were more pliable. My room had an adjoining bathroom with a tub, and it was the one true room in the apartment: she slept on one side of a partition that divided her living room in two. She liked her bedroom in the living room, preferring to sleep without shutting herself up behind a door—the same style as my shoe-designer friend's apartment where Eleonora stayed. This place was just as mysterious and beautiful: you could walk it in a circle via the V-shaped hallway, which led through three interconnected rooms and brought you to a second hallway leading back to the front entrance. And a narrow balcony ran along all three sides of the exterior.

The apartment's circular floorplan and long balcony gave the place a sense of possibility and made this older sister of mine seem even stranger, freer, than I'd expected. In one night, I'd not only discovered what had become of the apartment my parents gave her, I'd also learned about her preferences. Her doorless suite was simple and luminous, even with her square, crimson-red couch and her low, round cherrywood table covered with art books and stacks of photos evenly arranged, like hours on a clock. Two framed photographs—of the sky and industrial complexes surrounded by a natural landscape—reflected the light, and a very tall plant created its own shade. Irene never lowered her blinds; the windows and glass doors went all along the three outer walls, both lighting the interior spaces and displaying the outside, like in an Antonioni film, the cranes busy raising tall buildings. At night those sites were a planetarium of small flashing lights.

In that apartment, my sister's eyes were even rounder than I remembered, and she was covered in freckles, her skin clear and tanned from her last trip to the southern hemisphere in December. Her eyes grew excited when we sat by ourselves, at breakfast, or over evening cocktails. With others, she was more settled, sure of herself. She talked about fashion, money, Asian cities; if I tried to discuss our family, she'd lay her hand alongside mine, wait for our fingers to lace, hold my hand until I changed the subject.

One morning, she had to pay her rent to the landlady, who lived in the facing apartment, so she stepped onto the landing and I followed in my sweats, carrying my coffee, and the three of us chatted about hatha yoga, which the landlady taught. Finally, Irene handed her two five-hundred-euro bills. Back at my sister's, I asked where she got the money and she showed me a roll of bills in a rubber band that she'd just brought back from China: she'd worked like crazy for various customers there, in design sessions that went on for weeks, and in the end had been paid off the books, with wads of five-hundreds. To get them back to Italy, she had to hide them in different suitcases. For her rent, clothes, flights with travel agencies, she paid in cash. She paid directly, avoided online transactions, constantly recycling that part of her income which she didn't declare. While we were making our breakfast and I was slicing oranges for the juicer, she said: "Can I give you a little money for Milan? Then you won't have to withdraw any."

The five-hundred-euro bill was wide and stiff, the oranges sweet and delicious. If you find something you want to get for your wife . . . [I don't want to put her words in quotes anymore, like dialogue: I want to approximate the level of vanity to what she said, not hit the mark. In written speech, you lose the inextricable hodgepodge of affection and vanity in generous people.]

Her design work brought her more money than someone normally working at her level, and far more than someone at the equivalent level in publishing: I'd reached the top of my field and she was unknown, and now I had to face up to my bitterness as I clutched this bill.

Breaking another bill, we scheduled dinner with two friends. First, cocktails at Bar Basso, Negroni *sbagliati* in giant, blown-glass goblets, then dinner at a Chinese restaurant where Irene ordered the two of us turbot and potatoes, unseasoned but fragrant, an elegant dish, I thought, and she pointed out the artist Maurizio Cattelan, who was here in this unpretentious place having dinner with friends.

The couple we'd gone out with were originally friends of mine: I was going to publish a book of the man's before he started writing for television. He's one of those southerners who migrated to Milan for publishing and television; besides television, he's written cultural journalism, consulted for small presses, written for prime-time talk shows, and supervised sports shows and documentaries; he's the guy who runs a magazine for six months while it moves from one publisher to another because he knows how to handle transitions. He may have entered the media industry in the hopes of becoming a writer, but he never published a novel, because once on the literary scene, he discovered he didn't live there, and if he truly insisted on becoming an author, then he'd have to give up all the rest: the real home, the car, the children, the traveling to distant continents.

I'd known him for years, but I hadn't been the one to introduce him and his partner to my sister; one night, I'm not sure where, they all wound up talking and discovered this connection; they told my sister how much they liked me and she'd just gone with it, so to speak, talking about me like I was truly her brother.

That evening was the first time the four of us had gotten together. The gutted architecture of the turbot, the Italian white wine, some famous people being practical, upper-middle-class— even dinner was a frugal moment to get some work in—a productive atmosphere never found in good restaurants in Rome. My sister had none of my family's mannerisms: she was talking, she was witty, her mood never darkened over the course of the evening, as it did for my brother and me.

A beautiful dinner, he was nice, and so was she, and we all understood one another, a harmony that I'd missed for years; I could have a dinner like that every night in Milan, not to mention that Irene would always pay.

* * *

Two days later, I woke to find the woman, my friend's live-in girlfriend, in the kitchen. Francesca. My sister had already left. I was in sweats; Francesca, dressed to go, looked at me with the sweet expression of someone who'd prepared for this encounter.

"Come on—no need to blush now."

The windows partway open, the bracing cold. I studied the floor, it burst out of me: "What's going on here?"

She got up and made me an espresso; she set the table for breakfast. She didn't say anything right away. I nibbled on a slice of untoasted bread spread with cold butter from the fridge.

[I'm not sure, in the context of this experiment on how to talk about women, that there's any point in dragging things out and not just saying I was both excited and scared. The subject is my sister, and my sister had just spent the night with my friend's domestic partner. So, Francesca: in a white, partly unbuttoned blouse, a wool robe, no, more like a long cardigan, and black leggings . . . And so I catch myself turning this woman into a sex object. Was it me or her? Or just a moment of shared humanity? I know, I've already objectified my sister-in-law, and now Francesca . . .

I'll skip the tedium of constructing the scene, showing you that Francesca was slightly faded but attractive, and that we were alone (an Asian man would be in later to clean the apartment). It would be wrong to describe her body, or what I could see and sense about her body, still disheveled from that night.]

After we'd had our toast and talked some, after we'd giggled and smiled, and I'd told her I wasn't judging her, only then did she address my fears, assuring me that her partner, my friend, knew: he was completely okay with it, also because he didn't want to continue living with a woman who, at this point in their relationship, had become sexually frustrated. "I felt awful the first time he told me that. I was hoping to wake him up. But then I realized something I hadn't wanted to before: he was giving me what I wanted, and I suddenly felt so free that I decided there was something wrong and I started crying and told him I'd stop seeing her."

"But you guys still have sex?"

"Me and him?"

"Yeah."

"A little. But it's good, I think."

"You *think*?"

"Any way I put it, I'll sound like I'm justifying my actions. Only he and I know what this decision means for us. Everyone else is out there looking and offering opinions, but we've got it figured out."

"So, you guys are happy?"

"Well, otherwise I'd have split, moved here."

I raised my eyebrows, head tilted, frowning.

Irene did tend to lead straight women away from their partners: she provided a vacation in a world of tenderness, magic, sexual attraction, fun. I'd been aware of this pattern, but had never seen it in action—with someone I knew, no less. Irene had noticed this couple was having problems, and she found herself alone with Francesca at the end of an evening with friends, when my friend went home to relieve the babysitter; Francesca stayed out awhile longer, a safeguard they'd agreed on, to avoid feeling like they were primarily parents, in a period when parents are made to feel that since having offspring is a free choice, not a biological or social imposition, one must practice parenthood in a state of unerring self-denial. That same night, Irene got Francesca to walk the whole length of the Naviglio Grande Canal, all the way to her place. "Walking through the underpass, so much foliage, I entered another dimension. And then how a woman kisses you . . ."

"How?"

"Well. We went straight to her old apartment, where those friends of hers live now. She has the keys, she opened the door, we headed downstairs. The basement. I returned home at three in the morning and [my partner] didn't give a shit, hadn't even looked for me, was fast asleep. Later, Irene began giving me gifts. Keepsakes, pictures, posters. Things I hid under the bed. But [my partner]" [I just can't transcribe his name, it must be an Italian male bias when faced with a "cuckold," even when that cuckold seems to have arranged his life to get exactly what he wants], "it's like he wanted it even more than me. He was the one who really couldn't take it anymore, but he believed in family too much to make the first move—and maybe he's not seeing anyone else, though I act like that wouldn't matter, even if at times I feel incredibly jealous. I don't know if I'm making any sense."

Her partner had waited to tell her he'd understood everything since he'd seen her talking with Irene so intensely that first night. There came a point when she was getting depressed back at home—the initial effect of the affair was passing and she was starting to feel hungover—so he told her he hadn't seen her this happy in years, and he knew she was seeing Irene and she should keep seeing her. "He told me he loved me and that he didn't think we were lost."

Oh, that morning, that cold, that stink of burnt aluminum

and coffee. I can't remember if I just let her keep talking, or if in remembering, I've cut out my own comments, but I hope Francesca got the feeling that I was letting her talk; I hope I didn't interrupt too much, to tell her what I was feeling, to explain to her—me, who doesn't know a thing about it—what it was, exactly, that she was telling me . . .

It's only now, since I've been living here with Irene (I'll get to this later), that she speaks freely about letting me find out some things on my own during my first visit, so she wouldn't have to explain them herself. If she'd told me right then, tried to take a crack at it, it would have felt like she was fending off the invisible jury I'd brought along from Rome. For her, she told me later, it would have been like selling off everything she'd acquired. Letting Francesca tell me, as if she'd run into me that morning in the hall, was better than telling me herself, my rediscovered older sister, our speaking in clichés, like distant relatives use, and "I would have come off as terrible: self-absorbed, pompous. Full of resentment. Gratuitous, frivolous. Insensitive."

"What's crazy is that I hadn't really thought about you for years—decades."

"Such a pity."

In truth, I'd also escaped to Milan those two weeks so I wouldn't have to participate in Barbara's event at the medieval villa. Leone had been invited, and there was no way I was going to listen to him bring up his bestselling book, in front of Barbara or anyone else.

The morning of the event, a Saturday, Barbara called in tears and I remember leaning over the windowsill in my sister's room, the living room side, and looking out at the low sky over the distant cranes and asking myself why I'd never moved to Milan when I'd worked there all those years, and telling myself: "Because Eleonora was there, my sister was there."

My wife was calling from one of the office bathrooms, where she'd locked herself in, speaking breathlessly. A newspaper piece had come out by Gioia Longo, an old-fashioned polemicist from our generation, headlined "The Female Quota System to Mafia Capitale," in which she argued that the method my wife had used to organize the public notice for the mini-festival represented an abuse of power typical of the left and its laissez-faire attitudes.

Gioia Longo regretted having to write something like this, about a bright woman like Barbara, someone her age, who, like her, had probably dealt with all kinds of obstacles in her life, but she wouldn't side with the women's movement at any cost, "not like that—not at this price": it was more ethical to point out the problem.

A typical Gioia Longo piece: always trying to expose hypocrisy, the double standards of the left, with a typically loud headline, tailored to Roman readers who like their hyperbole, but it also put together the administrative problems Barbara had been telling me about for months.

She'd already taken twenty drops of anxiolytic and was sobbing. "What're they going to do to me? It's not fair. I was just trying to get this event going . . . They're the reason I did anything at all!" She was scared and couldn't explain why. "This isn't favoritism," she said, then her voice changed, becoming listless, "they're the most talented people in Rome. Everybody knows that." And then she was crying again: "I like them *because* they're talented! It's not favoritism! You have to believe me, Marcello!"

"I know, honey."

The grant winners had been notified before the results were made official. "Otherwise, we couldn't have them participate— there was a minimum amount of time necessary to write the pieces, get them prepared, and the region's delays in approving the public announcement made this a real problem. I would've had to drop the festival altogether."

"I know, I know."

"And she should, too—she should know I acted in good faith."

I started packing my suitcase while Barbara spoke. I told her

I was buying a train ticket and she screamed at me to just listen, instead of immediately mobilizing. "I don't need you—you can't help me right now. You don't have to resolve this. You can't."

I sat down on the couch but only for a moment—I jumped up again, slipped on my headset to free up my hands, and went back to putting my things in my roller bag. She'd be going out soon to meet with the administrator, the head of the company, and maybe the governor.

The night before, I'd smoked some pot with my sister, and it took me two hours to get to sleep; I kept sipping from the glass of water I'd cupped on my chest with both hands. I still felt exhausted. According to my wife, that article might lead, if not to legal action, then to her firing or forced resignation. She was by her car now and said she had to go: she didn't want to talk and drive, she was nervous, drugged out, it was raining, so it had to be shitty weather, too, like it wasn't enough the festival was going to be a disaster, why she ever agreed to do this in January was beyond her, "it could've been anytime in spring, we could've done it outside instead of in that fucking closed-up, dank hall," etc., etc.

I was waiting for them to announce the track for the 11:30 train when a man came up to me. "Would you mind getting me a coffee?" He wore a filthy sweater under an unzipped windbreaker. I agreed and we went into the main coffee bar, with its long, busy, somehow mournful counter. (One day, at Termini Station, when I was a teenager, a man had followed me; I was searching for a bathroom because I'd had an attack of colitis and this man was behind me, silent; I turned and our eyes met and I was more frightened than I'd ever been. These days, train stations are cleaner, functioning as shopping centers, with sliding glass doors to bathroom stalls that you can only get into with a euro coin.) This poor man got into line with me at the cash register, and I asked if he wanted a croissant; he accepted my offer and continued to tell me his story. He slept on the trains, begged to get money for his daughters. He gestured like a Neapolitan, but I don't remember his accent; I didn't look him squarely in the face. At the long, full counter I ordered a macchiato for me and an espresso for him, with a plain croissant. The barista set a small cup in front of me with a lot of caffè latte foam, very milky—not the macchiato I'd ordered: I accepted it, though, sliding the cup toward me. Then, the old barista took me to task: it wasn't for me—it was for my companion: "That's how he likes it," the barista said.

It was natural for a beggar and a station barista to know each other, but my immediate reaction was that I'd been scammed. The man tried to reassure me: "I'm not used to begging," he said. "It's very humiliating, and the only thing I can ask for is coffee. But it's really to have the chance to talk. I've had ten espressos today," which explained the added milk. "I get all this coffee when what I really need is money for my girls."

I listened, suspicious of his explanation. Strangely, at times, someone else's poverty can seem like a scam. Like when our cleaning lady told us her adult daughter was dying of heart or renal failure discovered right after she was born, and we couldn't seem to figure out if it was true, so we stopped trusting her in general.

I remembered that I only had four euros in my pocket and no bills in my wallet. I slowly slid my hand into my pocket while, out of the corner of my eye, I searched for the new security gates to the tracks, a glass dam to block all those without a ticket. I left the man a couple of two-euro coins, and we quickly said goodbye.

I felt very embarrassed and agitated as I squeezed into my seat on the train. It occurred to me that while I hadn't managed it with the poor man at the station, I could at least try not to be suspicious of Barbara and these complicated events of hers that made me feel excluded, like I wasn't on solid ground. Maybe her issue could be solved—it wasn't that serious—or maybe not, but while her fate was uncertain, I wanted to let her be, let her deal with the situation as she saw fit.

(Just before Florence, two policemen asked me to step outside the compartment, by the doors, to see my ID. One of them spoke on the phone, said my name, then seemed to be listening to something; when I returned to my seat, I had trouble breathing, and for the rest of the trip, felt the inhospitality of the world.)

The courtyard was wet, windswept. Inside, a shattered earthenware vase and some stripped ficus branches, leaves strewn over the floor in different rooms. A couple of novels had been torn to shreds, dirt smeared on one wall, a blind pulled down from the glass door. Coffee had spewed from the coffeemaker still sitting on the induction hot plate. The hot plate went off automatically when it came into contact with liquids.

I told my sister about the situation in a long phone call: "I kind of feel like laughing, and I don't know why."

"Poor girl. Is this normal, though? Does it happen a lot?"

"Well, no. It's that journalist who went off on her."

"So Barbara tears up the house a lot?"

"Well, you know. It happens. But way less often these days. Way less often."

There was a moment while we talked that I was surprised by Irene's voice: it was strange to feel like I needed her and could call.

On my cell phone, her number was listed under "Mummy," which was my mother's nickname back then, when we started saving numbers to the address book on our early cell phones. Fifteen years ago, the number belonged to our mother, then was handed over, along with the phone, to Irene, when she moved to Milan. That number had been saved on my SIM card for fifteen years and through maybe ten different phones, always in upper-case. All that time: MUMMY.

At the station, I hailed a taxi, and had it drop me by Barbara's office, where I knew she'd be leaving soon, on her own, in our car. When she came out of the Palazzo della Regione Lazio, the wind and rain had stopped scraping over the streets; the sky had cleared but everything was dripping, in that sudden blue chill. I had her give me the car keys.

The entire drive, she made me stay in the right lane. Via Pontina, narrow and dangerous, was exhausting for her; she wrung her hands and chewed her nails. I remembered driving through Jordan, where we'd begun to trust each other again and what might happen if we stayed together.

She told me about the latest. The councilman and head of the participating firm had said if Gioia Longo's paper didn't raise the issue again in the next few days, this tiny scandal would blow over. But she didn't have the strength to continue with her work after that attack: "She's made me feel ashamed of something I really believe was the right thing to do. She's insufferable."

"If you know you did the right thing, then why worry?"

"I don't know. Being accused like that . . . I can't help but feel guilty."

We muddied our shoes getting out of the car at the villa. Three young women, all in hats, took her aside and interviewed her. Their faces, showing above coats and scarves, were shining and clean, like the sky that had just cleared, before the sunset. I watched, standing back a bit. With everything going on that day, Barbara was justified in withdrawing from me, but I was tired and annoyed.

The villa was soaking wet and the public—the recognizable, the insiders—were in rain boots, while those familiar with this park wore hiking boots and were making their way through the garden.

That place . . . one small cloud, stalled over the mountain, waiting for nightfall. In the shadow of the mountain, a solitary tower. Below that, the castle with its gothic, double-lancet windows. And below that, the remnants of the medieval city, ruin after ruin in among the garden shrubs, with us in the clearing in front of the medieval town hall and workers coming and going, unloading folding chairs from a truck. In the hall, puffs of color sprouting below designer coats and simple windbreakers as Barbara's colleagues organized the black chairs, with the help of the men with their thick hands. The chairs were dropped, picked back up, set down like willful children; the organizers fished handkerchiefs from their purses and wiped off the water and mud spatters tracked in from the garden.

She'd come over to me eventually: I was a luxury, and she'd only see me when everything was in order. I couldn't help her, I'd reacted far too promptly to this crisis—I should have stayed in Milan. Maybe I came just because I couldn't stand hearing her cry. I stepped out for a walk in the dripping garden.

A gushing pond, water seeping through reeds and water plants, gathering in a clear pool . . .

I had to watch my step on the slippery grass. I turned and saw a tame green creek, zigzagging out from the lawn, toward a ruin crowned with trees of different colors. Moss, embrasures, arches, canebrakes. Wings of the castle, devoured by time. The music of the water. And below, sharp-leafed undergrowth, a uniform green. Water so clear you could make out the ripples over that sunlit surface, like a skin of pitted glass.

I'm lingering over the beauty of that moment, because afterward . . .

The river led to a musky, gently sloping bridge, its two arches like flirtatious eyes, half submerged in the water. Jasmine and wisteria climbed the wall.

By the bridge, the bare mountain was reflected in the water, in shivering colors. Fir trees and dwarf palms, pines, meadows spreading everywhere, the grass soaking wet, green interspersed with splotches of red leaves.

There was probably quite a crowd already, because many were in the park as well; I recognized a lot of them. I came closer and found Barbara; she was giving out instructions and greeting people at the entrance to the town hall. Some of the guests hugged her tightly. Someone standing beside me said hello, and I asked her for a cigarette, and then my stomach clenched.

Because I saw Gioia Longo. She was walking toward us, taking dainty steps, hand in hand with Leone. At the sight of them, I felt stabbing pains in my stomach—what did Leone have to do with Gioia Longo, waving now, expression blank, telling Barbara: "Leone's explained it to me. I hope I didn't cause you any real trouble. Sorry about that." Practically a realist scene out of Balzac, I thought, only heightened by the fact that a couple of colleagues were observing the scene at a distance. No—this was

Shakespeare, definitely a comedy, and everything would be re-solved after a number of misunderstandings.

Barbara's face was frozen in a smile. I tried holding her hand and could feel its coldness; the tendons and bones beneath her skin, I remember, made me think of frogs. She'd continued with her anxiety meds over the course of the day, in doses high enough to take the edge off without knocking her out; unfortunately, when she learned I was coming, she also had two glasses of white wine at lunch. She allowed herself the same combo on international flights, which always launched her into a different dimension, sometimes more severe, sometimes lovably cuckoo.

Since the two women couldn't seem to talk to each other, Leone intervened (his presence, for me, was a nightmare): "The paper can't afford to go on a witch hunt—their readers wouldn't like it. They can't push this any further. They only shook you up a little, but I don't think they'll actually do anything. The editorial staff has discussed it—they just wanted to make you feel like shit. It doesn't make sense for them to pick a fight when someone's struggling with bureaucracy, which is entirely how they view politics and entrepreneurs—actually, it's practically a fight they'd take on themselves."

It felt like he could be joking, and so I added: "Or not." And I automatically smiled at him, like sometimes happens with ex-friends during embarrassing moments, when all you can do is pretend that you're coming to each other's aid, like you used to. Leone caught my smile and his mouth settled into one as well, but his focus was on Barbara: "We could go on about this for days, but the point is, there won't be any follow-up piece. I've spoken with the senior editor, too."

Barbara kept smiling. (Much later, I found out she'd wanted to be alone with Leone, so he could more fully reassure her, without the embarrassment of having to face off with Gioia Longo, or having me there. She told me she was afraid I'd be jealous, lose my cool, and make a scene.) She looked squarely at Leone and said: "I'd like to go in now for the event, but thank you both for explaining this to me. I'm really so glad we spoke," and this last she directed, with a brief glance, at the journalist.

Then she turned and left. I could feel my eyeballs vibrate with rage (literally—I have no idea if this happens to others). I left without saying a word to Gioia or Leone, I saw a chair leaning against a tree and picked it up, pretended to check if it was broken, then I hurried off, the folding chair under my arm; I headed down a path, found a quiet corner and was about to smash the chair when I noticed two guys smoking pot and rubbing their hands together to keep warm. I leaned the chair against the stone dividing wall and waited, deadpan expression, until they turned to look the other way. That's when I picked up the chair—plastic and metal, cheap—and shattered it against the wall. I left it lying on the ground, the seat broken in three, and I walked off, almost certainly with them watching; I think I heard them laugh.

In the main hall, the event began: music, then a woman thanked the audience, read something, followed by applause. I knew this was Barbara's speech, that she'd asked someone else to give it instead. I stepped into the entranceway and looked around, at all those heads, to find my wife's, unmistakable, her short hair, always with her straight posture, a dancer and an actress. She was dressed in dark blue, sitting in the first row, beside the council member, a woman who now and then touched Barbara lightly on the back. I was exhausted, stunned at being there and not in Milan, where I'd woken up that morning. It was a good-size crowd, in the end, a lot of people standing around, like me.

A man stepped onstage dressed as a woman, his voice a husky baritone. I left, went for another walk.

I found a ruins, its arched window overlooking the river. I sat in that space, which somehow looked like a Japanese tearoom. The rock was wet. I took out my phone and started searching on the internet, copying down the names of the plants I mostly didn't know: yucca, weeping cherry, banana, South American acacia . . .

Leone was my monster. I sat and wrote some lines of poetry. Nature is there, the words renewing the world are here, and I'm in the middle, frightened of my monster. Chinese bamboo surrounding a spring lake . . . American walnut, Japanese maple, copper beech . . .

[For this next part, I have to use the same trick from before: I have to say what I've come to know, Barbara's point of view, which I eventually learned from her; I have to cobble together a sense of omniscience. I can't feign my ignorance from that night, I need a more ample voice, one that can reconstruct more faithful dialogue, one that's aware of other details, other intentions I failed to grasp at the time, lost in myself. Contemporary authors often play dumb: they take the easy road of privileging one character's limited point of view, even when they write in third person; they're trying to create a sense of chaos—that even as time goes on, characters—people—can't really learn a thing.]

Barbara found it annoying that I kept looking over at her while she shut the door and said goodbye. Leone and Gioia Longo had left before the end.

She felt compelled to speak with me, to tell me that I was taking myself way too seriously.

"Yeah, yeah, I spoke with the councilor—" ("It felt like you were grilling me"); "The way the two of them reacted, her and her assistant, made me feel bad."

"Why? How'd they react?"

"Oh, I don't know—like they were walking on eggshells."

"But they're such good friends of yours!"

"I don't know. I felt bad."

I stood near the villa stage, wanting to hear specifics. ("You kept pressing me.")

"Well, even so, it's not like it's your fault, Ba."

"I know, but Jesus. I didn't do anything wrong."

"Yeah, but it's politics, Ba, so it's just nonstop exploitation. They don't think it's your fault—they're just trying to figure out how to minimize the impact."

She'd bummed a nearly empty pack of cigarettes off someone: she handed me one, and we started walking, so we could talk without being seen.

Smoking brought on my stomach cramps. I took her to see the dilapidated cottage with its arched window over the river. The moon showed on the water. In manga, or in classic Japanese films, landscapes like these are where someone always gets killed; the serenity of nature and passionate violence make for the perfect couple.

We sat down on the brick windowsill, on my K-Way jacket, to keep from getting wet. I hoped she was settling down, that she realized I was only trying to help. ("Actually, I just thought you were being stubborn.") In her annoyance, she spoke without thinking: "It was my fault."

"Like I already told you, you had no choice."

"No, I'm not talking about the notice of the call for applications. That's not my fault. I'm talking about Gioia Longo—her article." She stared at the river like she was a tourist, and she told me that Gioia Longo was in love with Leone. So in love, in fact, that she was harassing any woman who had a relationship with him.

"What kind of relationship?"

Her long fingers holding on to her cigarette, her waving hand. "Any relationship." Friends, lovers, ex-girlfriends, anyone still in Leone's life, female writers he'd reviewed. Gioia followed them on Facebook, monitored them.

"Are you sleeping with him?"

"No. Are you crazy?" She was still staring at the river. "I'm not sleeping with him."

I believed her, but at the same time, I was certain they'd openly talked about it: they'd wondered about it, talked about it, god knows where, god knows when, to do it or not to do it, but they'd openly talked about it—"We can't . . ."—and so I was worth nothing.

"It's not that she's, like, a stalker," Barbara added. "Leone's sleeping with her. With Gioia."

"And how do you know?"

"Because he told me."

"He told you."

"Yeah. Because I went over to see him when this crazy lady started harassing me on Facebook."

"What do you mean 'harassing' you?"

"I mean she was writing me that she was going to go see you, to tell you that Leone and I were having an affair."

Legs weak, cramping up, I said: "If you ever speak to Leone again, I'm going to leave you."

"No, you won't," she said. "And I'll tell you something else, since we're finally being straight with each other and you just won't fucking let up about Leone, even though I've only been sweet to you after his book took off. There's a specific reason why I'll never stop hanging out with people like Leone. To stomach people like you, I need people like him."

"What's that supposed to mean?"

"People who listen!"

[The more I read this part and hone it down, cut the side details, the extraneous descriptions, making the dialogue as sparse as possible, the more I can see it clearly. Discarding the clutter, this moment grows sharper, clearer.]

I stood up, said: "All right then—this doesn't exist—our relationship doesn't exist. You want him. Just like I thought. Sorry—my life's crumbling right before my eyes. So, was it all an illusion? My life is literally crumbling. Right before my eyes."

"What the hell are you talking about?"

"You've just killed this relationship."

"Marcello, are you completely nuts?"

"I don't want to see you again. Take the car. Go back on your own."

"What!"

This exchange just kept building until I got to my feet, went for the car, my wife following after me, through the park, to the muddy parking lot: I got in, shut my door, she waited in vain for me to unlock hers, but I'd used the key, not the power locks, to open my side only.

I started the car with Barbara tapping on the window. I hoped the mud wouldn't make my feet slip on the pedals. "There," I thought, "the car'll jolt and I'll hit my wife." Such pointless madness. I managed to take off, the reckless, furious husband heading to Rome along the Via Pontina, guardrails on either side folded up from accidents, and bits of asphalt raised by the rain and cracked by ice the night before. I left her scared to death at the castle, and I didn't answer her calls.

How could I so suddenly lose every feeling, every certainty that went into the experience of loving and being loved?

In Rome, I parked the car by the front gate to our home and took my scooter, with the plan of hiding out at Francesco's. I was headed to his place when I realized my body was taking me somewhere else, and now my scooter was flying in the opposite direction, and soon I was parking on the next street over from Eleonora's.

She'd moved to Rome. In leaving Milan (I could tell from the cultural journalism pieces she wrote, more frequently now), she'd discovered a new world, the *salone dell'editoria sociale*, the debate on public housing, French writers of autofiction, "post-exoticism." I figured she'd broken it off with her hometown fiancé, but no one filled me in, so I also worried she was hanging around with Leone. She'd left her job at the large publishing house during those months our group and our competitor were going through the merger. Now in Rome, she edited Italian fiction and narrative nonfiction for a small publisher, a fiery guy who sent his old editors packing and drew her in along with other young people, in a complete overhaul.

She was living about a kilometer from my place, I knew, in a pedestrian zone full of restaurants and bars I didn't go to. When our paths crossed at literary functions, I tried to figure out if she was going to come talk with me, but she always just waved, and I'd stare after her, and as I couldn't interact with her, I'd start thinking about sex again. But really, I didn't much participate in that world since I'd stopped working.

During my days of unemployment, I would wander the side streets of that pedestrian zone, looking for her last name next to buzzers. From her Facebook photos, I finally recognized a narrow street, immigrants always hanging out on the corner, and then one day I found her last name in felt-tip pen on the mailbox of an apartment facing the street, a green-grate door in front of a frosted-glass door.

The idea that she slept there, one meter from the street—with all those strangers around, all those pushers on the corner—was both exciting and upsetting. A large potted plant blocked the view of the entranceway, a refuge, I imagined, where a lover could eventually survey those going by at night, searching for familiar faces, then escape the opposite way, to the consular road.

That evening, I showed up at her door without warning, just as the neighborhood was winding down for the night. To reach her green door, I didn't take the pedestrian walkway; I took the consular road, which narrows along that stretch and becomes a one-way street; only those waiting miserably for the bus saw me go by. I entered Eleonora's street and slipped among the immigrants idling outside.

It was well past midnight, and when she came to the door, saying, "Who is it?," I heard the fear in her small voice. Living on that street full of drug pushers was reason enough to be afraid, and she must have considered nighttime sacred, untouchable, to be defended, with the road so close. (A street that must be so intense for the daughter of a Northern Leaguer, for the sister of a policeman. There'd been squatters, for instance, in the ground-floor apartment, only ten meters away, but then they were cleared out and the door bricked over with large colorless bricks: to re-occupy it, some homeless person had shattered the lower bricks. So now instead of a door there was a partially caved-in wall, and where the wall was still whole, someone had spray-painted: RENT IS A RIP-OFF.)

I put my mouth close to the argyle grate and said into the glass: "It's Marcello—Marcello."

"Marcello? How'd you know? What're you doing here?"

"Sorry to disturb you."

She opened the door. Her hair was pulled back, and she wasn't wearing her glasses. I stepped inside, hugged her, kissed her, and I was pervaded by her smell, I'd missed it, but now I can't recall what her breath was like, to render that detail in the name of realism.

Standing there, I touched her ass, kissed her. I took down some notes of things to add, but I can't confirm they're what I remember: at one point, I felt her finger pressing down nervously, lightly on—I don't know—my shoulder? What do I remember? The only light in the room came from a reading lamp; before I kissed her, I shut the grate and then the inside glass door, the frosted glass of an ER. In the middle of the room, a queen-size bed, the kitchenette near the bathroom. And then a solid book-case separating the bed from the door and the street. I had the strongest feeling that I wasn't inside but on a furnished sidewalk, like in a dream. Both of us standing, I slipped my hand between her legs, inside her sweatpants. Her legs, the smell of this trembling woman, they said one thing to me: home.

"I kept hoping I'd run into you," she said. "But you weren't around anymore."

"I'm sorry. I couldn't go on."

"You left me because I was being promoted over you."

Still kissing, touching: "You slept with him. You realized I knew right away. You're the one who left me."

"Don't say that."

"Didn't you sleep with him?"

"No."

I lowered her sweatpants.

"You thought I was seeing him?"

"I still do."

"If I'd called and told you it wasn't true, would you have married me?"

"You really think you wanted to be with me?"

"You're the only one who understands me."

"I know. All you want is to work. I like the books you're buying. I like what you've written."

"Really? That makes me so happy." She started to cry, and I kept caressing her between her legs. "I really needed to hear you say that."

We stretched out on the bed, with me above her. I kept kissing her face, her mouth. I felt her pubic hair rubbing against my skin, she used to keep it shorter, but she was wet enough for me to enter her, and I did ("without protection," as might be said in a cautionary tale). And then, moaning, she said: "No, please, stop."

A couple of months later, so a few weeks ago, one of her female authors published a story narrated by a woman who has a sexual experience bordering on rape and doesn't report the culprit. After I read that story, my memories blurred with the narrator's point of view, and from there, thinking more precisely, I started to feel my offense was in those thrusts, maybe ten, while she said in a desolate voice: "No, I don't want to, please stop, get out, get out of me—and without a condom?—what're you doing, you're awful, you're awful."

Ten thrusts inside her, deeper, deeper, about ten times, and her saying, not violently, only asking, not loudly, only saying, "Come on, enough, get out of me," head turned to one side, she'd suddenly decided not to.

Shaken, I went into the bathroom to finish—this was all so crazy. I couldn't. I did manage to pee finally, then I washed around my genitals, my face, I found her mouthwash and quickly gargled, spat into the sink, all to the flashlight on my phone, because, it was crazy, but I didn't turn on the light and I carried out all these crazy maneuvers with my pants down around my ankles, furtive, slowing down now. I flushed the toilet, then stepped back into the room: Eleonora was curled up under the blanket. That thin blanket, swollen with her huddled form, seemed like something right out of Dostoevsky. I zipped my pants, picked up my T-shirt and my leather jacket; before saying anything, I stepped around the bookcase and stood by the two doors leading out to the street.

I told her I'd never forget what we had, and she said I'd managed to be even worse than when I left her. I asked if she really thought we could've been a couple, but by then, she'd stopped talking completely. I went back to the bed and touched the cluster of bones and muscles below the blanket, where I imagined her shoulders might be. She lay still. I wanted to say something, so she'd understand, but when she didn't respond, I was suddenly terrified that I'd forced her. I thought we'd been playing a game between lovers: she didn't want to have sex, but she was wet . . . She must have understood that I was starting to mentally dominate her again; so she played possum, pretending to be dead. I'd like to say I left out of respect for her pain, her confusion, but I left because I suddenly felt like I'd committed a crime.

Eleonora never spoke to me again. The few times I've seen her in Rome, at literary events, I put on a formal expression, like an ambassador.

[Months after archiving this manuscript because it was just too private, I'm returning to my file and inserting a note: in the spring of 2017, I was wrapping up this story about my marriage, my story with Eleonora accompanying it, like an embarrassing counterpoint. Why do this? Had I felt something stirring? The new feminist wave was already active, but it would still be months before that October of #MeToo and #quellavoltache, those public condemnations of private offenses like mine. The power of literature. So far, Eleonora hasn't exposed me to the judgment of public opinion; and neither will I. But I will say this to History: I did it. I won't destroy the evidence.]

I went home, but after opening the courtyard gate, I took the stairs for the roof instead of going inside. Barbara wasn't back yet. It was freezing cold; the rooftops and terraces were all empty. Below, cars drove by on the street beside the steep canebrake that closed off our private road.

Barbara returned and kept phoning me; it didn't occur to her to go up and check the roof. My cell was off and I listened to her calling and crying. [I think I was angry at her, but after endlessly revising this scene, I realized what I should write: I couldn't see her because I hadn't washed, I smelled like another woman, my underwear was wet, plus I ached from not having an orgasm. Addendum: and rereading this yet again after writing this note, I've realized something for the first time, something that splintered off right when it happened: I committed that act of violence against Eleonora on my return from a festival on violence against women. It's the first time I've realized, and I want to keep a record of this discovery, because it seems important to find every shred of evidence of the great divisions in the heart caused by love. It's upsetting to discover that even after spending so much time on this novel, I can hardly even manage to dig up the most obvious assonances, chances, flukes.]

Barbara stopped wandering around fretting; she must have taken another pill. I knew for certain that seeing both the car and the scooter would calm her down—she was terrified of accidents.

Two hours later, I came down and went in; the whole two hours I'd spent looking at insipid sites, sports and fashion blogs, while tiptoeing back and forth to stay warm. Inside, I kept the lights off and groped my way past the living room and kitchen, hit the corner of the low table but didn't scream, and the silence muffled the pain; I found the door leading to the basement room and tackled the steep stairs to the light of my phone; I'd shut the door behind me, locked it.

From below, that door seemed incredibly tall: and not just because it was at the top of those steep stairs; it rose, tall and white, hit by the light I'd turned on in the room below, with no doorjambs, sweeping, with an abstract architectural gesture, up to the ceiling.

It felt unreal being here. I took a shower, indifferent to the noise. I stretched out on the sofa bed down there (I'd put on my dirty clothes), and I fell asleep at dawn.

In the morning, Barbara woke me, knocking loudly: "Please open the door, let's make up."

Awake, I remembered what I'd done last night, and was terrified. I didn't answer. I couldn't check my messages, my emails, the phone. But Eleonora would never write to Barbara.

Meanwhile, my wife's mood had darkened, and now she was pounding the door so hard she scared me. "God, why are you being this way!" she said. "I haven't done anything—I didn't do anything with Leone! Not a fucking thing!"

For a short while, silence; then I heard her scream, start breaking things. For those minutes, I didn't exist. I was only a sigh in a space filled with filtered light drifting in from the cellar room near the backyard greenhouse.

The turntable was shattered, a chunk taken out of the parquet floor. A tile was loose.

I left with my roller bag full of T-shirts, underwear and socks, shorts, toiletries.

She texted me: "There's nothing you can do that will make me forget what you mean to me."

That day, a bit later, Barbara's company told her that, after reconsidering, it would probably be best if she resigned. She responded that she'd be staying anyway, that she hadn't done anything wrong. They accepted her decision and for a time gave her no new assignments; then, word got out that they were planning to transfer her to a subsidiary office focused strictly on administrative work.

Giò *and Francesco let me stay with them a few days. On* my folding cot in a corner of the kitchen, I watched this couple, up close, while what had happened not a kilometer from their eighth-floor apartment, the enormity of it, took away my hunger.

In the last year, Giò had started working for a comedy show, after all her years spent working with refugee aid. Her entire time on that evening comedy news hour, she never got over the pleasure of being able to work on a sofa in the control room, writing and talking things over, so not winding up with aching feet at night from all the walking from one problem to the next. During the broadcast, and only then, she stood holding a folder behind the camera. For Giò, in life, things both had worked, and they hadn't. She'd written the screenplay for a popular movie, and had walked the red carpet at the Venice film festival; she had a weekly column; opportunities came and went, but nothing was stable.

In September, the show shut down, even though it had already been renewed for a second season. The host received another

offer, still on television, a network channel that had fewer viewers but was also less controlling, and he only took along a couple
of veteran crew members. Giò went back, after so many years, to
working night and day, attempting to write a book, clashing with
Francesco, who was staying at home himself to write his own
book.

Perhaps Giò wanted a child and Francesco didn't, hard to say,
the issue didn't come up, like it might in a movie.

I compared my relationship with Barbara to theirs and was
unspeakably proud of the magical life we once shared. And with
this thought another, just as strange, would follow: that I left
home for Leone, to make way for Leone.

Francesco gave private English lessons to professionals, ages
varying from thirty to sixty. He would take them to a coffee bar
and I'd come along and sit at the adjacent table and write this
novel, attempting to find myself, reading (among others) books
about the end of human labor: someday soon, these books said,
artificial intelligence and personal robots would take over almost
all work performed by the middle class, which would then turn
into a geisha class, service providers for the uberwealthy. As a
poet, I've felt it in my blood, that through the ages, my work has
always been two-faced: a servant bowing and then, at the last
minute, betraying. Or just the opposite: objecting, objecting,
then suddenly, bowing and serving.

When he spoke with his students, Francesco's accent was
sometimes British, sometimes American. I watched them drink
espresso and glasses of water during their lesson, always in a bad
mood, as if learning wasn't the most invigorating activity on
earth. They'd listen and obtusely repeat and always end up somehow humiliating him as he sat hunched over, ill at ease in the

reading glasses he'd had for a few months now, with him taking cigarette breaks outside, in the courtyard, the collar to his windbreaker zipped and pulled up, then reentering the bar and explaining the same things over and over to these boorish, well-off men who never seemed to have the slightest suspicion that they could learn English by chatting about soccer or politics and not just repeating out-of-context sentences about going on vacations with their wives or about the weather in Rome.

At lunchtime, Francesco would go see the student who was reading his novels, and she'd kiss him, there in her studio apartment, but nothing more, out of respect for his partner—she didn't like playing the role of the younger woman *picking the older woman clean.* That her metaphor turned this respected older woman into a carcass escaped her, I think.

During that time, I found myself obsessed with my fate, and I discussed this with Irene on the phone. We sent each other hearts and other symbols all day long. Her emojis of choice were nail polish, the Easter Island head, the red rose, and various faces: shy, sad, modest, happy, and then the face with no mouth, because I told her when she was listening to me on the phone I imagined her without a mouth—she listened like no one else in our family, except maybe our grandmother, the one who'd paid for her therapy (these calls are where I learned that Grandma had done this).

I was sleeping in Giò and Francesco's guest room, and after a week, I took to paying them one hundred euros every Sunday, because I discovered they'd been considering renting the room out again. I was happy to have that space to myself: I talked on the phone with my sister in there.

I didn't want to go back to my place. I was waiting for Barbara to fuck Leone and perfect our punishment. I imagined them together at our home—then I'd have to let my father know that we'd separated and his investment in our place had been halved in value because she was on the deed. God knows what Leone was thinking in my home, with her. But my home wasn't mine: its substance was my family's, and its form was Barbara's. It must have been so easy for Leone to enter.

How immense she was growing, my wife, now that I could leave her alone. She was enormous, like everyone else I've abandoned. I didn't return her phone calls, and if she texted me I wrote back: "I'm not sure, I don't want to explain myself, I don't want to understand, I'm tired of constructing, I want something more natural, leave me alone, don't make me explain, you've got nothing to explain to me, don't tell me who you're seeing, don't tell me you're not seeing anybody, either . . ."

They were like Godzilla, Leone and Barbara, two giants wandering through the city, loving each other noisily in among the buildings, knocking them over as they went.

And we were already halfway through February. Barbara was still working. She'd resign soon, picking just the right moment to punish those who'd exiled her to that corner of the company, an administrative office far from the city center, while still exploiting her connections with artists, politicians, and officials.

I checked my bank account daily from my phone app, to figure out when I'd have to tell my family everything and ask for a loan. I stayed with my brother awhile and told my parents early on that Barbara was on a business trip and I felt like seeing my nephews.

Gionata had started talking, but slurred his speech a bit; he had a meek voice, always questioning, intelligent, but still went back to his invented language from when he was ill: "Kaku kaku katuto! Piko-pako!" We'd chatter together a few moments, voices bright.

"Piko-pako!"

"No!" he'd insist. "Pako-piko! Piko-pakuto!"

His ringlets were sparse; he was thin because he ate so little and was already talking about sex—he'd surprise you with: "I saw your *dick*!"

The twins: Giuseppe followed after Angelo, tiptoeing and laughing at the other's antics as if he weren't allowed to participate. Angelo was curious and would scramble onto furniture, but not Giuseppe, and sometimes he grew enraged and bit his brother; then, after a good cry, he'd go back to wandering around the apartment, waddling by, tagging after the other two.

My parents didn't come over to Luca and Daniela's anymore. They were frightened by my separation—they'd guessed it long before I was ready to tell them myself. For me, it was all an enormous gray bubble. I avoided them and left it up to Luca—that is, the most distant of us—to keep them informed. I did wind up telling my father what was going on, for just a minute, voices raised—

"Look, you can't argue once and just get divorced," I told him, pretending Barbara and I were fixing things.

"Well, yeah, but you have a history."

We dropped it. And I never discussed it with my mother. Luca and I sometimes started drinking at four; if we ate lunch together, two drinks, and I was out.

Whenever I told my sister that Barbara was Leone's now and I couldn't have her back, Irene would tell me: "Don't ever say Barbara belongs to somebody—or she'll kill you," or: "I understand completely—me, too—it's why I always send my girl-friends back to their partners . . . it's so sad . . . we really shouldn't."

Daniela spent her days in a downtown library working on a novel, and since we still weren't back to being friends, I didn't tell her I was writing one, too, this novel of my memories. She had an expert nanny watching the boys now, a Spanish woman who up till then had worked for people of a higher social class than ours, the kind of household where it would be considered a good thing for twins to be with the nanny as much as possible for their first year so the mother could "live." Faced with that old-fashioned, classist vision, I wondered if my not wanting children might be based on this contradiction warring inside me: that my being born bourgeois allowed for someone else to raise my children in the same way I took it for granted that my college degree gave me the right not to clean my own floors. Maybe raising children isn't so different from cleaning floors or cleaning the bathroom: I loved our home, but I didn't feel compelled to concern myself with it firsthand. Maybe, deep in my bourgeois heart, it was the same with children, and I refused to even conceive of becoming a wet nurse for any future offspring; this, from the moment that I'd been programmed, by way of Tolstoy and ancient Greek classes, to feel deep down that I wasn't "proletarian."

I was texting with Irene so often that I found myself beginning to resemble her, in a way. For instance, I wasn't really concerned if Luca's period of unemployment was turning into something serious or not. When Luca talked with me about his relationship with Daniela, I tried to be like Irene was with me, listening for minutes on end without giving advice.

At night we'd watch the game. When she came back at dinnertime, Daniela wouldn't comment on the state we were in—it had been quite the effort for her to impose her will for the first time, to begin writing, and she had to ignore what she perceived to be the direct consequences of this show of strength. More than likely, Luca was using me as the objective correlative of the neglected husband. As for Daniela, I felt certain Barbara was hiding behind her newfound tenacity. It was just a hunch—but later I found out I'd guessed right. Daniela was more independent, more methodically unemotional, and I could just see the two of them, on the phone or over coffee, and Barbara giving her advice on how to stand up to others and their demands and not let them tread all over hers. Two women from southern Lazio forced to deal with two brothers from Rome born into privilege and lacking a certain emotional resilience.

Meanwhile, Barbara and I had stopped texting. I'd begun to think that success was just an obsession. Couples must succeed! They only succeed if you put in the work! What a bourgeois crock of shit, the couple as a business venture, where every day you roll up the shutter door, then roll up your sleeves. I was resting my affective calves, like Giò had rested her muscles and nerves after quitting her job working with refugees, letting herself get wrapped up in the sweet uselessness of a comedy hour.

I liked thinking that Barbara influenced Daniela. I enjoyed watching Daniela come home at night, like a secret message from my wife. "Look at me, stupid, here I am, an independent woman, you'd never think this was your sister-in-law, would you? She can do it, you know. She's not here to make you a peanut butter and jelly—she's not here to seduce you like some concubine. You see my imprint on her?"

Then this dream became my nightmare: I worried that Barbara had found, in Leone, her elusive balance, had found that celebrated empathy, true partnership, as though, with that article of hers, poor Gioia Longo had gotten exactly what she was trying to exorcise, what I was trying to exorcise: Leone and Barbara, together, this decree I'd hoped I'd never hear and yet there I was, forcing myself to fuel it. Best-selling Leone; countercultural yet popular Leone; at "my" home (my father's home, Barbara's home), Leone; with her, "my" wife.

One day, while I was settling into my puddle of free time, I got an email from Irene's travel agency, with a train ticket to Milan.

She took me out to dinner with our friend, Francesca's partner, the "cuckold," in a Peruvian restaurant out past Centrale Station. [I still don't have the courage to give this friend a name, or describe him, because once a week, Francesca continues to sleep with my sister, and now that I'm living in Milan, we often have breakfast together. I couldn't publish this novel as is—I should change every detail, so revise it one more time, from the very beginning, but I love that everything's been saved. Could I preserve the fullness of my life if I modified these compromising details that I'd scattered throughout the book? Maybe yes, maybe the enzyme of fiction allows for this: first confess, then conceal.]

We all three ordered ceviche, and our plates arrived heaped with marinated fish and strips of red onion poking through, like oxidized bones: it looked like the kind of fish a civilized Hanna-Barbera cartoon cat might eat. It was very good, though not melt-in-your-mouth good. Pisco sour with egg white, letting go, relief, then the "cuckold" offered me a job writing for the television program he was developing. "The guy who created it with me decided not to do it in the end. I really want to, though—to dig in—but the others involved aren't particularly inspiring. I don't want to just work with someone—I want to be able to shoot the shit."

I was immersed in the piercing joy of fish and pisco sour and now he was offering me a job, a small job, but still, a job. "You mean right here in Milan? I'd come up here, live here?"

"Yeah, I know it would be a bit risky, but Irene tells me you like it here."

"And you thought of me?"

"You've already worked in Milan. I always thought it would be a good fit, you and me working together."

I didn't toss out some tasteless joke, like: "Careful what you wish for." It was just so affirming, what he'd said, so nice to hear, that my own response was just as enthusiastic, so he wouldn't regret being open with me: "It's true," I said. "Working with you would be a blast." I felt like someone who was running, vague shapes blurring by.

My sister was watching the small TV over the bar, a trio of Peruvian singers on a variety show. She looked bored and attentive at the same time.

He was pleased by my reaction and let himself go on: we could have all kinds of soup, try Soylent for lunch, go see a game, soccer, basketball . . . [In some alternate version of this novel, I could put different details in, to hide his identity, but I'd still be talking about the person I work with now; everything would have to be changed. I like writing about him in secret, referring to him affectionately as the "cuckold," understanding his soundness as a father, as a man.]

My sister and I asked our waiter to wrap up our ceviche

leftovers, and we finished them off at home, after smoking a joint. Sprawled on the living room couch, I started stressing about my friend, now my future boss, that he might be looking to start some kind of perverted love square between the four of us: him, me, my sister, and Francesca, an anxiety I kept to myself. (Now, seeing him daily, I know him as a man whose wants are illegible, who's so involved with his family that it's almost as if he has no desires of his own. He often gets free tickets to see AC Milan, and we've also gone to see Juventus play in Turin, sitting in a fashion house's skybox, with spumante and out-of-season strawberries in that lounge overlooking the field.)

My sister gave me the master bedroom and continued to sleep in her half of the living room, behind the dividing wall.

Her vulgarity in speaking of money, while perhaps her most annoying trait, is the golden glitter of freedom. When she was surviving in Bologna by working in coffee bars and sewing clothes, she'd already decided that she couldn't separate from the family without a pile of money. In the end, out of the three of us, she was the one who most resembled our father.

It would be easy to portray Irene as my savior. But a woman who saves someone is a woman who winds up punished on the following page; the role of savior that men apply to women in some narrative form is our wooden horse, concealing our desire to penetrate and destroy.

But if she doesn't save or damn someone, what does a woman do on a page written by a man? This is what I'm trying to find out. If she doesn't save or damn someone, maybe this female character wanders, appears, and disappears. Until, perhaps, I'm truly attached to them and stop feeling that they're only floating shadows . . .

After all, in the real world, a woman appears and disappears and wanders with the same moral freedom as a man. No—better—if she contains this freedom within herself, if she doesn't buckle to the model that insists she either save or damn someone, then nothing prevents her from moving about according to her own principles. Then we start to tell the story of her life and discover we're asking her what she does, who she belongs to, while the son gets to enter and exit the father-narrator's house as he sees fit. But what does a woman become if we treat her like a man, or like someone else, neither man nor woman?

The woman caught in our prose net is fixed to the paper with a pin. What's she free to do, now that I've pinned her in my display case, along with the others?

Her flight is so light, I'm not sure how to trap it under glass, to preserve that grace, or my impression of that grace.

I can't recall reading a novel by a woman, I mean a real author, that uses a man as a deus ex machina. Real male authors, on the other hand, are always using women. I know I've helped a lot of people, like my sister did for me: I've called a young, introverted writer to tell him he was good, that sooner or later, he'd get published; I've sent out email recommendations for people when I was the only one who could get them that dream job. But I'd never see a character like me treated as a savior in a woman's novel. There's everything residing in the person giving you a hand: affection, manipulation, calculation, compulsion . . . If a woman knows how to listen and is generous with her own money, why then must she wind up being either a savior or, ironically, a temptress?

I have to do for my sister what I've done for myself: allow her the privilege of being a person. Appearing, disappearing, minding her own business, showing sudden affection, boarding a plane without telling me, sneaking all my cereal at night, making me look like an idiot in front of her girlfriend because I'm being pedantic.

I've stopped telling my sister I love her every time we drink together. We've talked so much. I told her if I got back together with my wife, I'd want to kick out the couple living in her old place and move in there with Barbara. Irene said it was bound to happen sooner or later—a brother and sister living together after forty is pathetic (we had an old couple like that in my parents' building in Rome)—but until then, she was happy to have me.

*S*he came up to Milan in the spring.

She wasn't used to panoramic views, and she suffered from vertigo. But she did enjoy seeing the tall buildings at a distance, from my sister's living room. For ten years, she'd lived on the main floor, and in Anzio, she grew up on the main floor in two different places. At Irene's, she never leaned over the long balcony, to watch the boulevard. The railing was a neutral color, and we both felt it put us far too close to the emptiness beyond, and sometimes, just for the pleasure of feeling ill, we'd play at seeing who could stay out there the longest, huddled on the pavement, back to the wall. We'd goad each other to venture farther, to the point where it felt like we were floating. We didn't remind each other of that balcony where we'd made love the night we first met, when neither of us admitted to our vertigo.

She came up to Milan with her winter wardrobe, which she put away in the hallway walk-in closet, a space with shelves and two bars, all hidden behind a curtain.

She went out to network. A woman she knew had a publicity

agency for cultural activities. Events, book launches, film premieres. At night she told me about it. She never felt like going to
parties or bars or restaurants. After dinner, she played cards with
Irene, or went through the LinkedIn profiles of her many new
contacts in Milan.

We talked almost exclusively about work, comparing Rome
to Milan, the former in free fall, according to everyone, filthy and
irredeemable, the latter cruel, modern, and rich, its private foun-
dations constructing buildings in the business district, works of
art like the Feltrinelli-Microsoft headquarters: was this humanism or the end of humanism?

Right away we told each other that we mustn't pressure the
relationship to succeed, that we should just be together in that
apartment, in that city, and not force anything: and sometimes
she understood that we were getting along and starting to com-
municate again and then she'd grow frightened because deep
down she felt the urge to trust in us, but also not to. Then she
usually called her father, which put her in a bad mood, because
her father had no capacity to listen. Now bothered, she could
focus on that interminable problem and stop thinking about us
for a few hours.

Would we ever settle down? And what does settling even
mean—is it only a metaphor?

Sometimes we arranged to meet in Porta Venezia and we'd
head for home or stop for a negroni. While we walked, we'd feel
homesick for that hour in Rome, when the architecture was
soaked in yellow sunlight and then the evening, still yellow, with
pink streaking the sky and caressing the clouds. In Milan, negroni hour wasn't composed of light but of mid-century and early-
twentieth-century buildings, seen from the street, looking up, art

nouveau friezes, and rosemary gin and tonics. These days, the most beautiful sight for us was the blue and ice-white of the sky at breakfast at the coffee bar; but also the cold sun slipping through at lunch break . . .

(A conversation about the lights of Milan was the first one we had that felt natural, so I remember it.)

We didn't fight when we were drunk, but sometimes she cried and waved me off so I couldn't console her—she didn't want my tenderness to take her where I wanted her to go.

She'd buy an apple on the street, take a bite, then pour water over it from her water bottle. Those first days, I wasn't sure if I could tease her.

[I can't even call her Barbara in this chapter—now her name means something else entirely—deep down, I link it more to Leone's name than mine. While the woman I walked with in Milan, or sat cross-legged with on the balcony, that woman was something else, something unfamiliar, not belonging to me or Leone.]

Some mornings, from the bedroom, we hear the sounds of Irene and Francesca at breakfast. My sister has a large, five-cup moka pot. She wakes up in a good mood and the only trick to being a part of that happiness is not to talk, not to make speeches. A preference Barbara shares, and they both tease me about my tendency to groggily philosophize.

Barbara would get up and have coffee with Irene, or Irene and Francesca. I'd dress quickly and follow her out, sit down and start gabbing, or begin to make an omelet like I'd once seen done in a Cambodian hotel: tilting the frying pan, over the flame, the egg gathering there, solidifying.

Barbara and Irene would laugh. I'd protest, briefly. When Irene bragged about something—money, or trips, or people she hung out with—no one teased her, but if I put so much as three sentences together to tell them about something, I got teased; I was always the first one to leave the table.

I'd head out for work on my bike and wonder if Irene and Barbara might . . . Like a Dostoevsky novella, me in the role of the humiliated little man who wanders about embracing and insulting figures larger than himself, trying to destroy and to save them all at once, to destroy and save himself. But then I'd remember that I mustn't cut in on that budding relationship, to direct it where I wanted it to go, because that invisible place, where everything is within my control, is orange, and when life first appears in that orange shade, it dies.

Better to think about that television job, the idea of dedicating ourselves to earning money that we still get for entertaining a mass audience. Someday, we'll write exclusive TV programs for a public of two thousand, just the very rich, at least, according to essays I've read and at times reviewed for cultural magazines. But what a dream to work and get paid: in the office, the first meeting, always a light meal delivered by a South American kid on a bicycle. White light through the window, the silent courtyard. The writing room, a part of a multipurpose complex not far from the apartment my sister owns, the place I'd love to move to eventually, if Barbara and I can fully reconcile.

I was the one doing the guest interviews, I was good, even if the other writers had to keep reminding me to include questions about family or the interviewee's passions; if it were up to me, I would have only discussed work, that uncommon world, headed for extinction.

When my mind wandered, I'd relax by writing out lines from the website of the architects who'd designed this multipurpose complex: this poetry, the architects' and Milan's, transported me into the future, even while my job didn't matter to me.

Five white buildings around a courtyard
combining functions
(diminishing mobility)
new iconic form

Six conceived levels, double-width structural units
Each unit designed with an open floor plan, a mezzanine
loft, studios, stores, restaurants, and offices.

A hanging, rooftop garden
interior piazzas

geothermal utilization of underground water
radiant floor heating
ventilation
glass, wood, and vegetation
self-cleaning concrete to reduce smog
A flat strip of solid forms and spaces

white mesh screening
that rolls down and engulfs
the transparency of glass

One night I wrote down: "Love is the afterlife of plot—if the plot is too effective, how will we see the love shine through?"

Was I jealous of Barbara and my sister? I had to respect them, not ask too many explicit questions, avoid putting them in the position of feeling that they mustn't contradict each other. Sooner or later, Barbara and I would get to that other apartment and reestablish that sense of ownership that's practical for the life of the couple, but we weren't ready just yet.

One night, we were in our bed making love while Irene and Francesca watched a movie in their room, and after a bit, I asked if we were making love because we could hear them nearby. She said, "Yup," and I laughed.

Barbara remained physically distant, we weren't united, it was more like sex between strangers, and in the midst of this lack of involvement, I'd tell her my fantasies, a gesture which she reciprocated only rarely.

I was standing over her and I'd opened an erotic video chat on my laptop, so now I saw Barbara below me and there beside her, on the screen, was another woman, on livestream, unaware of us and the fact that she was lying there with her legs dangling just like Barbara and touching herself while I stood by the bed, one knee on the mattress, penetrating Barbara: "It's like I'm fucking you to get her off."

I felt her back arching, and she was squeezing my hips between her thighs, turning her head to check the screen.

"What do you see?" I asked, so she'd talk about herself.

"What do you mean? What do you want to hear?"

"Do you like what I'm saying, or are you just putting up with it?"

"No . . . I like it . . . but . . . yeah, I like it."

"What do you see?"

"Nothing. Us."

"And her. Come on—what do you see?"

"I see Leone, too."

I felt my fear rising and also that I was coming, and I was breathing slowly, on the bed now with both knees, pushing harder, my weight forward.

"Leone's there with the two of us and this girl." The girl in the video chat, who was trembling with a vibrator inside her, operated via internet by paying viewers.

"And Leone, what's he doing?" I asked.

"He's leaning against the doorjamb. He's watching us fuck."

"Oh, yeah? Is he naked?"

"No, I wouldn't let him."

"You told him he wasn't allowed?"

"Yeah. He asked and I told him: 'No, you only get to watch.'"

"And does he feel bad?"

"Yeah, a little, but he also likes that it hurts."

"He's hurting?"

"Yeah, and I'm staring right at him."

"You want to fuck him?"

"I'm staring right at him so he understands I'd like to, but I'm shaking my head, to make him understand he can't."

I'm listening and scooting her forward, a meter, toward the nightstand, and I get a condom from the drawer, tear off the wrapper, still listening to her elaborate, then I'm pulling away from her, slipping the rubber on, and I enter her again.

"And is he obeying your command?"

"Yes, he's obeying my command, but he's too excited now

and he starts touching himself while we're fucking, and he's staring at me, he wants me so bad . . . But he can't have me and I'm
coming and staring at him and you're fucking me."

My sister turned up the volume on the TV, then I was coming,
heart in my throat; I moved to my side of the bed, breathing
hard. I was calming down, then falling asleep.

We went back to Rome a number of times, and we always hated going to check on the house and our renters, a couple, some friends of friends. One morning, still wintertime, unforgettable, cold, the fog not yet lifted; the Virginia creeper had dropped most of its leaves, but a few curls remained, strawberry-red, blazing against green, like streaked hair, and in our home, another couple, a caricature of us, him with his beard styled like mine, her with her fashionable clothes.

But the time I wish to recall occurred in May. We showed up one morning, parked the car by the blooming Virginia creeper, the green wisteria; the jasmine had flowered, the planters were bursting with flowers in purple, indigo, red, yellow, orange.

They were preparing lunch, the smell of burnt butter. They were being lazy, eating inside instead of in the courtyard or on the roof terrace. I won't paint them in a disparaging light: Barbara thought they were okay—the kind of people who could appreciate the Mattotti painting hanging in the dining room. They invited us to take a seat at the table, well lit, perhaps the most well-lit spot in the house, under the skylight. They served American coffee from their automatic drip coffeemaker they'd crammed between the toaster and hot plate on the counter: Barbara seemed annoyed by this clutter. Holding a warm mug, our mug, Barbara looked up at the skylight and murmured, politely: "That stain . . ."

"Oh, yeah. You noticed?" the woman said. She was braless, in the light sweatshirt she'd slept in.

"I did," Barbara said, smiling, knowing, from her job, how not to appear angry. She spoke now as if the stain were our fault: "Look, Marcè, it's grown some," like this was my fault, though I knew that's not what she thought.

The stain appeared that winter, before we separated, and the work crew assured us it was gone for good. Now, it was a meter long and, at its broadest, about the width of an LP; a ribbon of paint had peeled away—we'd avoided that before. But our two renters hadn't let us know about the seepage.

"Yeah, I noticed it, too," the man said. He was wearing a long cotton cardigan over his pajamas, like a bathrobe.

"Oh, don't worry, call us whenever, no pressure. If you notice it reaching the walls, call us." Barbara had pegged them as rich, somewhat dense, accustomed to being served, but now, turning to them, she was trying to make sure they didn't feel like they'd failed.

Her reaction was no different, proportionately, to how she'd approached Gioia Longo. Before, I would have fixated on her not wanting to share how much seeing that stain upset her. But something had changed between us: I didn't feel excluded; I wasn't bothered because she wanted to retreat into herself. I knew she found the stain terrifying, a violation of her most private space, and she knew I only viewed this as a practical concern, something to resolve, not to anguish over.

The man assured us he'd text to keep us up to date: "I'll send you photos so you can see how it develops."

"Okay. Am I right you didn't talk to the workmen? Just so when I call, I'll know where we're at."

"But it's not like it's really rained," the man said.

"True, it hasn't, really . . ." Barbara was holding her coffee mug in front of her mouth. She stared at the cabinet beneath the skylight: "We'll get it figured out. Tomorrow, I'll come by with the work crew."

I didn't remind her that we'd be on the 8:00 a.m. train tomorrow, since I had to be at the office before noon. I knew this was her: she wore her mother's face, glued over her own.

But not intervening, I could feel my body imbued with pleasure, a sense of calm.

That expression of Barbara's, which only I noticed, lasted the rest of our visit. I didn't attempt to tear through that tight mask. I accepted that behind this expression was an individual I could never really know, who walked beside me through these rooms, escorted by the woman renter, to take a look at the usual key places that needed checking on. Though the house incorporated modern building techniques—to cut down on lost heat, for instance—that it wasn't waterproofed was starting to be a concern. Water scared Barbara: we didn't know why, hadn't figured out yet why she wiped her cheek if I kissed her after drinking something; she didn't like sweat, saliva, broth, coffee, bodily fluids—any liquid on her skin she immediately dried off—and she definitely didn't like the dampness at the edges of the parquet floor, or that mold spreading across the walls.

She discovered that they'd unplugged the dehumidifier in the downstairs room and put it out in the greenhouse, for aesthetic reasons. Since this was only a cellar space converted to a downstairs guest room, it had to be kept dry: now there was an inhospitable cold emanating from the room, and it stank of cellar. The being hidden behind Barbara's face spoke as if she were giving some advice: "If you want to have guests down here, it's best to run the dehumidifier."

I added: "Meaning, the dehumidifier should be on at all times, on the control timer."

Barbara said we'd be happy to get it going again, and three times the woman answered that this wouldn't be necessary, until Barbara stopped and changed the subject.

A stirring, nondescript and private, dark and subtle, beneath the mask of my wife: she noted all the mold climbing the walls, the cobwebs on the stairs. She pointed these things out, not speaking. I saw and followed behind her, while the renter, a forty-year-old brat in a sweatshirt, smelling nicely of incense, began to respond more curtly.

I knew Barbara wasn't up to adding that the wood table needed oiling, so I spoke up, talking like her.

The crucial room was the bathroom. More than any other problem in the house—and she would spot it every time we went over to somebody's place that wasn't very clean—she was most disturbed by the lime buildup when water would steadily, imperceptibly drip inside the toilet bowl.

Now, Barbara, who'd asked to use the bathroom, detected the first very slight trail of lime.

After all her politeness, when it was time to leave, she informed them that the workers would be by in the morning to address the various unsettled issues, as it was better to do it now than later, or "the problems will increase exponentially."

We walked in silence along the one-way road, toward the car my mother had loaned us. Barbara phoned the cleaning woman and asked if she was free the following day. The lady suggested her sister-in-law. They made their arrangements, and Barbara paused in front of me, as I held open the car door with excessive good manners, due to the tenderness I was feeling toward her.

Finally she got in, and clicking her seat belt, she squeezed her eyes so tight, the mask slipped, was swallowed up, and set free, she broke into tears and began to sob.

I started off, and got her out of there. From that moment on, I think, she became my wife.

My Mother

I was sensible how much gratitude I owed to her, but in truth, I never thought of it, and whether she served me or not, it would ever have been the same thing. I loved her neither from duty, interest, nor convenience; I loved her because I was born to love her.

—JEAN-JACQUES ROUSSEAU, *Confessions*

With springtime, my sister has opened her house to everyone, perhaps to help Barbara find a job: guests coming and going through the rickety glass doors, curtain rods slipping off their brackets, tumbling down, my sense of bourgeois order threatened, strange women sleeping on couch cushions tossed to the floor . . . Keys handed to girlfriends just returned from China or Belgium. Irene suddenly disappearing for a week, then reappearing one night, and I find her preparing a dinner with some men I don't know, one of whom is now in the kitchen with Barbara, chopping up onions, standing together, side by side. I know what he's after. But I've learned not to rush out of the house to get her attention, I stand in the corner and have a drink with someone, one of the girlfriends, and this skit between my wife and this stranger, seen from behind, makes me fiercely interested in everybody, I touch the others' wrists, laugh with this woman I don't know and mistakenly thought was one of my sister's exes; not thinking, I pull her close, all the women read like lesbians to me, they're combative, dry, short, all except

one silent, lanky woman . . . One night, in this perennial confusion, the doorbell rings, I check the peephole and, on the landing, there in wide angle, stands my sister-in-law, Daniela.

I open the door and Daniela, intimidated and shivering in the
cold, sets her turquoise roller bag against the door, leans forward
awkwardly, and kisses me near the mouth; I adjust my face, and
we brush lips, and a small breeze rises from the stairwell. I plant
my palms on her pink cheeks, she hesitates, and I kiss her on her
closed eyelid, and I'd like to kiss her entire face, I have the strang-
est sensation that I'm kissing Barbara, that Barbara's spirit has
migrated into Daniela's body.

This is no dream, even if I've written it like a confused dream.
There are moments when identities and meanings swirl about,
like dust beaten out of a rug.

Barbara's and Irene's voices draw us from the entranceway to
the kitchen, where we're greeted by mini-cannoli on a gold cardboard tray: they knew, "Ha ha, look at that expression, buried by
women," joking, further confusion, I can't seem to figure out why
Daniela's here in Milan, here with us, on the eighth floor.

I'm revising this as a confusing comedy scene, wordless, a
silent-movie placard for the one piece of crucial information:

"I have an appointment
with a literary agent!"

. . . They kept this surprise to themselves for a couple of days, so they could enjoy my reaction. Sunday night, windows closed, we'd just tried to cook a Southeast Asian dish, then realized we'd screwed up some of the ingredients; now we were waiting on our delivery order of pot stickers.

I washed the dishes with Daniela, standing side by side, and I felt the heat coming off her, from beneath her wool dress, and I drew closer, to feel her soft hip; she never pulled away. We made up the living room couch for her, and when she was lying down and I was brushing my teeth, I asked Barbara if it made any sense to go back and clear things up. My wife agreed that yes, I should, which I found exciting. Daniela was stretched out under an old blanket, the sheet beneath her barely covering the two hard, square couch cushions. She was reading a contemporary Italian novel. She'd pulled her hair back for sleep and was in one of my brother's sweatshirts, an old sweatshirt I used to steal. I sat down on the couch, sideways, an unnatural position, then, a powerful feeling in my chest, I turned but was afraid I'd wind up looking her in the eye. I managed to stroke her face. My hand on her cheek, she stopped me, turned my hand over in both of hers, and slowly, warmly, kissed the soft place on my palm, below my thumb.

The next day in the office, I asked if I could make a quick trip to Rome for personal reasons. Francesca's partner told me I'd have to take a couple of sick days, because I didn't have any vacation days yet.

I enter my parents' apartment and nod to my father in his easy chair, then I bend over and kiss him on the head, his white, fine hair tickling my beard. Emigrating makes you godlike—you can manipulate time, age your parents through montage, like a great director, transforming the continuity of life, the invisibility of time, into a series of portraits.

My father, deflated, arms thin, hairless; my mother, drowsy, weariness showing on her face, hair duller, frizzier; at one time, I think, it was completely straight: surprises, a combination of accelerated time and rediscoveries, paying closer attention.

She lets me kiss her on the temple and says: "You got some packages"—books still sent to their address, my packages from presses still come here, because living away from home, I've never had a doorman or a package room.

We go sit in the kitchen. Boiled vegetables and buffalo mozzarella for my father and me, my mother's already had some: we only manage to eat with her on important occasions—she's always "already eaten"—eating is shameful for her, like in that Buñuel movie where people have their meals hiding in the bathroom. She's standing, tailbone against the counter, back to the window.

To write about my mother, I take ten drops of benzodiazepine in water—it's the first time I've ever dared to write about her.

I've never described her, not here, not in any of my poems. She's a tall woman, just under five foot ten, with my same build, a bit overweight, like me. Strong shoulders, strong legs, a belly, a proud expression: evasive, amazed, superior, sidelong. She has a messy pageboy cut. I don't think she's ever spent more than ten seconds brushing her hair, including when she was a girl: I don't know if this is true, but my instinct says yes.

Once, seeing her on the sidewalk after Mass walking toward us, Barbara summed her up: "Here comes your mother—look how cute—a fur coat and a headband." No one had ever summed up my mother, or helped me to understand her. An extremely intelligent child who has refused to become an adult, who only pretends to be a lady when she talks to electricians and plumbers, and only truly seems like an adult when she's reflecting on religion and theology, which she studied in college after age fifty. She wears dark blue or turquoise flats, or moccasins. For a party, a ceremony: fine, loose-fitting slacks. In the winter she goes to church wearing a cape that billows as she walks. At home, her sweaters still smell like Mommy.

I remember her stretched out for hours on the living room couch surrounded by journals, books, plates with bits of cake, all lying on a bright tomato-red, black, and ocher rug. I was a teenager.

She had a benign tumor, has done postural gymnastics, sometimes walks with a limp. She's basically healthy, except for one real problem: phlegmons, abscesses that emerge in places I can't see, around her stomach, I think. Every time I ask her about her health she answers: "Oh, everything's fine, just those phlegmons . . ." We've never tied them to any particular illness, so they feel more symbolic, a memento that ills do exist. "You wouldn't believe how disgusting they are . . ."

She has a flawless complexion, and a weak chin like her mother and first grandchild. She loves wearing pearls, but she isn't the least bit vain, except when it comes to bragging about her sons.

[Characters in books get one description only, as if there's a starting point and then the changes inflicted by the plot. But in life, we're continuously taking stock of the people we know, describing them afresh, to see if we've understood something new. So maybe a character description should be left for the end of a book, a final sum-up. *Ecce* Mommy—she can't be "Mommy"—I have to call her "my mother," or my wife will think I'm a baby. The task in describing someone real, someone you know: there's so much to synthesize, year in and year out, endless discovery, fragments, I see a bit of who my mother is, with each passing month, the eye thaws a little, sees a little more, discovers moles, a twitching eyelid, a certain motion to the hip . . . Barbara, for instance, unnerved me when she pointed out that Gionata gestured just like his grandmother, and this felt like a conspiracy, not the detail per se, but that I'd never noticed before, the way someone might feel detecting an airplane contrail up in the blue sky, suspicious they might be spreading mind-controlling substances.]

After dinner we sit in front of the turned-off TV set; we're on two couches arranged in an L, my father and I on one couch together. My mother has her iPad beside her and my father, a mini in his lap. I ask him about his leg: rehabilitation's good, physical therapy's a trip, perfect for someone his age, he's always wanted to do it, he says, every day, some new method to get more out of life: "I'm very pleased."

I tell my mother: "I've got two tickets to the Auditorium, to something I'm sure you'd like, about the Gospel."

"Oh, wonderful, if I don't have to help out over there. If Luca and the nanny say I can, with Daniela away . . . I said I was available, so I have to be around."

I update them on Irene: she's doing great, she and Barbara just love each other, and I also got to see Daniela in Milan, an agent's interested in her novel, he's a good agent, I know him, not bad, huh, who'd have thought . . . (No, she didn't ask me to read it.)

"It's really thrilling," my mother says, "so unexpected, really, she's very brave to challenge herself like that, at her age." Then, we're onto another topic, politics, and they both start in with, "Of course that's not what you do . . . all of a sudden . . . being so unavailable . . ."

"Well, it's not like Luca's working."

"Still, the babies are used to a different routine."

"Yeah," I say, "but for Daniela, it was tragic having twins—she needed to think about something else for a change."

"What do you mean, *tragic*," Mom says in her usual voice, never letting anything past her: "A gift from God—you're saying a gift from God is *tragic*?" She asks this calmly, not dramatically, like she wants my opinion on a theological question.

"I didn't say that," I lie. "I mean, we have to be okay with it if she's working on something and is less available right now. Better than being depressed."

"*If* she's depressed," my father says. "I don't see it."

She backs him up: "Daniela has everything. Including a free home. These days, that's quite a lot."

She's wearing a dark blue raincoat. I've slipped into the driver's side of their car, I run my hands over the leather steering wheel; the smell, the detailing, the trills of the gauges tuned to the sound of the doors, a designer sound.

A friend has written me about the Auditorium show—he'll be performing a dramatic monologue. There'll be writers, journalists. North Rome is wet: rain from inside a nice car is more vivid than in a used compact car. The rich, low sweep of windshield wipers envelops the turn signal, which, little by little, goes out of sync.

She criticizes my parking. Under an enormous umbrella we

approach the three halls, three giant anthracite beetles rising above the horseshoe lobby.

We pick up our comp tickets at the box office, where I greet a blond woman I know, beautiful and sweet, her oval face covered in freckles, and I introduce her to my mother. We walk down the lobby, with its three wooden entranceways to the performance halls.

"See," I comment on the woman I just ran into, "she's certainly very nice."

"So, you two are always here," meaning me and my wife.

She's calm; she's walking slowly. I thought she'd be more nervous—she never goes to the theater.

"Yeah, well, Barbara gets a lot of free tickets."

"Nice. Very nice." She looks around.

The performance hasn't started. We're in the fourth row, the theater's filling up; my mother wants me to tell her who's who, and we discuss famous names, famous faces.

"I'm the only one who doesn't know anyone." She states this without condescension, embarrassment, neurosis: succinctly and nicely put.

The seats are cramped for the two of us and we haven't removed our coats; I note the kinship of our bodies, the same way we both rush to take our seats and then never quite settle in. She folds her arms and cranes her neck to look around, but she isn't frenetic, like usual. We never go out together, and we didn't used to, either, when I was a boy: I remember seeing only a handful of movies with my parents. And sometimes "going out for pizza." And trips abroad, the world opening up to us. But our life didn't feature fixed cultural engagements. My mother comes from a well-educated family—but Catholic—to the point of being, culturally speaking, anti-twentieth-century, averse, then, to rituals like theater or street demonstrations; my father escaped his lower-middle-class, politically right-wing, borderline-fascist background, but he worked so hard that he distanced himself from the intellectual friends of his youth, for whom, I'd imagine, entrepreneurship was essentially worse than the academic barony they'd chosen for themselves. In spite of the fact that, since their twenties, they'd been "politically engaged" and "great readers" (my mother still reads, but not literature: biographies, historical novels, newspapers, blogs on the Vatican and royalty), they've never been the type to take their children to the theater, which, as an adult, I found a bit odd, even eerie, because while I kept reading books and meeting intellectuals, I still held on to the belief that I was less informed, less educated than my parents were. Then, like in the movies, suggesting a night outside the norm, and finding myself here with my mother, waiting, indifferently, for the start of a performance, rediscovering how elegant she is, how shy . . . she won't mention—is poised enough not to mention—her fear that the Auditorium is a "vulnerable target" for a terrorist attack, the favorite subject these days. From her composure, I sense a different sort of life she might have led, a woman of the world allowing herself some of the pleasures this century has to offer.

Normally, if we meet some parishioners on the way home, my mother will criticize my clothing in front of them; today she didn't. And she's also not putting on the naive attitude of someone who's "too humble" to attend premieres—humble in the Christian sense of being meek, poor in spirit. She's comfortable, in her own way, anxiously waiting for the lights to dim and for the writer to appear onstage, my friend, the writer whose book inspired the monologue, which she's read. Apparently, my mother knows how to be at the theater, understands the proper etiquette, though she hasn't been in decades. I'm mesmerized by this. I don't think I've ever gone with her. The Auditorium is five minutes from her home.

The lights go down, the writer makes his entrance, microphone twig against his cheek, and starts talking. My mother listens closely; she listens like an intellectual, nodding, following the cause-and-effect relationships in the monologue, approving with comments like "Right, right . . ." I can't look at her straight on, but every time she shifts in her seat, I feel it vibrating in my legs and back. I also tend to nod and whisper, "Right, right," and tonight, we both wind up saying this at many of the same lines. This tendency to nod and whisper that I got from her has shaped my life and world, my relationships, work, habits, lovers. In my mother, it's a curiosity that's survived her moral and religious choices, like people who stopped playing tennis after adolescence but immediately regain their form if they play again.

At intermission, we eavesdrop on the depressing conversations going on around us.

I mutter: "They're all talking about people who are either sick or dead."

"We're an old country."

When it's over, we leave, and I greet some famous writers, happy for her to see. "Oh, that's X, right?" Outside, in the cold of the colonnade, by the bookstore windows: "This was nice— thank you. And the Auditorium's so close to home."

Clipped sentences, restrained, fleeting, orchids that don't flower every year.

I was sad to see her walking even a little slower than the last time I'd noticed her gait. Other times, I would've tried to raise her hackles: "Why are you being so normal today? So it turns out you *do* know how to be civilized?" I didn't do this, and as I write now, I take some pride in knowing I refrained from lecturing her on her behavior that generally annoys me.

She lets me take her home. I park the car in their garage, hand over the keys, watch her take the stairs after the gate, down to the main entrance. I head for my scooter and, feeling emotional, I peel out in the freezing cold. Piazza Ungheria, piazza Fiume, Castro Pretorio, San Lorenzo, all the traffic lights still operational.

[I'm editing this section while wrapped in the embrace of benzodiazepine; it holds me, muffles the keys on the keyboard, and there's some soothing digital music coming from my noise-canceling headphones—I absolutely need this cocoon to talk about her—I feel like I'm back in my father's luxury car.]

The day after, she was sweet on the phone. The way we spoke to each other left me feeling like we'd had a relationship that was different, better, in the distant past, and she was remembering.

And the day after that, I called her from the train: "What would you say to us all celebrating my fortieth birthday here in Milan?" Because I wanted Irene to be there.

"How could we, though?—no, come on—and bring the babies? It would be so complicated."

"Well, then we could all come down to Rome."

"I don't know. I need to check if Dad has plans—but sure, sure—why not—we could—what were you and Barbara thinking of?"

I'd made her nervous, so I said we'd talk about it later.

I tried again one night after my third gin and tonic, standing on the sidewalk of a Milanese street, trams and cobblestones, talking to her on my headset, glass in hand, a few meters from the crowd drinking outside, at twilight, on an exceptionally cold evening. I really felt like hearing her voice.

My mother was the one who brought it up: "About your birthday . . . Dad's really tired, let's do something normal, simple. Come for breakfast. Barbara, too, maybe, if you two come to Rome the Saturday before, or stay afterward. Dad's tired."

"Why? What's wrong?"

"No, it's nothing. You know. It's just complicated right now."

And as she spoke, I reconsidered and told her she was right. I remembered a recent conversation I'd had with my father:

"I know how I caught this chill. But I'm always sick lately."

"It's stress."

"Maybe I have a tumor in my esophagus. I have this acid reflux, I keep coughing."

"You should go see the doctor who cured mine. He gave me a connective-tissue massage."

"Maybe. When things aren't so busy."

I agreed with my mother, I had the same impression lately about Dad, and we hung up, having decided on a breakfast the morning of my birthday.

On the following day, during cocktail hour at a different bar, I started thinking about it again, and left a group of colleagues to give her a call, again using my headset. My mother told me: "Marcellino, why are you dwelling on this?" She never calls me that. "It's your birthday—nobody else's. Figure out how you want to celebrate your fortieth birthday and stop trying to engineer something else."

I wish it were truly possible to have a major scene at my house, a time when you truly hit the mother lode—excuse the pun—but it just doesn't happen. I heard myself saying: "For a gift, I'd like to have a party with you and Irene." But I didn't say this. "Okay. But these last months in Milan, things have changed for me, and I'm happy about it."

"That's wonderful, the best thing a mother could hear. But really, you mustn't concern yourself with how others are getting along. We're all adults and have made our own choices."

And then I went ahead and said—cryptically, respecting her wish to be vague—"Sometimes a person makes a choice, other times he doesn't—it's just turned out that way." I purposely used "he," to be extra vague.

"I sometimes think," she said, twisting my meaning, "that certain choices are made because they're in style."

The way she said "style" brought me back to myself, standing on a sidewalk in Milan, among people that only a few months before I didn't know. My mother's voice came from Rome—my city.

"In style?" I said. This was the same woman who'd sat, so dignified and pleasant, on a red orchestra seat in the second performance hall in the Auditorium.

"Certain life choices are also meant to wound," she added, of course referring to Irene. But it feels forced for me to explain that exchange: it would betray her nature: religious, allusive, serpentine. Like an oracle, you could take that comment as referring to the two of them, my parents, instead of their daughter. "Certain life choices are also meant to wound." What a heroic admission that would be. Or maybe it was intended as a universal truth to

contemplate. As I write now, I can visualize both my sister's thin
hair under her wig and my mother's hair, so dull. I jot down:
"incomprehensible incomprehension."

I don't remember what else we said on the phone, but I remember my mother's small voice, strange, not my mother: for
the rest of the call I kept thinking this wasn't my mother.

Irene joined me and my colleagues in that bar, then Barbara
joined us, and I did something I'm ashamed of. They could tell I
was sad, and I told a group of colleagues, along with my wife
and sister, that I'd just gotten off the phone with my mother. As
you do with people our age, joking that parents can be such a
burden. This bad habit of exorcising the mystical journey you
take in your relationships with your aging parents . . . I said they
didn't feel like throwing a big party. I'd already asked Irene if she
might organize something in Milan and invite the family and she
suggested having it at a restaurant, having lunch together (I
hadn't brought up that our parents thought Barbara and I were
renting something on our own, not staying with Irene, and I also
hadn't explained to them that Irene wasn't living in the apartment she owned), but anyway, she agreed to my proposal about
a family celebration. Now, in front of everybody, I told her: "They
don't feel like coming to Milan. Maybe we'll just go down to
Rome, but I don't really know if we're going to do some organized thing with them."

"Some organized thing"—what a stupid thing to say. At these
words, my sister, who's shorter than me, her hair cut short right
now, like Mia Farrow's, dressed a bit more butch than usual, a
wild boy, maybe because she's hanging out with lesbians more
than straight people, my sister seemed to shrink in size, and she

stared ahead with the same expression I saw on Gionata's face at Christmas, when my mother asked if he was happy about his brothers being born.

But different from Gionata: Irene's furrowed features smoothed over into a docile smile with such fluidity, it was painful to watch. She said: "Don't worry. I'll come down to Rome anyway for your birthday. If something happens with everybody, great." She'd adopted that same vagueness typical of our family, but a sweeter version. "Otherwise, plan a nice party at some bar, and I'll make sure to be there."

An exchange lasting only a few seconds, that I've homed in on, out of a trivial conversation about parties and getting drunk. While the conversation resumed its cheerful tones, I felt like a hit man sent from Rome to break my sister's heart. I'd prepared her for months, reassured her, manipulated her into opening up, and now that she was open—in just a matter of seconds—I'd stuck a knife into her gut. Maybe, as a son, I had no choice but to obey, and I was the scorpion on the frog's back, letting the frog carry him across the river, promising not to sting her, but doing it all the same, because it's his nature.

I *went back to the Auditorium with my mother and Barbara.* Pappano, the music director, was performing Brahms on the piano accompanied by the first violin and first cello of the Santa Cecilia Orchestra.

At intermission, Barbara got up to greet some ex-colleagues and collaborators. My mother and I chatted in our seats.

"What do you think? It's a nice space, isn't it?"

"Dad would like it," she answered.

"So next time, we bring him, too."

"He'd gladly come," she said, "from Heaven."

Her father's been dead for thirty-five years, so generally when she uses this word, she's referring to my father. The tenderness in her voice embarrassed me.

When the performance was over, while we slowly took the stairs, among the crowd, I slipped my hand in my jacket and discovered the toffee, softened now, that Gionata had given me that afternoon and that I'd dropped into my pocket and forgotten. I was holding the candy by one of its little yellow paper ears, waiting for it to harden in the cool night air. I started to unwrap it, and my mother asked: "Is that the toffee you offered me?"

I said it was, handing her the unwrapped candy.

"You have more, don't you?" she asked, and popped it in her mouth and started chewing.

All those moments will be lost in time, boats against the current, borne back ceaselessly into the past.

The night before my fortieth birthday, Francesco helped carry the party supplies from my car up to their apartment. He was in between jobs; I was free to return to Rome that week because I was preparing interviews pretty much on my own; Barbara was starting to take on individual projects with a Milan agency; and Giò had no steady job. We joked about my fortieth birthday party being held at their place—we still had renters—at such an unusual period in our lives. The party was set for tomorrow but the four of us, dear friends, would wait for midnight together.

Out on the balcony, Barbara and Giò were kissing and hugging and asking questions, sharing news, while Fra and I set the cases in one corner of the living room–kitchenette. Then the two of us went out to have a smoke on the porch swing: Barbara went into the living room, taking over, discussing with Giò how things should be arranged.

From the eighth floor, the view was artificial yellow with broad blue bands of light stretching from the city to the Castelli

Romani hill. Ahead, to the left, the massive wall of a working-class area.

"For a month," Francesco said, "I felt awful after turning forty. I keep thinking about dying."

"I remember your party. It was really touching." I got up, went in, and took some martini glasses down from the shelf and put them in the freezer to chill. Then I stood there a moment, thinking I'd never wished my sister a happy birthday on her fortieth, but then Francesco came in and distracted me, handed me the large glass shaker. He opened the fridge and took out a fat lemon, already missing some of its rind.

"I'm on my third gin Campari." He was grinning, his eyes very round, dark, haloed by yellow skin. His skin tone isn't usually pink or anything, but it's never been that yellow.

"I didn't realize . . . You carried up all those cases . . ." I was checking for ice in the freezer.

"I've been drinking all week—at lunch, too. I keep thinking about how I felt last year. That this was the start of my golden age."

"So my party won't make that go away for me?"

I ran water over the ice tray, then smashed the ice on a plastic cutting board and put it in the shaker, incredibly happy to be there. One morning when I was a kid, I realized I could make my own breakfast with cold milk and cereal: I still remember that feeling of satisfaction, that if I opened the refrigerator for the milk, the one cupboard for a bowl, the other for the corn flakes, and the drawer for a spoon, then I could feed myself. Living in a neighborhood that let me just walk over to my friend's, enter his home, I knew about putting the glasses in the freezer and when to take them out, I knew a real secret to life. So, this topic under discussion, this sadness my friend felt, was so strange: how is it possible, my friend, when you make me so happy, how can you be sad? And tonight, of all nights?

He handed me the bottle of vermouth while draining his Campari; I poured a little over the ice in the shaker, stirred it with a wooden chopstick; strained the vermouth into a glass; poured the gin into the shaker, over the soaked ice.

He grabbed the gin bottle from me before I could set it on the counter, unscrewed the cap, poured a splash into some Campari. "I don't know, Marcè, I'm feeling pretty miserable."

"Is it something in particular, or are you just feeling bad in general?"

"Both. I don't know. I'm forty years old and I've got nothing to show for it. Here at home, things aren't so great."

"You want the keys to my place? I could boot the tenants."

"No, no, the last thing I need is somewhere else to go."

"Well, in that case, maybe we could start letting my sister-in-law write there, too, you could meet her there, give her some brilliant advice on writing, she'll fall in love with you . . ." I stirred the gin with the chopstick, told him to take out the two chilled glasses, white now with condensation. I cut off some lemon rind and rubbed it along the rims of the glasses; I poured in the cold, diluted gin.

"Maybe I really should do something nuts like that—go after your sister-in-law. Would you kick my ass?"

"Cheers."

"Happy birthday, my friend." He set his glass on the counter and hugged me.

I could feel his big, warm body, and about a third of my martini sloshed onto the floor.

Afterward, he was drying the floor with some paper towels, almost the entire roll spread out, leading to the fridge, and I joked: "Better you, anyway, than my brother. But the children! The kiddies! What about *the children!*"

"See? One wrong move, you ruin somebody's life."

The girls knocked on the window by the porch swing where they were sitting and gestured that they wanted a drink: I downed mine in one gulp and started making more.

Two hours later, Francesco and I were slurring our words, and we'd both turned morose. Barbara and Giò got up from the couch (I was lying on the floor), and said we were incredibly boring, so they were heading to the bar now, to wait for our toast at midnight. It was only ten.

As soon as we were by ourselves, Francesco said: "It's very simple: I don't have a family and I don't have a job."

Just then, I realized that my mother would be turning seventy that summer, because I was turning forty, and we had always turned the same number, thirty years apart, every single year. *And how bewildered is any womb-born creature / that has to fly.*

My mother was the oldest of five, very attached to her father, an engineer for the Enel Group. She was born in Terni, spent her childhood between Genoa and Milan, and then in the early sixties, moved to Rome when she was beginning high school—too late to adapt—she never learned to start her words with double consonants.

Even when she was little, she considered herself a leader in any group: she made the other kids sing and play, children, friends on the beach, on vacations in Liguria. One boy, a dear friend, died of TB, I think. The other day she told me: "It's true, I practically didn't have a childhood. I lived in a city where I didn't grow up, and I grew up all over the place."

She was her father's favorite, the only one who truly seemed to be his, both of them: abstract, moral, elusive, playful, silly, tall, childish.

She always finished her dessert before anyone else. When it comes to her childhood, the story I know best is that her brother, the next oldest, liked to savor his treats and would still be nibbling the edge of a pastry or taking little licks off his gelato cone, and she'd be done, and eyeing his.

At seventeen or eighteen, she took a whole bunch of kids to France, on a cultural-religious trip. "Uncle Paolo came, too, and we all slept on trains parked overnight at the station. I gave him a wonderful classical guitar as a thank-you gift."

They lived on a street named after a composer, at the edge of the African quarter, by Prati Fiscali, where there still wasn't much development. Down in the valley, the shacks of the Abruzzians who'd come to Rome to work in construction after the war. They scraped those shacks together from rubble. My mother's group of friends, all graduates of the same high school—all still Catholic back then, I think—would gather by the shacks and assist people with their practical concerns and try to bring some cheer to this shantytown. One time, she told me, "I was stroking this little girl's hair, I don't know why, and ugh, so gross, they were crawling up my fingers—lice? Bed bugs?"

They read Mao's Little Red Book. They listened to Inti-Illimani, Joan Baez.

She was the one who oversaw the work with the people there, and a number of the boys from the group were interested in her, including a somewhat homely boy four years her junior, just starting his engineering studies, very ambitious, the son of an Abruzzian no less, but from a middle-class, fascist family, which no one discussed. He wore a "poop-brown" sweater and courted her just like the rest of them. He snuck out to work with this group, bringing along a change of shoes so he wouldn't return home late at night in a pair covered in mud.

Meanwhile, my mother's siblings were engrossed in a new Catholic movement founded by a Spanish artist who'd had a vision of the Madonna on the wall of a building and started "announcing the Gospel" and forming groups inspired by the first Christian communities, so they could live, "breaking the word together," announcing the Gospel to others and subsisting off mutual aid. My mother also "entered the community," but one night she wanted to go "celebrate Mass" instead of celebrating my father's birthday, and he told her: "If you don't come celebrate my birthday, we're through." Which her siblings took as a lack of faith.

From that point on, my mother practically lost her two brothers and two sisters: they became more and more involved in this group, colder and colder toward her. Or more precisely, they were formal with her, and treated her like a stranger. They were only close to their "communal sisters and brothers"—my mother was generous but also unapproachable, I think I got this, and this collective decision on the part of her four siblings was because they'd finally found some structure to their lives with this community (Grandpa, their father, grew up in boarding school, and Grandma, their mother, was the daughter of an army officer), and this somehow justified shutting out their unmanageable, magnanimous older sister. They'd answer: "Let the dead bury the dead," because the scriptures are full of cruel one-liners.

The president of the Catholic union was my mother's godfather. She worked for him; I know she translated documents from four different languages. She flew to Russia to attend a conference, for the university, I think. These are our family legends. She studied sociology and political science, then argued with the young professor she was working for as an assistant. Too pure, she couldn't work for glory or for money: often, at the end of a job, she'd feel angry, wounded, and would arrogantly say: "Then I'll do it for free—keep your money."

She played guitar and sang, but then she lost her voice. After an operation on her vocal cords, she had to be silent for a month.

She stopped riding her scooter because it scared my father.

She worked to support him while he started his career as an entrepreneur, then she stopped working, to raise us. She fought with people at the university, stopped taking trips like the one to Russia.

I remember when her father died; the funeral was held the day she turned thirty-nine. I spent the night with my paternal grandparents, and when I arrived at the church, I saw her standing with strangers all dressed in black, and I rushed over and wished her a happy birthday. One of my uncles explained to me then that my mother was unhappy because her birthday was on the same day as her father's funeral. But I really couldn't connect the two, and all I said was: "But it's still her birthday . . ."

When I was a teenager, my grandmother, whom I loved very much, would drop these comments like: "You know, the problems between your parents, your mom's problems with your dad." And I'd say: "Okay, Grandma, what does that even mean . . . Problems, sure—what does that even mean?" but I didn't want her to explain. To us, it felt like our parents couldn't be with anyone else.

On our vacations to the beach, my parents' friends always teased my mother for her complete lack of irony. She clobbered their Catholic University professor-friends at Trivial Pursuit, which they didn't take very well. She didn't like the sea but made us stay for three months. She loathed the beach. She'd shuttle us back up to the house after lunch, in our scalding-hot car, before we'd really started enjoying ourselves, before the informal soccer games starting at six, when the sand was tolerable.

In the nineties, she was spending way too much time lying on the sofa, and then we learned, after she had a long discussion with our grandmother, that it was decided Mom could do what she loved most—study. She enrolled in Pontifical Gregorian University to study theology.

She became friends with a Brazilian nun, a psychologist whose dark face was perfectly round. She didn't complete her dissertation because the professor assigned her Habermas, and she wasn't interested in Habermas.

I don't know much about my mother. At times she's expressed particular hurts by doing things carelessly. Once she dropped some eggshell into the custard she had in the mixer; out of sheer laziness, she didn't do it over and served us crunchy custard. She pretended this wasn't annoying.

But talking about my mother, my language is muddled, imprecise—it's all hearsay.

One afternoon, we were talking together in our new calm manner. "I decided not to pursue my teaching license because I didn't want to leave you by yourself." She wasn't complaining when she said this, just owning up to her fears. "Maybe I could've done it after all."

I don't remember much. Bags from La Standa stuffed with junk food, handed out to us and polished off in an afternoon. And incredible trips to America where we bought all kinds of crap at drugstores and ate it in our motel room. And the apartment in Rome where nothing happened, and I'd read, write, play music.

When Dad came home at night, he felt like an outsider; we were already deep into our own slow rhythm.

My mother can really provoke my brother: he'll be talking about something he finds important, and she'll always ask the wrong question, be rude to him. With her grandsons, too, like that time when Gionata was nervous, and she shut him up inside a room with a glass door. On the other side of the door, he was anxious: "It's all closed! It's all closed!" And she stood there, arms crossed, telling her grandson she wasn't going to open up for him. I stood behind her. And it's not lost on me that the only time I really portrayed her in the preceding sections was in that Christmas scene when she drove Gionata crazy with jealousy, asking him if he was happy that the twins were born.

Still, her grandsons adore her, look for her, climb all over her, always want to sleep with her, are desperate if she takes a trip to the Holy Land. She's a baobab tree, all three of them will climb her. She'll sit rigidly on the couch, wearing lace, and let the twins scramble onto her. Then she'll lean way back against the couch, while they hold on tight, laughing, mumbling, turning to leap, and Gionata, already down, returning to grab and squeeze the twins, to try to pinch them and pull them off, and all of this happening while in my mother's arms

Gionata's like her, weird, an end-in-himself. He says to her: "Grandma, always in church. Too many Masses. Let's not go anymore."

My mother will go around the neighborhood during the day giving Holy Communion to the sick.

I talked about my mother a long while. We wanted to get some fresh air, but I asked Francesco if we could stay inside, not go out onto the balcony: I was afraid of falling. We'd turned on the stereo; *A Love Supreme* was playing. I was stretched out on the floor again, with him on the couch. We were separated by a coffee table. We'd stopped drinking a half hour before.

"What's your mother got to do with anything?"

I thought about it. "Because you said you felt like you haven't done much and my mother's story is beautiful, moving—it makes you forget about those patterns."

He got up and made two gin and tonics and brought them back, along with some *caciotta* and *pane carasau*. He knelt and set these things down next to me, on the floor.

I rolled onto my side and nibbled a slice of *caciotta*.

For me, I said to him, being forty meant only two things: not getting worked up when you're judged; and for the first time, feeling aches and pains and knowing they're only going to get worse.

Rather than some inspired monologue summing up what was being said even while it was drifting away, forgotten by both of us, I want to talk about what sort of body I had just then:

If I drink too much, my heart trembles in my chest. I no longer get acid reflux, that went away with the physiotherapist's massage, but I feel a pressure on my sternum and I know my tissues are breaking down, even if it doesn't hurt. When I go out dancing, if I get into a rhythm, after a while my heart starts pounding, and I get scared and have to slow down. Running to catch the tram takes a lot out of me, and then, once on board, I break into a sweat. The physical therapist tells me I clearly have thyroiditis—I sweat an unnatural amount, like someone with a fever, unrelated to real exertion. I take a pill every morning for the thyroiditis. I have lumbar problems, and they say I need to stop playing soccer. An andrologist told me my sperm count's low. I ruined my right arm playing soccer—I took a shoulder charge, and the contusion caused nerve damage, and ten days later, my right arm shrank to half the size of my left. I had physical therapy and regained part of my muscle mass, but my right arm has never been completely rehabilitated: it has way fewer nerve endings now. Mornings, I'll stretch in bed, and a nerve twists in the crook of my arm and I'm shocked by the pain. I notice how weak that arm is when I wash my face. For two years now, I've had to eat much slower, because I can't seem to swallow properly. Maybe it's psychological, tied to the fact that when I was six months old, I was rushed to the hospital for an inguinal hernia; they intubated me and left me alone for a long time without my mother, so I've always been terrified of choking when I eat. But now I have to strain to get my throat to work, and sometimes I'll sneak into the bathroom and spit out the remnants of what I've been exhaustedly chewing. But I'm not sure if this problem is physical or mental. It might be physical: I've read that too much acid reflux can weaken esophageal movement.

That night, too, I felt an irregular pulsing in my chest. This was something new that happened when I drank too much or had too much sugar.

"But there's a difference here," Francesco said. "There's your mother, this intelligent woman who's lived through such a contradictory time, then seen this period devolve into the eighties, the nineties, the new millennium, and now the decade after that." He paused. "And then," he said, "there's me. Just some ahistorical dumbass."

At times, when Francesco's pessimistic, I'll get worked up and give him an alternative vision of the world, where everyone is redeemed. I started telling him about my grandmother, whose story might be even more inscrutable than my mother's, so even more salvific for us, in our situation that night, an hour or so from this important birthday, when I'd be launched into the sunset of life, into darkness.

My grandmother was a member of a group who worshipped the tabernacle; it was their mission never to abandon the Host. They took turns worshipping it, constantly. When it was her turn at night, on her knees behind a pew in the nave, the Host nearby in a protective display case in a wall niche, the church, I imagine, would be locked.

Her father died in her arms. That's how I always heard it. And right after she lost her husband, at sixty-three, she decided to enter the Neocatechumenal Way to try to understand the faith choices of four of her children and their spouses, to be closer to them. She let the catechists send her to London and Taiwan, where she worked as a volunteer cook for young men in seminary, aspiring priests from all over the world.

She was dignified. She didn't like permanent home care. She didn't want to be seen naked or in the various awkward positions the elderly must endure daily. Her toilet, for instance, had an elevated seat because she couldn't stand up from a normal toilet, and I'm sure she didn't want others to go into the bathroom and see it, this explicit indication of bodily weakness.

She reached ninety after twenty-five years of arthritic pain and countless sleepless nights spent reciting the rosary in bed or in her easy chair. She'd tell me, "I see the devil, he's right there," and from her easy-chair recliner, she'd point to a corner of the living room, by the TV set. She felt the temptation of the devil, and she lived with her arthritis brought on by her two frugal years as a cook in London and Taiwan.

In the few years before she turned ninety, she grew steadily more confused. I'd go see her about once a month, not even, and I was one of her favorite grandchildren. As she grew less and less coherent, I learned to hold her cold hand, fragile from cortisone, and caress it. At first, this felt indecent, but I'd leave her apartment crying my eyes out, and I'm crying now as I write.

There came a time when she was no longer aware of things, and then we could only connect through our hands: one of the last times we tried to talk, she stared at me, looking lost, raising that wide, receding chin of hers, just like my mother's, just like Gionata's, and she said: "I'm sorry . . . that story . . . I didn't tell you . . ." She was referring to a friend of hers who'd married her own stepfather after her stepmother died. When she first told me, I said that she'd have to get me to write down all the details sometime, but then we never got back to it, and that afternoon she said she was sorry because she didn't have enough of her mind left to tell me.

Our interactions grew more intense, all caresses and kisses.

Recently, I'd learned something new about her from Irene, as I told Francesco, reflecting on what made someone mature, an adult, a realized person, and how uninteresting I found these concepts to be. Before she became completely unaware, my grandma went through an angry phase and complained incessantly about her past. Whenever Irene came to Rome, she'd visit her. Grandma told Irene that the happiest time in her life was after she became a widow.

My grandfather was a saint. At night he'd carry his daily prayer book with him down the hall. He led a permanent catechism in his parish. He was tall and thin, owned some large cameras and a console stereo. He listened to the Beatles and knew the basics of orchestra conducting. He was an engineer.

Grandma told Irene the story of how she and my grandfather were engaged. This was the early forties and she had two suitors. My grandfather, slated for the Eastern Front, saved himself by joining the Civil Engineers. He was an engineering student: serious, devout. The other suitor was a poet from a large Roman family. I don't know how Grandma managed to lead this great life in Rome: her father had died in her arms when she was just thirteen, in Naples, I think, then I know she attended high school in Rome, at Liceo Torquato Tasso, behind Via Veneto. She was beautiful, we know this from a single framed picture of her: blouse, wavy hair, tilted head.

She didn't know how to choose between the two boys. She went to see her spiritual advisor, the priest who heard her confession and gave her guidance, and she asked him what she should do.

The priest said: "If your faith is strong, marry the poet, who loves you. If your faith is weak, marry the saint."

Totally biased—what pious Catholic would ever dare claim her faith was strong? "Blessed are the meek . . ." So my grandma married the saint.

Irene says that in her last angry, lucid moments, Grandma told her more than once: "I should have married the poet . . . I'd be happier . . ."

Our grandfather was a handsome man: sad, bighearted, modern.

For Grandma's ninetieth birthday, her children and oldest grandchildren organized a mass in her living room. She couldn't talk anymore; she used to be sturdy, almost as big as my mother, and now she was shrunken, but she was still present, you could see it in her eyes. Still proud, above everyone, yet somehow modest. During the personal reflections, after the officiant's sermon—a Neocatechumenal custom—my relatives declared that even in her tribulations, Grandma was strong "and wrestled with God."

They tried to put a good spin on something that had never really been explained: how was it that Grandma's faith had been so strong and yet so unruly at the same time? No one could ever presume to be more devout than she was, but if her children went out of their way to stress their own confirmation, she'd never been impressed by her faith. To me, an impassioned twenty-year-old who wanted to reconcile snobbery and the spirit, elegance and spiritual exercises, she said with a serene disquiet all her own: "You're a poet, you'll never get along with Catholics. You're too sensitive." "Come on, I'm not that sensitive," I protested, "I'm completely normal." "You'll see. You'll see."

Her four Neocatechumenal children tried to make sense of a story that was hard to make sense of, a story, however, that they found splendid: the story of a woman of the Old Testament, of violent faith.

While my mother, trying not to cry, said that now that Grandma had grown smaller, more delicate, she smelled like Mommy again, the smell she went searching for in her parents' closet, breathing in, nostrils wide, when she was a little girl and her mother was away.

Back to the poet. After my grandma refused him, he decided to take his own life. Grandma told Irene that a friend of the poet's family, "an important philosopher," told the boy if he no longer valued his own life, he might as well enlist and donate it to the country, since they were at war. The poet died "carrying the flag in an assault" (we'll never know if this is true—it feels like a World War I anecdote, and my grandma was born in 1922, which makes me think the story she told Irene happened to a friend of her father's that she conflated with her own story of failed love).

My back against the cool granite floor, I was waving my arms around while I spoke, lying beside the glass and plate with the remaining *caciotta* and bits of flatbread. "My grandma was studying political science, but as soon as they got engaged, my grandfather decided she had to change her major to literature, which was more suitable for raising refined children . . . My grandma waited until she was eighty-eight to mention the poet again— whatever the real story. A half century in the blink of an eye. To be born, to die."

"Mother of god," Francesco said, "such tenderness."

"Yes. Such tenderness."

Then one of us, checking the clock, said: "Let's go hit on some girls at Hop's."

"Yeah, let's."

"If that salesgirl's there, let's make sure to talk with her."

We got up, stiffly, and each of us had our turn in the bathroom.

We took the stairs, because I didn't want to be shut up in the elevator for eight floors. But as soon as we were outside, Francesco said he needed more time in the bathroom. "You go on ahead."

I thought maybe he wanted to call some woman. "Be there by midnight, though."

Walking to the bar, I started laughing, thinking that in less than an hour, I'd be "someone headed into his fifties," while right now I was "someone headed into his forties": the power of words, figures of speech. A decade in an hour, like something for sale at 99.99 euros.

I'd put my headphones on and was listening to a song, rich with distorted, compressed guitars, recorded in the nineties, when that music meant everything to me, and now it was pounding in my older ears, my fragile eardrums, through a pair of noise-canceling headphones that cut me off from the consular road I walked along, chuckling, pensive, out of breath.

Under the cloudy orange sky, interrupted by a row of buildings, I stepped into the intersection by the grocery store, walking against the light: first the lane of cars moving toward me, leaving the city; then the two sets of tram tracks, going their opposite ways; then the lane to downtown. I kept an eye on the approaching cars, headlights shining, and was almost to the other side when I said something out loud, and I felt like I'd spoken to my mother—it gave me the shivers. I know the exact words, because when I was back on the sidewalk, I stopped and wrote them down on my phone, convinced I'd never said anything more true: this is who I am, someone crossing the street, listening to music, headed to the bar.

Acknowledgments

Draft by draft, this book was born thanks to the critiques of Edoardo Albinati, Mattia Carratello, Massimiliano Catoni, Arianna Curci, Gabriele Di Fronzo, Natalia La Terza, Francesca Mancini, Lorenzo Moretto, Alessandro Piperno, Nicolò Porcelluzzi, Rebecca Servadio, Fabio Severo, and Laura Spini.

My thanks as well to Anna Stein, Mark Krotov, Marion Duvert, Matteo Falomi, Marcello Pacifico, Stefano Cipolla, Christian Rocca, Tiziana Scalabrin, Michela Iori, Francesca Casalino, la Segheria, Citofonare Interno 7, Matteo De Simone, Cristina Gerosa, Molly Walls, and Elizabeth Harris.

"We are the ambiguous forms.": This line on page 51 is from "Le forme ambigue," by Edoardo Albinati, translated here by Elizabeth Harris.

"Our extremest pleasure has some sort of groaning and complaining in it . . .": This sentence on page 170 is from the essays of Michel de Montaigne, translated by Charles Cotton.

"And how bewildered is any womb-born creature / that has to fly.": This line on page 252 is from "The Eighth Elegy," by Rainer Maria Rilke, translated by Stephen Mitchell.

In memory of Anna Maria Bertolli Marciani.